D0910912

First Impressions

"Charity and Mercy Ackerly, I'd like to present you to Lachlan Kimball, the Marquess of Asheburton."

Both girls executed halfhearted curtsies. Mercy nodded briefly in Lachlan's direction before turning her full attention and a dauntingly bright smile on her hero, the Duke of Blackthorne. Charity, though, was focused on Lachlan. Unusually focused. She took a step closer, peering at his polite smile, which was rapidly fading.

"Your teeth are beautiful," she said in an accusatory tone.

Startled by her odd statement, Lachlan raised an eyebrow. "Thank you."

"I don't suppose you have an unsightly wart or a disfiguring scar?" She scanned the rest of his face and then actually reached for one of his hands, as though she intended to inspect it, before she remembered herself and snatched back her arm. "Guess not," she muttered, tossed him an irritated look, and walked away.

Other *Leisure* books by Deneane Clark:

FAITH
GRACE

Deneane Clark

Charity

Dorchester
Publishing

DORCHESTER PUBLISHING

December 2010

Published by

Dorchester Publishing Co., Inc.
200 Madison Avenue
New York, NY 10016

ISBN 13: 978-1-4285-1125-5
E-ISBN: 978-1-4285-0940-5

The "DP" logo is the property of Dorchester Publishing Co., Inc.

Printed in the United States of America.

Visit us online at www.dorchesterpub.com.

For every teacher, coach, administrator and school counselor with whom I have ever, during my education or that of my children, been associated, especially:

- *Elizabeth Lamulle,* who taught me and taught me and taught me how to type. I think of you, and thank you, every time I place my fingers on a keyboard.
- *Joseph Buccaran,* my high school principal, who managed to make high school both rewarding and fun . . . a giant accomplishment, dwarfed only by his many others.
- *Jane Parrish* and *Brenda Keeling,* two of my children's elementary school teachers who beautifully engaged my daughter, my son, and me when it mattered the most.

And for a very special woman named *Connie Lee Campbell,* who is both the strongest and the kindest person I have ever known. I can't tell you how many times you helped me at the very moment I needed it most. You are a gift to the world.

I cannot thank any of you enough.

Charity

One

Patience?"

"Mm?"

Charity Ackerly plunked down on the blanket next to her fourteen-year-old sister and looked up, her little brow furrowed with concern. "What does 'homely' mean?"

Patience stopped sorting stockings into matching colors and sizes, and peered at her closely. "Why do you ask?" Her tone was cautious. Charity was the most volatile of all her sisters, which sometimes seemed odd, given the girl's fragile beginnings. Patience recalled in vivid detail the day her twin sisters came into the world, although that was five years past and she hadn't been called in until late in the delivery.

Amity had been born first, surprisingly small to the mind of the midwife from the village who cleaned and tended the newborn, but apparently healthy and whole. She was just wrapping the baby to place in her mother's arms when she heard Marie Ackerly gasp in sudden renewed pain. Quickly she'd knelt and placed a hand on her patient's belly and then ducked her head beneath the blanket. She'd emerged, white-faced. "Find someone to send for the doctor . . . quickly!" she commanded the girl she'd brought from the village to help.

Frightened by the midwife's tone of voice, the young

woman scurried off, no questions asked, and found the ten-year-old Patience playing with her two young sisters in one of the large rambling country manor's bedrooms. "Run," she'd said, "as fast as you can to the village for the doctor. This baby is bad."

So Patience had run, her heart in her throat and tears streaming down her face, unable to do more than stammer something about her mama having a "bad baby" when she arrived. The doctor, well-acquainted with the growing Ackerly family, put Patience in his carriage and drove her home. Once there, he'd disappeared into her mother's bedroom and did not reappear for hours.

The household went from a worried uproar to a tense, still silence. Even Grace and Faith, only five and three years old at that point, were oddly quiet. Bingham Ackerly, who seldom drank more than a single brandy at a time, was well into a bottle.

When Dr. Pettishaw finally reappeared through the bedroom doorway, the first person to whom he spoke was not Bingham, who surged to his feet, but Patience, who stared up at him with round, frightened gray eyes. He knelt in front of her chair so that he could look her in the face and said, "Your mama is doing well, Patience. You were a very brave girl to come and get me so quickly. She is tired but fine. I promise."

Patience nodded, bit her lip, and looked down at the floor so he wouldn't see her tears.

Hiding a smile at her little-girl bravado, Dr. Pettishaw stood and reached out to shake Bingham's hand. "And you, sir, have two rather small but beautiful new daughters."

Relief blossomed on Bingham's face. He started to go to his wife's bedside but was brought up short as he registered what the doctor said. *"Two?"*

"Yes, two. Twins!" Pettishaw chuckled. "The second baby had to fight her way into the world, but she made it. A bit scraggly looking, but strong for all that. Go and see all your girls."

Charity, as it turned out, the younger, smaller twin, was not quite finished fighting. Amity filled out and thrived, a peaceful easy infant, which was fortunate indeed, for Charity both needed and demanded much of Marie Ackerly's attention. She did not eat well, did not sleep well, and was frighteningly prone to illness. Time and time again they thought they were on the brink of losing her, but she always managed to fight her way back to health.

By the time the twins were a year old, Charity finally matched Amity in development. They were inseparable. Their mother was often heard to fondly declare that one couldn't live without the other, and that Amity had shared a measure of her own good health so that her sister could catch up.

The twins looked so much alike that even family members had difficulty distinguishing one from the other by sight. They remained smaller than the other village children their age. After spending their first year without any hair at all, they suddenly both grew a thick mop of unruly strawberry blonde curls. Their eyes were wide and of an odd shade somewhere between blue and green, and within hours of the first time their faces were exposed to the sun they developed a smattering of freckles across their cheeks and noses. That, however, was where the similarities ended. They were polar opposites in personality.

Amity was the embodiment of her name: friendly, happy, kind, serene. Charity, on the other hand, having fought her way into the world, seemed bent on enjoying every single corner of it, and woe to anyone who sought to curb her enthusiasm or determination. From a very young age she displayed a fiery temper that became legendary, and she had seemed the most affected by their mother's death three years ago.

Because of this temper, it was with understandable trepidation that Patience sought to understand what had prompted Charity's rather odd question.

"Robert Benton said his mama told Mrs. Ingram at the apothecary that, with my temper, it's too bad I'm such a homely little thing." Charity wrinkled her nose. "I was going to kick him when he said it, but I didn't know what 'homely' meant so I told him to wait while I came to ask you."

Patience carefully suppressed the urge to laugh. "Robert is waiting for you to decide whether or not you will kick him?"

Charity nodded and rubbed her freckled nose, leaving a smudge of dirt across the bridge.

Patience eyed her sister, garbed in a dress that no longer fit Faith but into which Charity had not yet quite grown. The six Ackerly girls weren't always turned out in the best frocks, but as long as they were all decently covered Patience counted it a good day. Although they were certainly not poor, Bingham Ackerly was often so involved in his scholarly pursuits that he failed to notice it had been a while since he'd last paid the butcher or collected the rents from his various properties. Patience had learned long ago to practice frugality even during the more prosperous times, and the younger girls found their own ways, often preferring comfort to fashion. Grace seldom wore anything other than hand-me-downs from the Beldon brothers on the next estate, and while Charity was content to dress in female clothing, it seldom saw a full day without becoming smudged or torn. Three-year-old Mercy, curled up and napping on the blanket beside Patience, was barefoot.

She struggled to keep the expression on her face pleasant. Most of the villagers were friendly and understanding, but there were a few, like Robert's mother, who were more vocal about their disapproval of Bingham Ackerly for entrusting the care of the younger children to his eldest daughter. "You go tell Robert that 'homely' can have a great many meanings, but in your case it must mean that you look like you come from a home where you are very, *very* much loved."

Charity's tiny face cleared, and she smiled brightly as she stood and began to run back to her playmate. She stopped in her tracks, thought a moment, and then returned to throw her dirt-streaked arms around Patience's neck. "I'm *glad* I'm homely," she said. "And I wouldn't have minded being homely at all, even if it were something bad. I was only going to kick him for Amity's sake, because she looks like me and I won't let anyone say anything bad about her." And off Charity ran, shouting Robert's name as she disappeared.

Patience returned to sorting socks and smiled at the cheerful sound of her sisters playing with their friends, her irritation with Mrs. Benton entirely forgotten.

Ashton, Scotland

"Gregory?"

The older gentleman seated on the other side of the single-room cabin looked up from his writing, his bushy white eyebrows raised in inquiry. "Yes, my young lord?"

The boy with the perpetually serious expression was paying little attention to the book Gregory had given him to read. Instead, he was strumming his fingers on the rough-hewn table, an oddly adult gesture for a ten-year-old boy. The learned old man hid a fond smile.

"What does 'homely' mean?"

Gregory set down his quill. "Well, that depends upon the context in which it was used." He searched his brain, trying to recall if there were any passages in Homer's *Iliad* that dealt with someone being described as "homely." None came to mind. "Why do you ask?"

"Papa took me with him to the village this morning, and while I waited for him outside the blacksmith's shop, I heard two women talking." His brow furrowed over a pair of large, startling gray eyes. "They said it was fortunate the next Marquess of Asheburton would not be quite as homely as the current one, unless I died and Lewiston lived to inherit."

Gregory pressed his lips together and shook his head. "Those ladies were unkind, Lachlan. They meant that your father and your younger brother are not very attractive, which has little to do with one's ability to be either a good or a bad lord. The idea of judging a marquess by his attractiveness, well . . . it's ludicrous."

Lachlan's brow cleared at the explanation, but the expression in his silvery eyes remained troubled. "I don't think my father is a very good lord, Gregory," he said haltingly.

"Why do you say that?" The retired vicar kept his voice carefully neutral. He very much wanted Lachlan to come to independent conclusions about his family. It would never do to lead the boy to form a negative opinion of the people who were raising him; he himself was only here to ensure Lachlan had every opportunity to grow up with all the tools he needed to someday be a proper marquess.

The boy glanced around the small, neat cottage. "Our

home—the keep—is not well-tended, the servants never stay for very long, and the villagers don't like us."

Gregory nodded. "All could be signs that your father is not managing well, but do you think he is a good man, my boy?"

The fledgling marquess thought a moment and then nodded firmly. "I do."

"Well, in that case, perhaps you can learn to help him manage what will one day belong to you."

Gregory watched the boy carefully for a response.

After another moment's consideration, Lachlan turned back to his reading. "Perhaps," he murmured.

Two

London, 1814

Mercy Ackerly leaned over the banister and watched the two men disappear into the study with her brother-in-law. She sighed with happy adoration and turned back to her seventeen-year-old twin siblings. "Sebastian came to the wedding with some man I've never seen instead of bringing another woman."

"'Another' woman?" Charity laughed aloud. "You mean a woman other than *you*? You're only fourteen—not even a woman yourself, much less one with whom Blackthorne would consider being seen."

Mercy glared at her. "I'm nearly fifteen," she corrected hotly. "And, besides, Sebastian is going to marry me."

Charity rolled her eyes and opened her mouth to retort, but Amity spoke up, doing her best to keep her sisters from arguing on Faith's wedding day. "You said he came with a man you've never seen?"

Mercy waved a dismissive hand in the air. "Tall, dark, powerful. The usual. Doesn't Trevor have any short, ugly friends?" The three girls pushed away from the railing on the landing and continued their descent to the first floor.

"Maybe this mysterious new man has bad teeth or something," said Charity, her eyes glinting with fun. "Let's wait here in the foyer for them to come out. That way, Trevor will have to introduce us, and we can inspect the new person for flaws."

"Oh, for heaven's sake! These men are peers of the realm, not boys from the village." Amity pointed a stern finger at her twin. "Whatever you're planning, don't you dare ruin Faith's wedding," she warned.

Charity gave her a look of exaggerated innocence. "I'm just going to get to know him. It'll make the poor man feel welcome. After all, he's amongst strangers." She sighed with an air of mock tragedy. "He probably feels lost and alone."

They stopped outside the closed study doors. Mercy stared longingly at the panels of polished mahogany, wishing they'd open so she could see her beloved duke, and Charity linked arms with her. "Let's walk up and down the hall. It will look like we were just strolling by, having a harmless little chat, when they come out."

Amity shook her head and backed away. "I'll just go see if Grace and Faith need any help. I'd rather not be anywhere near here when those doors open."

Inside the study, the hapless victims of Charity and Mercy's intended ambush were having a comfortable conversation with their host, Trevor Caldwell, the Earl of Huntwick, who had just finished explaining the necessity for the day's rather hasty wedding. "So you see, since Faith has compromised poor Gareth quite beyond recall, the only possible solution was for her to make an honest man of him."

"I thought Faith's debut might go a bit more smoothly than Grace's," remarked Sebastian, who was both the Duke of Blackthorne and Trevor's best friend. "She seemed more logical and less headstrong than the other Ackerly girls we met."

"That logical streak is the very reason for the haste. Gareth is not at all sure that, given time, Faith won't find a reasonable way out of the situation. And he seems rather set on having her for his wife." Trevor laughed. "Besides, I don't think 'smooth' is an adjective one would ever apply to a relationship with one of my wife's sisters. Something you should bear in mind as Mercy grows older." He gave his friend a pointed look.

Sebastian looked unconcerned, although a small smile played about his lips. "I suppose the urchin is in town, too, running amok somewhere in your home?" He was reluctantly fond of the youngest Ackerly sister, who had been the inadvertent reason the family even entered their social circle. Had he known the impact his decision to continue traveling that day, despite the late hour and diminished visibility, would have on both his life and his sense of peace, he might well have decided not to take the risk; but he'd overridden Hunt's warnings, and now the second of his friends had fallen prey to the snapping jaws of matrimony. Both surrenders had stemmed directly from that one foolish decision.

"Last time I saw her she was whispering with one of the twins—I haven't a clue which—while watching the front door for, I believe, your noble arrival." Trevor's green eyes danced with amusement. "I'm not sure how you managed to make it in here safely."

The third man in the room, listening quietly up to this point, finally spoke. "Twins? How many of these Ackerly creatures exist?"

Lachlan Kimball, the Scottish Marquess of Asheburton, was related to Sebastian, although neither man could publicly claim kinship. They bore a startling resemblance to one another, and most of the *ton* suspected some sort of distant relationship. It was far less distant than people imagined. They were cousins.

Both men had come into their titles through rather tenuous connections. In Sebastian's case, he'd discovered he was heir to the Duke of Blackthorne's estate through a letter sent from a solicitor, and he'd been anything but pleased with the development. Or, more correctly, he'd been displeased with the history he'd discovered. The elderly duke, it turned out, had disowned both of his sons—and with good reason: the pair was undeniably handsome and charming but spoiled by their mother and utterly lacking in principles and morals. After being banished from the estate, the elder son married the daughter of a respectable country squire, breezed through her small dowry and then abandoned the young lady, never to be spoken of or heard from again. Shortly after her husband's defection, she gave birth to Sebastian. The old duke had kept tabs on his eldest son for a period of time but, considering him a lost cause, decided to turn his attention to his grandson. When old age set in and his health began to fail, he contacted Sebastian, now a young man of considerable independent fortune, and named him his heir.

The younger son—Lachlan's father—had gambled his way through most of England, using his considerable looks and occasional luck at the tables to charm his way into the hearts and bedrooms of many a young lady. Eventually he'd ended up in Scotland, in a border village, where he impregnated the beautiful daughter of a successful merchant. With his debts following him from England and new ones mounting in Scotland, and faced with the prospect of becoming a father, he also disappeared. Lachlan's title had come . . . somewhat differently.

Sebastian had learned all this after hiring discreet investigators, something he'd learned to do in his successful early days as an investor before his elevation. He had then contacted Lachlan and satisfied himself that the man was indeed the son of his father's younger brother. The two had become immediate friends and, later, business partners.

"There are six sisters," said Trevor, giving it a moment's thought. "Patience, the eldest, whom you will discover was very aptly named; my wife, Grace; and then today's bride, Faith; followed by the twins, Amity and Charity; and finally little Mercy, who fancies herself betrothed to your cousin here." He glanced at the clock on the mantel and stood. "Gareth and Jon should be here soon."

Sebastian and Lachlan also stood. "Should I be afraid to leave this room?" joked the marquess.

Trevor opened the doors and glanced out into the hall. He pushed the doors wider and gave his friends a wry, apologetic look. "Absolutely," he said, his tone colored with amused irony. Mercy and Charity were walking down the hall, arms linked, pretending an absorbed interest in their conversation.

Trevor cleared his throat. "Good morning, Mercy."

When he raised his eyebrows and regarded the second girl in mute inquiry, she scowled at the realization that he didn't know her name. "I'm Charity," she said, then added in a dampening tone. "For the *second* time today."

Trevor appeared unrepentant. "Charity and Mercy Ackerly, I'd like to present you to Lachlan Kimball, the Marquess of Asheburton."

Both girls executed halfhearted curtsies. Mercy nodded briefly in Lachlan's direction before turning her full attention and a dauntingly bright smile on her hero, the Duke of Blackthorne. Charity, though, seemed more focused on Lachlan. Unusually focused. She took a step closer, peering at his polite smile, which was rapidly fading.

"Your teeth are beautiful," she said in a tone that sounded accusatory.

Though startled by her odd statement, Lachlan merely raised an eyebrow. "Thank you."

"I don't suppose you have an unsightly wart or a disfiguring scar?" She scanned the rest of his face and then actually reached for one of his hands, as though she intended to inspect it, before she remembered herself and snatched back her arm. "Guess not," she muttered, tossed him an irritated look and walked away.

"Unlike Patience," Sebastian spoke up, "Charity is *not* so aptly named."

Mercy giggled.

"I heard that!" Charity called from down the hall.

"You might want to cut your losses and just leave now," Trevor advised Lachlan. "You might even consider going straight back to Scotland where it's safe."

The marquess, however, was staring thoughtfully down the hall. "Interesting girl," he remarked. "I think I can handle it."

Two hours later, Lachlan found himself standing on the steps in front of the Caldwell town house, a somewhat bemused expression on his face. "That may well have been one of the oddest experiences of my life," he announced. The wedding itself had been a brief, somewhat strained and awkward affair, as had been the reception. Additionally, every time he looked around he found Charity Ackerly watching him. If that weren't disconcerting enough, she steadfastly refused to look away when he caught her eye, leaving him with the distinct impression that *he* had somehow inconvenienced *her* by catching her staring.

"Welcome to the unconventional world of the Ackerlys,"

replied Sebastian, pulling on his gloves. They descended to the street and climbed aboard his coach, settling comfortably across from one another into the deep burgundy velvet squabs.

"I found Patience and Amity quite pleasant," remarked Lachlan when they were underway.

Sebastian looked unimpressed. "Gareth Lloyd," he said, referring to the rather grim groom, "would once have said the same thing about Faith." And with that, they lapsed into silence for the rest of the drive.

Three

Though the Ackerly twins had once been described as homely by the women of Pelthamshire, time had worked its magic and seen fit to bestow the two of them with exceptional beauty. Parasols and time spent indoors had faded the hated freckles, and their complexions were now a creamy alabaster with just a hint of glowing peach on their high, sculpted cheekbones. Their eyes were of an odd cerulean blue, fringed with russet lashes, wide and shining brightly with intelligence and humor beneath delicately winged brows a shade or two darker than the hair on their heads, which had remained a lovely strawberry blonde despite everyone's prediction that it would darken. But beauty was not everything.

They were also the next pair of Ackerly sisters to make their debut in London. That Season the village was abuzz with speculation, and everyone wondered if it were possible for the girls to make matches as advantageous and connected as those of their older sisters Grace and Faith. Those two respectively had married an earl and a marquess, which had greatly elevated the stature of the family in the small community. The connections had landed the two girls in Madame Capdepon's School for Girls with half a dozen of their peers, most of whom would never even venture outside the village, much less see the inside of a London ballroom.

"Charity Ackerly!"

Startled, Charity dragged her eyes from the enticing view of the beautiful spring day outside the window and focused on the disapproving face of Madame Capdepon. The room had fallen silent.

"Y-yes, Madame?" Charity's voice was hesitant. She truly *hadn't* been paying attention to the lesson. It was all Mercy's fault, of course. The wretched child kept appearing at the window, making faces and taunting her with the evidence of a freedom to enjoy the day as she saw fit. Charity had tried—truly she had!—to pay attention to the etiquette classes her elder sister Patience insisted she and her twin sister Amity attend before they went to London for the Season. But the classes had droned on for hours, and Madame Capdepon quite obviously did not like her.

"Am I expected to believe, Miss Ackerly, that you're so adept at knowing which utensil is the proper one to use at every course of a formal dinner, you have no need for further instruction?"

Charity bit her lip. She most certainly knew no such thing. And, while she recognized the fact that knowledge of this sort might come in handy at some point in her life, she had full confidence in her ability to adapt to any given situation without the necessity of enduring this wretched, endlessly boring class.

Unable to respond with anything except an admission of her ignorance, Charity raised her chin, stared belligerently back at her nemesis, and did not answer.

Amity groaned inwardly. When backed into a corner, Charity would come out hissing, and Amity recognized quite well the militant look in her twin's eyes. She hastily spoke up before Charity could say something to fan the flames of the developing situation. "We will go over the lesson at home tonight, Madame. Papa likes to see us apply what we've learned." She hoped the insinuation that they demonstrated her invaluable instruction to their learned parent might mollify the older woman.

Not a chance. "I'm quite certain, Amity Ackerly, that you have *not* been addressed." The imposing matron stalked around the circular tables at which the young ladies of Pelthamshire were seated, bearing down inexorably on the twins. "Class!" she boomed out, the spectacles she kept hanging on a ribbon around her neck bouncing off her rather ample bosom as she moved. "Gather around, please. Quickly." She fixed Charity with a triumphant glare. "Miss Ackerly—Miss *Charity* Ackerly—is going to astonish us with her extensive knowledge of formal place settings."

Charity knew next to nothing about place settings. She sent Madame Capdepon an imploring look, but the angry instructor was not to be appeased. In desperation Charity tried to visualize the way the table had looked at her older sister Grace's wedding a couple of years earlier. A plate . . . she was quite certain there had been a plate, and that the utensils went on the sides of the plate.

She stood and walked to the front of the class, chewing on her lower lip. She'd simply have to bluff her way through.

"Well, the plate is, of course, the most important piece." She picked one up and put it on the table, then surveyed her silverware options. A couple of girls in the front row stifled giggles. Charity glared at them. They simmered down as she reached hesitantly toward the utensils. Her eyes found those of her twin, hoping she'd receive some guidance.

Amity shook her head slightly as Charity's hand hovered over a stack of forks. She moved her hand toward the spoons, a bit to the right. Again, Amity shook her head.

Madame Capdepon crossed her arms. "Enough stalling, Miss Ackerly."

Charity grabbed a fork.

"No." Madame's voice was sharp.

Charity reached for a knife.

Madame sighed. "No," she said again.

Charity scowled, grabbed one of each and plunked them haphazardly to the left and right of the plate. She looked at the place setting and recalled something resting horizontally at the top. She picked the longest utensil, moved it above the plate, and then stepped back.

Madame Capdepon didn't even look at her handiwork; she stared directly at the younger girl until Charity began to fidget uncomfortably. When she'd made her student suffer a sufficient length of time, she delivered her sentence with the daunting finality of a bewigged judge at trial. "Miss Ackerly, I would like for you to leave my class and not come back."

A collective gasp rose from the room. Charity lifted her chin, glared back at the older woman, and then grasped the sides of her skirt to sink into a beautiful but incredibly mocking curtsy. Without a word, she straightened and left.

All eyes swiveled to Amity, who, blushing hotly, picked up her things and Charity's, nodded coldly at the instructor and followed her sister from the building.

When Amity emerged into the sunshine, Charity already had a good lead, her anger making her strides almost impossibly long. Mercy appeared out of nowhere and took Charity's reticule and lesson book.

"Come on," she said to Amity with an impish grin. "You don't need those silly lessons anyway. Neither Grace nor Faith had etiquette lessons, and they did just fine."

Amity looked grim. "Grace was lucky. And Faith was born knowing how to behave correctly."

Mercy shrugged, utterly unconcerned.

They caught up to Charity, who'd finally realized they were behind her and stopped to wait. Amity took one look at her sister's face and knew she was already beginning to internally berate herself. She felt a twinge of remorse for second-guessing her sister's headstrong ways. "Don't even *think* about apologizing to me, Charity. There's no way I was staying in that horrible woman's class after she kicked you out."

Charity smiled gratefully, but the guilt didn't leave her eyes. "She hasn't liked me since the day we learned how to dance, anyway." She scuffed at the dirt with the toe of her shoe, sending up little puffs.

Mercy laughed. "Well, you showed up dressed as a boy!"

Charity looked indignant. "Because there are only girls in the class. How would we ever learn to dance with a boy if someone didn't play the part?"

Amity smiled. "Come on." She tugged Charity's arm. "We'd better get home and face Patience." Their older sister was not going to take this well. "I'll go in first and tell her. Maybe she won't be quite so angry if I give her the news and explain what happened instead of you."

They all turned when they heard a vehicle coming down the lane. It was Madame Capdepon's curricle. She'd obviously decided to let class out early, and was now apparently headed to the Ackerly home.

The sisters stepped aside to let it pass, then stood in the swirling dust and watched the vehicle disappear around a bend. Mercy linked an arm through Charity's. "Maybe, when we get home, you can ask her to stay to dinner." Her lips twitched. "You can tell her it will be no trouble to set an extra place."

Charity lunged and swatted at her, but Mercy ducked and took off running, musical laughter trailing behind.

Charity chased her a few steps, then gave up and returned to her twin.

Amity hid a smile and tried to keep from laughing as they walked. She glanced at Charity out of the corner of her eye and bit her lip. Her blue eyes danced. And then, because there was nothing else they could do, both girls succumbed to the hilarity of the situation and continued on their way home, wiping away tears of mirth.

"She is a hoyden, entirely undisciplined, and I will not have her in my class! Furthermore, Mr. Ackerly, I have to say that I despair of her ever making a decent match, despite the fact that her older sisters have been so fortunate in their marriages. I can't imagine anyone of breeding accepting her as his wife."

Charity pressed her lips together in an effort to control her temper. Seated on a bench outside her father's study with Amity and Mercy, she held herself stiffly erect, her head high. In her mind, however, she was drowning in mortification at the etiquette instructor's harsh description.

They couldn't hear their soft-spoken father's reply, but the modulated, gracious voice of Patience came to them quite clearly. "I'll be happy to show you out, Madame Capdepon." The doors to the study opened and Patience appeared with the still quite indignant woman. Neither spared a glance for the trio seated on the bench.

After a few moments, Bingham Ackerly stepped out and stopped, regarding the three girls steadily for a moment. He shook his head and smiled. "Well," he said. "I suppose that is that."

Charity chewed on her lower lip and stared up at her father, her cerulean eyes filled with remorse. "I'm sorry, Papa."

He smiled fondly and shook his head. "It was likely a

mistake to send you to those classes in the first place. Patience meant well."

"I don't have to go to London, Papa. Amity can go without me." Even as she said the words, though, Charity felt a pang of regret. She really *did* want to have a Season, to dress up in beautiful gowns and be presented to Society. And she knew—she *knew*—if she tried hard enough, she could manage to play the part of a demure debutante for three whole months in a row.

Bingham reached down and rumpled her hair. "I have every confidence that Faith will steer you in the right direction. Of course you can still go to London." He wandered back into his study, his mind already back on his current writing project. To his way of thinking, the problem with Charity was resolved.

She watched him go, her expression troubled.

"Why are you still frowning?" asked Mercy. "You heard him. You're going to London."

"I know." Charity sighed heavily and looked at her twin. "Do you think what Madame said is true? That I'll never find a husband?"

"Don't be ridiculous!" Amity slipped an arm around her sister's shoulders. "We're going to find a couple of lovely gentlemen with whom we'll fall hopelessly in love, we'll have our perfect double wedding, and they'll build us quaint little country homes right here in Pelthamshire so that we never have to be away from one another or our family. Just like we've always planned."

Charity gave both of her sisters a smile that only wobbled a little. "Yes. Just like we've always planned," she echoed, but there was still a tiny shade of doubt in her voice.

Four

Scotland, 1815

Asheburton Keep, after a couple of hundred years of neglect and misuse, was once again a sight to behold. A jewel nestled in the emerald hills above the small Scottish village of Ashton, the ancient castle managed to be both intimidating and stunning. It was a far cry from the near ruin in which Lachlan had been raised.

Mounted on his favorite stallion, Apollo, aptly named for the god of the sun because of his glowing golden coat, the Marquess of Asheburton gazed across a small valley at the home he'd restored. So regal was his bearing, pride stamped into every inch of his powerful frame, one could easily have pictured him in full armor, preparing to storm the castle upon which he set his sights. It was time to think of the future.

Well pleased with the empire he'd created, Lachlan now longed for more. He wanted the laughter of children ringing through the hills surrounding the keep. *His* children. He would wait no longer.

Two years ago he had almost married, choosing a young girl from the village named Beth Gilweather, daughter of the blacksmith. She was a beautiful young woman with the coloring prominent in Ashton, pale hair and light eyes, but in her case her hair was the golden blonde of newly minted coins, and her eyes flashed a brilliant green that rivaled the emerald hillsides of Scotland. He'd fallen hard for her, but when he approached his parents with his intentions, his mother's reaction had been instantaneous and negative.

"Out of the question! You will not marry a commoner from the village."

He'd bitten back the retort that rose to his lips. It would not do to remind Lady Eloise Kimball that she was once a villager herself. Not when the stakes were so high. Instead, he'd looked to his father, who shifted uncomfortably in his seat.

"Perhaps if you traveled a bit first, my boy. Go to London, or Edinburgh. Meet women of your class."

"I don't consider Beth below my class, Father."

"Then you're a fool, Lachlan, who cannot see past her physical beauty and understand that she sees you as nothing more than a way to improve her circumstances. Especially now that both the keep and the village are prospering." Lady Asheburton had folded her lips and stared at him. The marquess had looked as though he might speak, but Eloise placed a restraining hand atop his. He'd closed his mouth and given Lachlan a look of apology.

Without another word, Lachlan left the room. He'd stalked out to the stables, saddled Apollo, and rode to the village. When he saw Beth sitting outside her father's shop, he'd reined in the stallion and swung down. He approached and knelt before her. "Marry me, Beth. Today."

She laughed softly. "Lachlan, my goodness! You look like a thundercloud. A girl likes to be asked for her hand in marriage, not have it wrenched from her arm."

He stood and ran a hand through his hair. He turned and looked back up the hill to the distant keep that overlooked the village. "I know," he said. "My parents oppose the match, Beth."

The blonde girl paled. "So if we marry . . ." She left the sentence unfinished and frowned. Such an eventuality apparently had never occurred to her.

"We could live anywhere—here in the village, or we could go to England if you like. I'm not afraid of hard work, and I'm sure I would be successful eventually."

When he turned to face her, she pasted a supportive smile on her face. "Perhaps they'll come around if we give them time."

He tilted his head and studied her expression. His mother's words rang through his head. *Understand that she sees you as nothing more than a way to improve her circumstances.*

Seeing his expression darken, she'd hastened to explain. "I don't like the thought of our marriage dividing your family, my lord." She laid a soft hand on his cheek and raised soft eyes to his. "I'll marry you no matter what happens, Lachlan. But let's give them some time to come around." He didn't respond, so she took his hand and began to draw him inside the cottage. "My father is in Edinburgh for two days," she said with a coy little smile.

Lachlan flicked a glance up and down the street. Nobody was about. "Apollo," he'd said, indicating his very visible stallion. He didn't want to sully Beth's reputation.

"Take him around back," she suggested. When Lachlan still looked dubious, she laughed. "We're engaged now, silly. There's no reason for us to wait, is there?"

No longer able to resist the entrancing promise in her bright green eyes, he'd nodded and did as she suggested. They'd had a wonderful time. Three days later she broke off the engagement. He pressed her to learn why, but she never would say. It had thankfully killed all romantic instinct in him.

So that wedding had never happened. But another would. One that was practical, one that was all about need. His love for Beth had been a serious mistake. How could he love a woman and not tell her all truth as he knew it? And he couldn't imagine Beth responding well to the truth of his parentage or to his onetime determination to abdicate his position as marquess. No, marriages were better things of convenience.

Apollo danced beneath him, bringing Lachlan back to the present. "Had enough of the view, have you?" With a smile, he urged the horse down the hill and across the wildflower-strewn glade at a gallop, only slowing when those hooves beat a sharp staccato on the bridge that had once crossed a moat. Now one could merely see the gentle indention of land circling the castle where the moat had been, and the lush grass grew right up to the surrounding walls.

Well pleased with his ride, Lachlan dismounted and handed over Apollo's reins to a waiting groom. He crossed the courtyard to the massive doors of the main entrance, which stood open, allowing the breeze to carry indoors the intoxicating freshness of the mild spring day.

Unfortunately, the marquess's pleasant morning ended the moment he stepped inside. Eloise Kimball's shrill voice uncoiled and lashed him like a whip.

"I don't suppose you've given any thought at all to getting us some *decent* help around here."

Lachlan grimaced and bit back a sharp response. "Our servants are perfectly competent, Mother, and most of them are quite skilled." He continued toward the stairs without glancing in her direction, anxious to escape to his chamber and change out of his dusty riding clothes.

"They most certainly are not," retorted Eloise, her voice filled with indignation. She followed him up the stairs. "That valet of yours looks like a common criminal, and Cook is quite beyond the age at which one should be working. She barely manages to construct a palatable meal."

"The fare may be simple, Mother, but it is good. Cook's husband has become infirm, and I refuse to put her out of work when she is the sole provider in their family."

"I don't understand why you insist upon hiring only people from the village."

"Ashton is their home, and I am their lord. We've discussed this many times. For too long the lords of this castle held themselves aloof from the people of the village and surrounding area." He gave the older woman a stern look. "Do not forget your beginnings, Mother. You were once a villager yourself. Now, if you'll excuse me?" Without waiting for a response, he stepped inside the master chamber and closed the heavy oak door.

Summarily dismissed, Eloise stared at the solid panel of wood that stood between her and her infuriating eldest son. His ingratitude for the sacrifices she'd made for him stung. After all, had it not been for her quick thinking when his scoundrel of a father impregnated and abandoned her, he'd be nothing but a villager himself, and a bastard to boot.

She turned and walked slowly back down the hall, lost in the past. As a young woman, Eloise Gardner had been considered the most beautiful girl in the village. She was the only child of the richest merchant in town, and she could have had her pick of the men who came from miles around to court her. Or, more correctly, *tried* to court her. Eloise had looked at none of them. Her mother despaired and her father blustered, but she steadfastly refused to even consider anyone who came to the door of their modest home on the outskirts of the village. She turned up her pretty little nose at all of them, judging them nothing more than ill-mannered louts and instead insisting over and over that she wanted to go to London for a Season.

"Out of the question." Her father refused to budge on the issue, and Eloise, at first cajoling and then tearful, had finally resorted to an angry little tantrum.

"Why not?" she'd demanded, when he first insisted they didn't have the funds available for even a modest trip to the capital. "Am I not worth it?"

"Even if we could afford it, we don't have the connections required to gain entrée into the social circles you seek, Eloise. We could purchase you the most beautiful gowns and obtain a fashionable address, but you still wouldn't be invited to a single event. Not without a noble connection to sponsor you."

Eloise had frowned and looked out the window. Her eyes settled on the keep that overlooked the village, crumbling away up on its hill. The Marquess of Asheburton, she knew, resided there, unmarried and alone. He never came into the village—was in fact rumored to be a complete recluse, never leaving the keep at all. There were rumors he suffered from periods of instability, black moods, and an irrationality long established in the Kimball family do to tragic consequences, but nobody in the village really knew if it was true. He was, however, a peer of the realm, and that was precisely what Eloise required. Her thoughts had turned speculative.

The very next day found her climbing the hill to the dilapidated old keep, picking her way carefully in her best frock and nicest shoes. "I'd like to see the Marquess of Asheburton," she demanded when she reached the massive front doors. The dour-faced servant who answered her knock didn't say a word, just opened the door wider and turned away. Eloise took that as an invitation to come inside.

The castle was as unkempt on the inside as it was without,

and gloomy besides. The structure was built to withstand siege, and none of the lords of Asheburton had seen fit to modernize it since the middle ages, so there were no windows in the place. The only light filtered weakly in from arrow slits high up in the walls, supplemented by the occasional sputtering torch.

She followed the servant down a dank hallway until they reached a door which stood ajar. He indicated that she should go inside. Eloise did so and then stopped after a few steps, waiting for her eyes to adjust. Once they did, she looked around.

"You are . . . ?"

Startled, Eloise looked to her left. Seated in a corner of the room in a cracked leather chair was a nondescript balding man, rather younger than she'd imagined. She cleared her throat and turned to face him. "I am Eloise Gardner, my lord. F-from the village." She curtsied prettily.

"Why are you here?"

There seemed no point in beating around the bush. Gathering her courage, she said, "I seek a Season in London, but don't know of anyone who might sponsor me. I hoped you might do so, my lord."

"London." It was a statement, not a question, and Eloise waited for him to say something else. He seemed lost in thought. After a few moments, she began to wonder if he'd even heard of the city.

Just as she was about to offer explanation, he spoke again. "I've never been there. And I cannot sponsor you."

Eloise's face fell, and she looked down. She'd been so sure he would help once he saw how beautiful she was. It had always been thus.

Unbeknownst to her, Andrew Kimball had watched disappointment cloud the ravishing girl's face. She'd obviously dressed her best for the arduous climb to the castle and yet managed to arrive looking fresh. Her hair was a light gold, and probably glowed when she wasn't in such a dull setting, and even the dim light couldn't hide the brilliant emeralds that were her eyes. For the first time ever, he felt the stirrings of desire.

"Why do you seek a Season, please?" he asked.

Eloise looked up, her eyes probing the shadows for a better look at her host's face. She couldn't read his expression and said, "I do not wish to marry beneath my station."

Her bearing was indeed regal; almost haughty. Andrew rubbed his chin. "And what *is* your station?"

"My father is the most successful merchant in the village," she explained.

Unfortunately, Andrew knew what her father had already tried to impress upon her: a merchant's daughter, no matter her wealth, would never be accepted by the aristocracy. He sighed. "I cannot sponsor you," he repeated.

Eloise curtsied. "Thank you, anyway," she said, and turned to go.

"If you haven't—" The marquess stopped midsentence, then continued in a rush, as though he had to force his words out quickly or not say them at all. "If you find yourself without a better alternative for wedlock, you might consider me."

Eloise froze. "Consider . . . *you?*"

The man in the corner said nothing.

She thought about it for a bare second and then lifted her chin. Inside, she shuddered at the thought of marrying the odd, unattractive man with the thick loathsome Scottish accent. Certainly he was titled, but he had no apparent connections, his home was ghastly, and his appearance, from what she could tell, was less than desirable. "Thank you, my lord. I will give it some thought." Carefully keeping the revulsion she felt from showing on her face, she curtsied again and left the room, walking swiftly down the hall and out the door.

Once she'd gained the open air, it was all she could do to keep from breaking into a run. She was far less careful on her way down the hill and, as a result, stepped on some loose rocks. Her ankle turned, and she fell, crying out in sudden shock and pain. Overwhelmed by the events of the morning, though she wasn't seriously hurt, she sat on the side of the hill and cried. She cried for the death of all her hopes and dreams, for the knowledge that she would really never be anything more than the prettiest girl in the village, and for the futility she'd refused to accept in the first place. And then, when her tears dried up, she just sat, glaring up the hill at the old building from whence she had just come.

"Are you okay, miss?"

Surprised, wincing at the twinge in her ankle, Eloise scrambled to her feet and turned to face the person who had spoken, realizing as she did that the voice was male, cultured, and decidedly English. "I'm fine," she said, and took a step back.

Her mouth fell open in shock. Coming toward her on the path was the most beautiful man she'd ever seen. He was tall, very tall, with dark hair and flashing dark eyes, and his amiable smile revealed a row of the whitest, most perfect teeth she'd ever seen, made even more striking by his tanned face. He looked rugged and fit but every inch the aristocrat.

Suddenly, she was acutely aware that, despite how hard she had worked to obliterate all traces of her hated Scottish accent, she would never sound as cultured and sophisticated as this man. "I was just on my way home," she managed to say, when she finally realized she was staring.

"You don't live in that castle?" He pointed up the hill behind her.

Eloise shook her head. "The Marquess of Asheburton lives there. He's . . . rather reclusive."

"Too bad," the stranger mused. "I was hoping to prevail upon him for hospitality. I'm in the area for a while, you see—taking a walking tour of Scotland, you might say."

No wonder he looked so fit. Aloud she said, "And you are . . . ?"

He smiled, dazzling her again. His face transformed from one that was merely handsome into a visage that was breathtaking. "Oh, I'm sorry. I'm Oliver Tremaine." He held out a hand into which Eloise automatically placed her own, and he raised her wrist to his lips for a kiss. "My father is the Duke of Blackthorne."

Her wrist still tingling, Eloise absorbed that bit of information, and her entire demeanor changed from cautious reticence to the calculating coquette. Oliver instantly noted the change and pressed his advantage. In no time they'd both agreed that the castle wasn't at all a viable option. Instead Oliver agreed to accompany her home, and Eloise had promised that her father would be more than happy to welcome him.

She was right. Her father extended an invitation for Oliver to stay as long as he liked, and Oliver easily managed to charm all the members of her family. Eloise herself fell for him like a rock. It took him less than twenty-four hours to seduce her, and before the month was out she was pregnant. At first she didn't realize why she felt so tired and ill, but by the time she'd missed her second monthly flux, she knew. When she fearfully told Oliver, he held her close, whispered promises that he would marry her, that everything would be just fine, and then he convinced her to go to sleep. Together, they would speak to her parents in the morning.

When she woke up, of course, he was gone—along with all the money in her father's till.

Terrified and alone, Eloise didn't waste any more time feeling sorry for herself. For the second time in her life she climbed the hill to Asheburton Keep. Presenting herself to the marquess she announced, "I'd like to accept your offer, my lord."

Andrew Kimball had eyed her steadily. "Why?"

"I am with child." She lifted her chin and bravely met his gaze.

"The father?"

"Gone."

"And you'd like me to give the child my name. What if you bear a son? He would become the next Marquess of Asheburton."

She nodded.

The marquess tapped a finger against his lips and appeared to be deep in thought. Eloise waited quietly. When he spoke, his voice was soft. "It might not be a bad thing for the child you carry to inherit the title. I have . . . reasons for this, reasons I do not feel comfortable discussing. Though you have heard the rumors." He stood and walked a few paces away. It was the first time she'd seen him rise from that cracked leather chair, and she realized he wasn't very much taller than she. "I ask two things of you," he said without turning. "First, that you never let it be known that our marriage is anything other than one of affection."

Eloise pressed her lips together. "Agreed," she answered with a decided nod.

"Second . . ." He finally turned to face her. "If the child you carry is a boy, I'd like a son of my own."

Her face paled, but she nodded once more.

"Very well. Go home. I'll come speak to your father this afternoon."

He'd kept his word. They married quietly at the keep with only her parents and his few servants attending. Her father settled a dowry on her that she applied toward renovating the spaces in the keep she frequented, and she never entered the village again. Before long, Lachlan was born. Because she didn't leave the castle, the date of his birth had not become known in the village, nor was it questioned. She'd kept her word, too. The Marquess got a faithful wife and also a son of his own, and their years together had been tolerable if not everything of which she'd once dreamed.

"Mother?" Caught up in memories, Eloise hadn't heard her youngest son enter the room. "You look like you're a hundred miles away."

She smiled. "Just woolgathering, Lewis," she said, and presented her cheek for his kiss.

Short in stature and already balding in his early twenties, Lewiston Kimball so resembled his father it was astonishing. The differences between the brothers had eventually been noted and whispered in the village, but the family had held its secrets close, and when Andrew Kimball died the year before in a hunting accident, Lachlan had assumed the title without challenge. Lewiston, who had been with the old marquess when a boar charged and forced him over a cliff, casting him to his death in a deep ravine, had not seemed to completely recover from the incident, in any case. He began to suffer from periods of depression, sometimes disappearing into his chamber for days at a time, which seemed to remove any question of suitability.

Besides, everyone agreed, Lachlan just *looked* as though he should be the marquess.

Five

London, 1815

"Ah, Thorne." The Marquess of Roth smiled with genuine pleasure and stood, extending a hand to his good friend. "What brings you here? You're typically nowhere near London during husband-hunting time."

Sebastian chuckled at Gareth's description of the glittering social whirl that was the London Season, shook his hand and pulled out a chair. "I'm meeting Asheburton, who will be staying in my town house for a while. He intended to purchase one of his own, but I offered mine, since I so seldom use it."

"Ashe is coming to Town for the Season?" Gareth raised a brow. "That can only mean one thing."

Sebastian looked decidedly grim. "Exactly. I've done all I can to dissuade him."

Gareth laughed softly. "Well, you won't find help from this quarter. Marriage, after a bit of a rough start, is treating me just fine." He reached for a deck of cards on the green baize-covered table and began shuffling them. "Hunt and Jon should be joining us shortly. They're dropping their wives at my place for the afternoon. The Ackerly twins have just arrived for their debut, and there is, apparently, a great deal of planning to be done. Gowns and such, I'm told."

The duke grimaced. "No wonder you're here instead of

there." He looked up and smiled. "White's is an excellent haven."

The Marquess of Asheburton appeared, walking up to the table with Trevor Caldwell and Jonathon Lloyd, the Earls of Huntwick and Seth. The men exchanged greetings and then sat down, oblivious to the stares of the club's other patrons. It wasn't often one could find such a powerful and influential group gathered around a single table.

A footman arrived with drinks, served them and then disappeared, allowing the five men to get down to the serious business of trying to relieve one another of bits of their rather considerable fortunes.

After thirty minutes of solid play, Gareth pushed back his chair, stretched out his legs, and reached for his glass of port. "Thorne tells me you're looking for a wife, Ashe."

Lachlan raised a brow. "Indeed. One hopes the market is favorable."

Trevor grinned. "You make it sound like a business transaction. As if one were proposing a limited partnership in, say, a shipping venture, or purchasing a new property." The men all chuckled.

Lachlan smiled. "But isn't that precisely why one marries?"

His perspective, they knew, was the prevailing one. Most *ton* marriages were either arranged to increase the fortunes of one or both families, or they took place simply to add a new title to the family tree. Love, for the most part, was reserved for those below their social circle. Even extramarital affairs, commonplace in their set, were seldom about emotion.

Gareth shook his head. "Not if you marry an Ackerly."

Trevor just nodded.

Sebastian gave his cousin a level look. Sighing, he said,

"If you insist on ignoring my advice to eschew marriage altogether, at least be reasonable enough to avoid the mistakes Roth and Hunt have made." Both men laughed, taking the statement without rancor. The group had all gone through the rather tumultuous courtships and weddings of Grace and Faith Ackerly together, so there was little arguing with the comment.

Lachlan had been party to only some of the drama surrounding the marriages. "To be quite honest," he said, "I was hoping—since I haven't a clue who is and who is not available—to enlist your guidance."

"My guidance? Typically," spoke up Sebastian, his voice sardonic, "there's no difficulty distinguishing the available young ladies. The instant you step foot inside a ballroom, they'll flock around you like a gaggle of very colorful geese."

Jonathon Lloyd shook his head at the duke's jaded viewpoint. "Our wives would likely be of more help in that capacity." He looked uncomfortable. "Perhaps you might tell us of your requirements and we could see who they know."

Sebastian snorted. "A list of requirements? He's not purchasing a horse."

Lachlan looked thoughtful. "Well, if you think about it, in a way I actually am." He signaled a footman, who scurried quickly to the table. "A round of drinks for the gentlemen, please, and a pen and paper."

The man hurried away to retrieve the requested items, and Lachlan glanced around the table. Trevor and Gareth looked amused. Sebastian merely looked bored. Jon frowned. "Surely you're not planning on making an *actual* list, are you? You're really going to write it down?"

Lachlan shrugged. "Why not?"

To that, the men had no response. Possible damning evidence aside, this was, when one considered all factors, a rather sensible approach—much more sensible than the approaches used by Trevor and Gareth.

Jon, whose marriage to Amanda had been arranged before they'd even met, shook his head. "I don't know that I quite expected an afternoon of cards to culminate in *this*."

Trevor spoke up. "I, for one, am enjoying it immensely. Tell us, Ashe . . . what qualities do you seek in a wife?"

The footman returned with their drinks. He served everyone, placed the pen and paper at Lachlan's elbow, bowed, and disappeared.

Lachlan considered. "A woman of strong mind and fortitude."

Trevor grabbed the writing implements and jotted that down.

"Fortitude?" Gareth tilted his head quizzically.

"You haven't met Ashe's mother," Sebastian said. "Fortitude is a necessity."

"Someone biddable and sweet," Lachlan continued, as if he hadn't been interrupted. "I don't want to spend the rest of my life arguing over dinner."

"Well, that narrows the list of possibilities significantly," Trevor said. He shook his head at the developing profile and gave a hoot of laughter. "Strong but obedient. Does such a creature exist?"

Lachlan ignored him. "An impeccable and unquestionable lineage. Wealth is not a requirement, but I want no aspersions cast upon my children, nor do I wish there to ever be speculation as to my son's right to the title."

The men all fell silent. They were among the only people in the world who knew the truth about Lachlan's father, and to a man could be counted upon to take that knowledge to their graves. Jon cleared his throat. "Is that all?"

Lachlan nodded and then added, almost as an afterthought, "Someone who wouldn't mind living in Scotland instead of London. I do not care at all for the social whirl." He paused. "Any ideas?"

Trevor glanced at Gareth and then Jon. As the married members of the group, they were the most informed about the statuses of the *ton*'s daughters. The list of available candidates was staggeringly small. "Lucinda Harcourt," he offered in a dubious voice.

Sebastian shook his head. "Her mama has shoved her beneath my nose for the past three Seasons. The poor girl is a complete henwit. Attractive, but no substance whatsoever."

"Katherine Davis," suggested Jon.

"Well, she's certainly intelligent, possesses the required fortitude, and appears biddable and sweet," said Gareth. His voice shook with suppressed laughter.

"And," added Trevor, grinning widely, "her lineage is unquestionable."

Lachlan raised his brows in mute inquiry then glanced at Sebastian.

"She's everything they say she is, and attractive as well," his cousin confirmed.

"Then what is so amusing about her?"

"If your goal is to marry in order to beget an heir, you'll want to consider someone a bit younger. She's at least forty, and she's already buried three husbands."

Lachlan sat back. "I can't believe that, out of the hundreds of young ladies paraded before Society every season, the four of you can't come up with anyone except a henwit and a thrice-over widow."

Trevor looked apologetic, then brightened. "Your best bet might actually be one of the Ackerly twins." His green eyes sparkled. "Charity and—"

Lachlan grimaced. "No, thank you. The word 'biddable' should never be mentioned in the same sentence with that young lady." His eyes turned thoughtful. "Amity, though . . ."

Trevor nodded. "If you can stand being around Charity while you court her, I agree that Amity would make you a very suitable wife." He smiled and glanced at Sebastian to include him. "They'll both be attending the Corwins' opening ball with me and Grace this evening, if you'd like to join us."

"I'll pass," said Sebastian, not at all interested in fighting off hordes of desperate debutantes and their even more maneuvering mamas. He pushed back his chair and stood up to leave. "I'm sure I have something suitable for you to wear at the town house," he told Lachlan, "since you've not had time to unpack, and I know better than to leave the decision with that bulldog you call a valet. I'll meet you there." He nodded at the rest of the table. "Good day, gentlemen."

Lachlan watched his cousin go and sighed, resigned to taking the plunge into London's glittering social pool and praying he wouldn't end up all wet. Turning back to Trevor, he asked, "What time?"

Six

"*I* think the simplest thing to do is to order two of everything."

Charity was standing near the long table, staring in wonder at the brightly colored bolts of rich fabric, but she whirled around in sudden horror. "Heavens, no!" she exclaimed. "Amity's taste is far different from mine. *So* dull." She smiled at her twin to soften her words. "I mean, she always looks lovely, but she's a bit more conservative than I am."

Faith gave her sister a no-nonsense look from her comfortable seat on the sofa. Dr. Matthew Meadows, a physician and friend of her husband, who had traveled from his home near Gareth and Faith's country estate, had given her strict orders to stay in bed until her child was born. Her pregnancy had been difficult to this point, and Gareth feared for the health of both his wife and first child.

"Now, Charity," she reasoned. "Debutantes traditionally dress in demure, conservative colors. After you've made your bow and found a husband you'll be able to dress as you wish."

Charity's brow furrowed, the obstinate look her sisters knew well marring her delicate features. "If we both wear the same bland clothing, nobody will be able to tell us apart!"

"She has a valid point," put in Grace. "And it isn't like she'll set Society on its collective ear by wearing brighter hues. After all, I did it."

Amanda Lloyd, the Countess of Seth and Faith's sister-in-law, laughed musically. "You *did* set Society on its ear, Grace."

The Countess of Huntwick looked entirely unrepentant. "Yes, but not because of my clothing." She smiled at a sudden memory. "Well, except perhaps that one time I dressed up as Trevor's male cousin so that I could go play cards . . ." She trailed off as Faith cleared her throat and gave her a dampening look.

"Charity did that, too," put in Amity with a fond smile. "On dance-lesson day at Madame Capdepon's Etiquette School."

Amanda looked impressed. "She's either braver or more foolish than you, Grace. At least you did it at night, when the odds of being caught were slim."

Everyone laughed.

"Well, then," said Charity, giving Faith a triumphant look. "It's all settled. Brighter colors for me."

She picked up the book she'd brought along. Although she had very much looked forward to the Season, she hadn't counted on all the preparation that went into the blasted thing. Gowns, shoes, wraps, hats . . . She'd been posed and stood and measured within an inch of her young life, and she was heartily tired of it. This morning she had been on her way to the garden to read for a bit when Amanda and Grace cornered and herded her into the sitting room for more gown measurements.

"Since Amity and I are the same size, you won't even need to measure me," she suggested.

Faith folded her lips and looked as though she intended to say something, but Amity spoke first. "That's right," she agreed. "You just go on out and enjoy the sunshine. We'll choose everything for you. Madame has some truly lovely laces and ribbons, and I'm positive we can make your color-ful gowns quite . . . extraordinary."

Madame Toulesant nodded with enthusiasm. "We will make Mees Charity sparkle like zee jewel!"

Charity, halfway to the door, stopped in her tracks. Although she favored brighter colors, she also much preferred a plain, simple line to her gowns, utterly eschewing ribbons and other such frippery. Amity knew this. She turned slowly and glared at her twin.

Amity smiled back sweetly.

"Oh, all right," Charity groused, tossing her book on a chair upholstered in a bright marigold silk. "Let's get on with it."

With Charity properly corralled, the modiste and her assistants got to work. More measurements were taken, colors chosen, and new patterns discussed. Day dresses, walking dresses, morning gowns, ball gowns, wraps, hats, accessories, and accoutrements were all in order. While the work was going on around them, the married ladies discussed the latest *on dits,* of which there were relatively few, since the Season was just getting underway.

"Therese Thomasson-Sinclair is going to try, yet again, to find a husband this year." Grace shook her head. "Twenty-five years old, and still she comes out every Season with impossibly high standards."

"Why hasn't she found anyone to meet them?" Charity fingered a sumptuous cobalt silk and sent a questioning look toward Faith, who nodded approval.

"She wants nothing less than a marquess," replied Amanda, adding, "and she has precious little to offer in return."

"Is she ugly?"

"Charity!" admonished Amity in a gentle voice.

Charity shrugged. "It's a legitimate question. If nobody has wanted her in all these years, and she has no fortune to offer, it stands to reason that she must be ugly. Men still marry pretty girls who don't have money."

"She's not ugly, though she's definitely not the prettiest girl in any given Season," said Amanda. "And it isn't as though she hasn't had offers. It's just that her family has only moderate wealth, and her conversation isn't at all engaging. Still, she sets her cap, every year, for only the Most Eligible."

"Which means," said Grace, her blue eyes dancing, "that she'll be after Lachlan Kimball this year, if what Trevor told me this morning is true."

All eyes instantly swiveled her way.

"Supposedly," she continued, "the Marquess of Asheburton has come to London to find a wife, after which he intends to whisk her off to that castle of his in Scotland."

Amity stared. "He doesn't truly live in a castle, does he?"

"Nobody really knows. Only Sebastian has been there, and getting him to talk about anything is like pulling teeth."

Charity wriggled impatiently while one of the poor seamstresses tried, in vain, to measure the length of her arm from elbow to wrist. "It's probably some crumbling old medieval keep with dirty floors and ventilation problems. One is perpetually cold in the winters and hot in the summers."

Amity laughed. "Be nice. The marquess is a good friend to this family."

Faith looked bemused. "He *is* rather reclusive, though, which means visits to Town might be few and far between. Imagine going to live in that godforsaken place forever, completely out of touch with everything and everyone you have ever known." She shuddered delicately. "How far do you think it is to Scotland?"

The women all looked at one another. "I don't think it's *that* far. People elope there," said Amanda slowly.

"Yes, but that's just to the border." Grace frowned. "Does anyone even know where in Scotland Asheburton lives?"

The room fell silent. Finally, Charity spoke up. "Oh, it doesn't matter. It's not like anyone in this room is going to marry him, anyway."

"I'll be in Town once or twice a month during the Season. Other than that, you have the place to yourself." Sebastian walked into the downstairs study. "Brandy?" he asked over his shoulder.

Lachlan nodded. "With any luck, I won't be here the entire Season."

Sebastian made a snorting sound that could, by a great stretch of the imagination, have been considered a laugh. "You'll find yourself beset by matchmaking mamas the moment you step inside that ballroom." He handed his cousin his drink, and they sat down.

"Well, as inconvenient as that sounds, at least it will allow me to come up with a list of prospects fairly quickly."

The two men sat in silence a moment, and then Sebastian cleared his throat. "I'm afraid most of my staff is at Blackthorne. Feel free to hire whomever you need."

"Thank you. Given the temporary nature of my stay in London, both Roth and Hunt have offered to send competent help from their own staffs."

Sebastian raised a brow. "Is that so? Don't be surprised to see a rather short footman in Huntwick livery show up."

"Oh?"

"A favorite of Grace Caldwell's. The man actually made it inside the doors at White's under her orders. Have Roth tell you *that* story sometime."

Lachlan smiled. "So the wives will plant spies?"

Sebastian finished his drink and stood. "You can be certain of it. Now, shall we go see what my valet left in my wardrobe? We can't have you looking for a wife without making sure you are properly turned out."

Seven

Stop fidgeting, Charity." Cleo Egerton glowered from across the coach.

"I can't help it. Something's poking me." She tried reaching around to the middle of her back with no success and wriggled some more.

The twins were clad in gowns borrowed from Grace for the occasion, as they hadn't anticipated going out until the Season officially began, which wasn't for another week. When the men returned from their afternoon of cards, however, the wives learned Huntwick had invited the Marquess of Asheburton to meet them at the Corwins' ball, and that he had specifically mentioned Amity and Charity would be there. At this point, the sitting room had erupted into a flurry of frenzied activity. The men quickly and wisely retreated to Gareth's study.

Grace dispatched a footman to the Caldwell town house to have her maid send a selection of gowns, as Faith was far too tall to lend any of her own. While they waited, hair, jewelry, and other accessories were fussed over. When the gowns arrived, Grace spread them across the bed in which Faith was now comfortably ensconced, leaning on a collection of freshly fluffed pillows. After some deliberation, two gowns were chosen and the rest sent back.

Amity had handled it all with her usual quiet good humor. Charity, however, was cross.

"I don't even *like* the Marquess of Asheburton. He's

unpleasant," she muttered as the carriage rumbled along. Her twin hid a smile and managed, just barely, to keep from pointing out that Charity was being rather unpleasant herself. "And this dress is too frilly."

"Nonsense," soothed Amity. "There's only one bow on the whole dress, tied in the back, and you won't feel it anymore when we get out of the coach. Just sit forward a bit until we get there."

Aunt Cleo, who had picked them up in her carriage since Grace still had to go home and get dressed, shook her head. "I hope you're not going to be this much trouble all Season."

Charity bit her lip, instantly apologetic. "I'm sorry, Aunt Cleo. I don't mean to be trouble."

Her expression was so contrite that her relative couldn't remain put out. "I know you don't, child," she said, then reached over to pat Charity's knee. "Just try not to say everything that pops into your head before you think it through."

Charity nodded and looked out the window, wondering again why she had wanted so badly to have a London Season. The stories Grace and Faith told had seemed so glittery and fun. She'd had no idea there were so many rules and standards, or that everything one did was so closely watched and, worse, commented upon.

Amity slipped an arm around her shoulder and gave a squeeze. "It'll be fine," she whispered. "We'll simply stick together."

The smile Charity gave in response was grateful, if a trifle wobbly.

Before the twins knew it, the carriage slowed and then came to a stop. The doors opened and a footman appeared to help them down. They joined Grace and Trevor, who had also just arrived, on the walk outside a large town house teeming with activity.

Charity tilted her head back and stared in wonder at the building's sparkling facade. Her eyes filled with awe and she instantly forgot her trepidation from moments before. "It's so magical," she murmured.

And it was. Couples floated like bright tropical birds by the bank of windows at street level. Others strolled in groups, ladies laughing gaily behind ornate fans. The men were just as colorfully garbed, in satin breeches, embroidered waistcoats, and intricately tied cravats, some starched to such stiff points Charity feared they might nick the undersides of their chins.

"Come on, Charity!"

The group had started up the wide marble steps to the entrance. Reluctantly, Charity tore her fascinated gaze from the view and hurried after them.

An hour later, her most recent dance partner returned her to her family, breathless and flushed with laughter. A group of young men was gathered around Grace and Aunt Cleo, waiting for an introduction to one of the twins and the chance to add his name to their dance cards. In mock desperation she held up a hand.

"No, please," she protested with a smile. "I need a few moments to rest."

Amity, no less besieged, linked an arm through her sister's. "Perhaps a short stroll on the terrace is in order." When instant offers of accompaniment were offered, Amity laughed. "*Alone*," she clarified.

Charity tossed an apologetic glance in the general direction of the assembly but allowed her sister to pull her toward the row of double French doors through which could wander guests who desired a breath of fresh air. She and her sister strolled to a quiet spot and stopped.

Charity fanned herself vigorously. "My goodness! I hadn't expected such a crush of people!" But her eyes glowed with happiness.

Amity nodded in agreement. "Grace says it is far worse than during her debut, when nobody really knew our family. I suppose the possibility of a connection to a marquess and an earl makes us all the more desirable."

Charity frowned. "How does one know, then, if the interest is genuine? In us rather than our connections."

"I guess one doesn't straightaway." Amity's voice was soft. "I'd imagine it becomes evident over time, however." She stared out into the garden with a dreamy smile, her eyes reflecting the dancing light from torches placed at intervals along the walkway.

Charity gave her sister a long, slow look. "Good lord, Amity. You're going to go all sheep-eyed over the first man who figures out to act like a stray dog. That's all he needs to do to worm his way into your heart, isn't it?"

"Most certainly not," protested Amity, but she laughed, knowing the accusation wasn't entirely unfounded. She had filled their household with rescued pets from the time she could walk far enough to find them. All any animal, including those of the human variety, had to do was look at her with wide, soulful eyes, and she was instantly lost.

Charity opened her mouth to continue, but she was stopped as someone opened a door nearby and the muffled sounds of the ball grew louder. She turned to see who had come out on the terrace, a bright smile of greeting on her face.

The smile slowly faded. Walking toward them, his steps slow, measured, and deliberate, was the Marquess of Asheburton. He was dressed all in black, unlike most of the other male guests, who preferred styles more flamboyant and colorful. Where the other men mostly wore breeches, Lachlan Kimball chose unfashionable trousers. His coat was of a dark superfine instead of a more garish embroidered satin, and his cravat was tied in a loose, simple style at his throat.

It was a style of which Charity found she reluctantly approved, until she realized he'd stopped before them and that she was staring. Embarrassed, she scowled. "What are *you* doing here?" she asked.

Amity poked her in the side in silent admonishment for her rudeness.

"Well," Charity said crossly to her twin. "Trevor said he hates London, he hates balls, and I'm pretty sure, given the way he acted at Faith's wedding,"—she swung her gaze back to Lachlan—"that he hates me."

Lachlan bowed slightly from the waist, but his eyes never left Charity's and he did not deny her accusation. "How fortuitous, Miss Ackerly. You've spared me the awkwardness of trying to identify one twin from the other."

Despite there being no specific insult in his wording, the obvious indication that he felt he could tell them apart based purely on demeanor was not lost on Charity. She colored and drew herself up as tall as she was able, her eyes spitting blue fire. "I think I'll go back into the ball, Amity. It has become *quite* crowded out here." She brushed past Lachlan without addressing him and disappeared inside.

Lachlan gave Amity a rueful look. "Your sister and I seem to have difficulty communicating," he said, a note of apology in his voice.

Amity's eyes, unlike her sister's, were alive with fun. "Oh, I think you both did fairly well. You managed to say

precisely what you think of one another in very few words."
She grinned.

Lachlan let that go. He smiled at her instead. "How are
you enjoying the Season, Miss Ackerly?"

She smiled back. "It's the first ball for me and Charity,
and it's been very nice. A bit more active than I expected."

"Quite a change from Pelthamshire, yes?"

She nodded. "As it is for you from Scotland, my lord."

His eyes, which had been a flinty gray seconds before,
softened to a liquid silver, his love evident for his home-
land. Amity caught her breath and then felt her heart warm
as he spoke, his voice low, vibrant, and resonant. "Yes, very
different," he agreed.

Silence fell. After a few moments Lachlan cleared his
throat. "Would you care to dance with me, Miss Ackerly?"

"Why, I think that would be lovely," she replied, and
placed her gloved hand on his proffered arm.

He escorted her inside and returned her to her family for a
proper, public introduction. To his relief, Charity was nowhere to be found. Lachlan grasped Trevor's hand and gave
it a hearty shake, and then he clapped his friend on the shoulder. "Good to see you, Hunt. I encountered Miss Ackerly on
the terrace, and hoped to gain permission to dance with her."

Trevor grinned broadly. "Barring any disagreement from
the ladies, I think that's a capital idea." He stepped to the
side and swept a hand toward Aunt Cleo. "I believe you've
met Lady Cleo Egerton?"

Lachlan bowed over the older lady's extended hand. "My
lady," he said. "It is a pleasure to see you again."

When he straightened, she was giving him a probing,
assessing look. "So it's to be Amity, then? I can't say I expected that. I suppose it is fine, though it won't be nearly as
entertaining for me."

Lachlan raised his brows, not quite sure what to say to this harridan's odd and outrageous statement.

Grace choked back a gasp of horrified laughter. "And, of course," she said hastily, stepping forward and extending her hand, "there's no need to introduce me. I'm very happy to see you again, Lord Asheburton."

"Likewise, my lady," Lachlan replied. He turned to face Amity, and held out his arm once more. "Shall we?"

Hundreds of eyes followed them to the dance floor, all speculating about the unusual appearance of the Marquess of Asheburton at a Town event. Even those who had never made his acquaintance knew him by description and reputation. Most came to the immediate—and correct—conclusion that he sought a wife. *And,* it was noted with narrowed eyes by the matchmaking mamas, it appeared for the third Season in a row an Ackerly sister was well on her way to knocking the Most Eligible off the list of prospects.

One particular set of eyes widened in surprise and then immediately narrowed. Charity Ackerly watched her twin sister step into Lachlan Kimball's arms, and felt a surge of . . . what? She furrowed her brow, unable to identify the curious feeling that was making her stomach twist itself into an ever-tightening knot. She gripped the railing of the balcony that encircled and overlooked the teeming ballroom below. Her sickened feeling increased until she finally looked away, her eyes skipping over the crowd. They collided with those of her aunt, who stood just outside the circle of people that comprised Charity's family. Cleo Egerton was looking up at her niece with unconcealed glee.

The gnawing feeling in her gut forgotten, Charity lifted her chin and stared back until the older lady looked away, only to lean over and whisper something to Grace, who glanced up at Charity and laughed. She gave her younger sister a wave.

Instead of waving back, Charity pushed away from the railing and walked along the balcony until she reached the curving staircase that led to the ballroom. She lifted her skirts slightly and began a swift, graceful descent. Once she'd gained the main floor, she crossed the ballroom, making her way through the milling throng with quick, dainty steps. She stopped when she reached her destination and frowned as she glanced from one smiling face to another.

Aunt Cleo laughed. "You'll never find a husband if you intend to stand around on balconies looking like a thundercloud instead of dancing, my dear."

Charity opened her mouth to respond but then bit back the retort. Behind her assembled family she saw Anthony Iverson, the young and dashing heir of the Earl of Endlecourt, making his way toward them, an inviting smile on his handsome face.

"Excellent advice, Aunt Cleo. I shall dance with the very next gentleman who asks."

With Lachlan Kimball's mocking grin and her aunt's words prominent in her mind, she turned a bright, dazzling smile on the approaching young man. She waited while he requested an introduction from the Earl of Huntwick, then curtsied gracefully and accepted his invitation to dance. The couple glided off to the dance floor just as Lachlan was returning with Amity.

Amity smiled in her sister's direction. "Who is that dancing with Charity?"

"Anthony Iverson," Grace replied in a distracted voice. She looked troubled, and turned to Aunt Cleo. "Wasn't there some rumor last Season about Iverson and someone's wife?"

Cleo furrowed her brow. "A duel, if I recall correctly," she mused, then lifted her cane to point it accusingly in Trevor's direction. "Why in the world did you introduce Charity to that blackguard?"

Trevor eyed the end of her ebony walking aid with understandable trepidation, having been its target on more than one occasion. "I know his father. Good man," he replied. "Don't you think 'blackguard' is a trifle harsh for someone you only *think* 'may have been involved in something or other with someone's wife'?"

Grace ignored that bit of logic and glared at him. "How could you not know better than to send my sister off to dance with someone of questionable reputation?"

Trevor snorted. "In the first place, finding anyone with an unblemished reputation in Society verges on the impossible. In the second place, it is entirely likely that I missed large chunks of gossip from last Season, since I spent the bulk of it trying to keep *you* from interfering in Gareth and Faith's marriage."

Grace colored and looked a bit sheepish. "Well, I suppose there's nothing to be done about it now," she said, "except to wait for their dance to end." She watched the couple glide around the floor with anxious eyes. If Charity's bright eyes and animated face was any indication, she was enjoying the dance very much indeed.

Lachlan listened to the exchange for a moment, but his eyes weren't on the dancing couple like everyone else's. Instead, they swept the crowd that ringed the dance floor. Women were nudging one another and whispering, some with obvious malice. It had not escaped his notice during his dance with Amity that the young ladies in attendance had a less than favorable opinion of the twins. And while he knew it was largely due to jealousy because of the matches their older sisters had made, he also knew that something had to be done to distract the crowd, and quickly. The only way he could think to accomplish that was to give them something else to watch and discuss.

He turned to the eldest member of the group. "Lady Egerton?"

Cleo didn't even spare him a glance. "Not now, young man."

Lachlan almost smiled at her impatient dismissal. "Oh, but I really feel as though this cannot wait."

She gave him an irritated look. "What is it?"

"Well," he began, and sketched her a gallant little bow, "I hoped you might honor me with a dance." He straightened and sent her a speaking look, his eyes willing her to accept.

Surprised, Grace glanced away from Charity and her partner. "Aunt Cleo doesn't dance!"

At that, Cleo snorted. "I most certainly do!" She thrust her cane at Trevor, who took it from her with a wide grin.

"Yes, Grace," he said solemnly. "She most certainly does."

Lachlan hid a smile at the old lady's indignation. He extended an arm, which she took more firmly than he would have imagined possible, and then walked along beside him with surprising agility. Lachlan had to shorten his strides only a little, and he found himself wondering at the actual depth of her need for the cane.

When they reached the dance floor, she turned to face him and they fell quite neatly into step. "That was brilliantly handled, young man." She looked reluctant to part with the compliment.

He smiled. "What was, my lady? Managing to convince a beautiful woman to dance with me?"

"You are altogether too charming, Asheburton. Flattery

will get you nowhere with me," she chided, though she flushed with pleasure. She looked over his shoulder, scanning the crowd, most of whom were now staring in fascination at the unprecedented spectacle of the large, powerfully built marquess dancing with a lame old woman. Lachlan had to jerk his head back quickly when she turned her head in order to avoid being smacked by the lime green feather bobbing helplessly in her magenta turban. A smattering of laughter rolled through the watching crowd.

It went unnoticed by Cleo. She continued, "Strategy, however—*that* will get you an open invitation to visit my nieces."

"You are gracious, my lady." He could tell, despite her stalwart effort to hide it, that she was tiring. Luckily the music was drawing to a close.

"Bah!" Cleo made a face. "I am many things, young man, but 'gracious' is certainly not one of them."

Satisfied that they had drawn the attention away from Anthony and Charity, Lachlan smiled and drew the old woman's hand through his arm, offering his strength and support in a way that wouldn't be obvious to the crowd of onlookers. As they left the floor, a few people began applauding. Cleo smiled and acknowledged the accolades with a regal nod of her head, first to the left and then to the right. By the time they reached their group, the ovation was deafening.

Lachlan saw Trevor hand Cleo her cane. His friend gave the woman a grin of admiration and a little bow of respect, then he intercepted Charity and Iverson, who were returning from the dance floor as well, largely unnoticed. Smoothly Trevor escorted the young buck away from the others. "Iverson, I'm so glad you're back. I wondered if I might entrust you with a message for your father."

The men's voices faded, and Lachlan watched their retreating backs.

Grace breathed a sigh of relief, tossed Lachlan a grateful smile and turned to the twins. "I think," she declared, "we should call it a night."

Eight

"Charity, you really shouldn't lie like that," admonished Faith quietly from the bed.

"I know," her sister agreed pleasantly. Her voice was muffled by the pillow she'd pulled over her face to keep out of her eyes the morning sun that slanted in through the window, and she lay on the floor with her feet propped on the seat of a chair, her skirts inching up her calves. "But there's nobody here except you, me, and Amity."

"And Gareth, who could walk in at any time, and the servants," said Faith.

"And Dr. Meadows," came a male voice from the doorway.

Surprised, Charity peeked from beneath the pillow and then rolled onto her side. She scrambled to her feet, hastily shaking the wrinkles out of her skirt, her legs now decently covered. "Good gracious," she muttered.

Dr. Matthew Meadows, the young physician Gareth Lloyd had befriended through the frequent injuries he suffered while "helping" renovate his estate, strolled into the room with a smile, his brown eyes twinkling. "Just stopping in to check on my favorite patient," he announced cheerfully. Winking at Charity he said, "It's okay, I'm a doctor. I've seen my fair share of female ankles."

Amity laughed. Charity colored, stammered an excuse about reading in the garden, and promptly escaped.

Faith shook her head. "Sweet of you to call me your favorite patient. Especially since Gareth dragged you from Rothmere to London to dance attendance on me. I believe that currently makes me your *only* patient. And I'm doing quite well," she added.

"I'll just step out into the garden with Charity," Amity suggested in a quiet voice. She turned to leave the room.

"No need," replied Matthew. "I can already see that Faith is right where I've told her to stay, and that she's looking as radiant and healthy as ever." He grinned at Amity. "You and your sister keep her from becoming bored."

"We do our best." Amity smiled. "Charity pops in and out to make her laugh, but she can't sit still for very long. Still, Faith and I have enjoyed one another's company very much."

"Excellent." The young physician stared down into Amity's bright eyes, and he seemed to forget, for a moment, that Faith was even in the room. Faith glanced back and forth between the two, noting Amity's heightened color and the intensity of Matthew's gaze. She almost hated to spoil the moment but knew it would become awkward when the pair realized they'd been staring.

She delicately cleared her throat, and then stifled a laugh when her sister jumped in reaction. "Amity, I don't suppose you'd be kind enough to walk Dr. Meadows out, would you?"

"Of course." Her sister covered the blush that was stealing across her face by ducking her head and pretending to straighten the extra blanket folded across the end of Faith's bed while Matthew said his good-byes.

Downstairs, unbeknownst to the trio in Faith's bedroom, the Marquess of Asheburton had arrived. "I'd like to see Miss Amity Ackerly, please," he told the butler who'd wrenched open the door after his second knock.

Desmond scowled up at him. "Have you been announced?" he demanded.

Lachlan, who rather thought it was the butler's job to announce him, remained nonetheless patient. "Well," he said, "I've only just arrived."

"*Un*announced," declared Desmond, and he sighed heavily. He turned away, muttering something under his breath about constant interruptions, and then looked back at the marquess, who stood just outside the open door. "Are you coming in or not?"

His patience rapidly fading, Lachlan raised his brows and gave the butler a dampening look, and then he stepped inside, wondering why Gareth Lloyd continued to employ the man.

Desmond, who had seen Charity slip out to the back garden and steadfastly refused to try to distinguish one twin from the other, led Lachlan through the foyer and into a lovely solar. It was glassed on three sides, with doors that opened out into the back gardens, and Charity sat across the lawn on a blanket, quietly reading, her back to the house. The butler pointed in her direction and walked abruptly away.

Irritated by the servant's utter lack of professionalism, Lachlan watched him go and then stepped outside. He stood a moment on the terrace, hoping the girl would look up and see him. She presented a fetching picture, clad in a simple cobalt morning dress, her strawberry blonde curls caught at the nape of her neck with a jaunty matching ribbon. She twirled a wayward strand of hair with a graceful finger and continued reading, utterly unaware that she was being watched.

When she didn't look up, Lachlan descended the wide, shallow steps and began crossing the grass. He cleared his throat lightly as he drew near, loath to startle her, but Charity, completely absorbed in her book, still did not sense him. He stopped a few paces from her blanket.

"Good morning, Miss Ackerly."

Charity glanced up in surprise to see the man with whom she had sparred from the beginning of their acquaintance. This time, however, the expression on his face contained no trace of censure, disapproval, or annoyance. Instead, he looked unexpectedly amiable and quite handsome. Her heart skipped a beat, and then began pounding at twice its normal rate, as if to catch up. She bit her lip, oddly at a loss for words.

"Good morning, my lord," she finally managed in a quiet voice.

Lachlan took a step closer. "I was hoping I wouldn't startle you," he said, then indicated the space beside her on the blanket. "May I?"

Charity nodded and closed the book, her finger marking the page she'd been reading. Inexplicably shy, she looked down for a moment, and then chanced another peek at him while he was getting settled.

The Marquess of Asheburton was different from all the men of her acquaintance. Tall and powerfully built, he exuded an aura of barely leashed strength and subdued fury. Every time she was near him, she felt as though she had to hold her breath, almost as though something spectacular were about to happen. It was the same feeling she got when a storm was about to break. The very air was charged with crackling tension, soaked with energy. It made her ache for . . . She frowned. For what?

Lachlan stretched out his legs and leaned back on his hands. His gaze roved the garden before returning to settle on the girl who sat beside him, her legs curled beneath her skirts, her wide blue eyes locked on his face. The moment his gaze found hers, which was filled with an odd yearning, he was lost.

Charity held her breath and then let it out slowly on a single word. "Gray," she whispered, unaware that she'd spoken. His lips curved in a soft smile. Something lurched inside her, and she felt the odd knot of tension that had settled in her midsection unfurl and spread outward, warm, liquid, and comforting. Because, when the Marquess of Asheburton smiled, the world fell away beneath her. His face, normally stern and cold and forbidding, seemingly chiseled from icy granite, thawed and became a visage of sheer male beauty. His eyes melted from a flinty silver to a soft pewter.

The book she'd been holding slipped from her grasp and landed on his hand, causing him to glance down and break the spell. He picked it up and handed the volume back to her. "I'm afraid you've lost your place, Miss Ackerly."

"Oh," she said, her voice a bit dreamy. Her eyes widened. "Oh!" she repeated, and composed herself. "I shall find it easily enough later." She took the book. "How clumsy of me. I hope I didn't hurt your hand."

The skin at the corners of his eyes crinkled as his smile broadened. "No," he assured her, a tinge of amusement in his voice. "I'm quite uninjured."

She tilted her head to the side. "Why do you not have a Scottish accent, my lord?"

"A couple reasons," he replied. "First, my mother refused to allow it, although my father's accent was decided and pronounced. Second, I was educated by an Englishman." He met her eyes. "My accent manifests occasionally. Typically when I am tired or provoked."

Charity cast about wildly in her mind, searching for a topic that would preserve the unspoken truce that seemed to have arisen between them. "Do you have plans this evening, my lord?" she blurted, then felt her face grow warm. Now it would seem as though she were prodding him to offer his escort.

Sure enough, Lachlan's smile faltered. "Why, yes. As a matter of fact I'd hoped to ask if you would care to accompany me to the Upshaws' ball."

Charity's blush intensified, giving her alabaster cheeks a becoming peach glow, and causing the aquamarine color of her eyes to intensify. She closed them and pressed a hand against her hot cheek. "I'm so sorry, my lord," she said, stifling a groan. "How unutterably rude and leading of me." She covered her mouth with her other hand in an effort to stem the tide of embarrassing statements pouring forth, and stared downward, no longer able to meet his eyes.

Lachlan thought she was adorable. He sat up straight and reached for the hand that was covering her mouth, pulled it away, and then crooked a finger under her chin and lifted her face to his. "It really *was* my intention to come here and ask you to join me this evening, Miss Ackerly. Will you?" His voice was husky and low. "Please?"

Charity held her breath and leaned toward him, drawn by some force she couldn't explain. She looked up with vulnerable eyes, her lips slightly parted, soft, open, and inviting. She nodded agreement.

Lachlan smiled and smoothed his thumb along her jaw line. "So sweet," he murmured, then cupped her chin and, dipping his head, brought her mouth to his. Lightly, softly, he brushed his lips along hers, drawing out the moment, delaying his first taste of her, tormenting himself with the barest of touches.

Charity's heart was pounding as she waited for the kiss to engulf her senses, to carry her away on gossamer wings of passion until she swooned with delight. Because in every description of a first kiss she'd ever read in the silly romantic tales she preferred, *that* was precisely the way it happened. But first kisses weren't quite the amazing, wonderful things she'd always imagined—not that she ever would have thought her first kiss would be with Lachlan Kimball in her sister's London garden in the middle of the day. Lachlan hovered just out of reach, teasingly separate. And when his lips *did* touch hers, it was only to brush lightly across them. He immediately pulled back. In frustration, Charity leaned forward and pressed her lips fully against his.

Lachlan laughed softly, surprised by the unexpected move, and he caught her face between his hands. Amity was usually so sedate, so quiet. He pulled away a fraction of an inch, just enough to look into her eyes. They were as bright as the morning sky, wide with expectation and something else. Was it disappointment, he wondered? He released her face and watched as she settled back, a tiny frown marring her expression.

Silence stretched between them. Charity glanced at Lachlan out of the corner of her eye. He seemed to be waiting for her to speak, so she smiled politely. "Thank you."

A glimmer of humor touched his silver gaze. "You're welcome," he returned with mock gravity, then added, "Is something amiss?"

"Oh, no," she assured him. "It was really a very"—she paused, searching for just the right word—"*nice*, um, kiss."

"Nice?" Lachlan cocked his head to the side and captured her eyes with his.

Charity squirmed, wondering why he was placing her in the awkward position of trying to reassure him that he kissed well, especially when the kiss hadn't been at all what she expected. Uncomfortable with an untruth, she finally said, "Well, I mean . . . perhaps they do it differently in Scotland."

Thoroughly entertained and charmed by this young lady who, he was learning, was far more unconventional and open in a private setting than a public one, Lachlan leaned back on his hands again. "Ah, I see." He raised his brows. "How do they do it here?"

Charity had the grace to blush at the question, since she didn't have an iota of expertise on the subject, but she charged recklessly ahead. "In books, the girl almost always gets all swoony and breathless."

"Mm? Is that so? In books, you say."

The way he was looking at her, eyes half-closed and speculative, was doing odd things to her stomach again. Nervously, she smoothed her skirt over her knees and bit lightly into her lower lip.

Lachlan watched Charity's even white teeth sink delicately into that tempting, plump bit of flesh and, doing so, decided he could not possibly allow her to think that, in all of Scotland, there wasn't a single man who could kiss with the passion of a literary Englishman. In fact, he convinced himself, it was his patriotic duty as a Scot to persuade her of the exact opposite. He caught her arm and gave it a little tug so that she fell against him. "Perhaps then, Miss Ackerly, *you* can teach *me*."

He slid a hand into the sun-warmed curls near her temple, tilted her head back, and took her mouth with his. The kiss was anything but gentle or hesitant. His lips slanted across hers with hot insistence, and Charity felt suddenly as though she'd been tossed into an unknown sea teeming with feelings she'd never encountered. His tongue slipped along the crease between her lips until she whimpered and opened her mouth. She couldn't think, could only feel and react and simply be in the moment. Right now. Here. With him. Her hand crept across his midsection to curl around and cling to his waist for support as the world spun away beneath her.

Lachlan hesitated a bare second as she opened to him. A tiny voice inside his head whispered at him to stop, to think, to wait; that something wasn't quite as it should be. But then she wriggled and fit herself against him, and that voice faded until it was lost.

Charity gasped as his tongue invaded her mouth, but the gasp ended in a low moan filled with aching need. Tentatively she met the next foray with one of her own, and then began imitating his movements with growing confidence. She kissed him back with blossoming ardor, igniting a fire that quickly raged out of control.

Lachlan had never been so aroused by a simple, single kiss. He felt his lust mount, knew he should stop and try to regain his equilibrium, but when Charity began mimicking his movements with her tongue, his rampaging desire consumed him. He felt himself swell and harden with need. As if of its own accord, his hand slid up her rib cage to curve around the soft fullness of one breast. The hard little bud of her nipple, puckered with desire, jutted proudly into his palm, and he knew she was as aroused as he. Her unexpected ardor filled him with a sense of pride, of warmth and caring beyond anything he'd imagined.

A distant door slammed, jerking him abruptly back to reality. He remembered with a groan that they were seated on a blanket in the garden of his good friend's home, in full view of anyone who chanced a look out of the many windows on the back of the town house, and he struggled to bring himself and the girl curled against him under control. Reluctantly he relinquished his claim on her lips, kissed her gently on the forehead and tucked her curly head beneath his chin. There would be no need for him to look any further for a wife.

"Amity," he said softly.

Charity stiffened in sudden shock. With a strangled cry, she pushed herself back and away from the man into whose arms she'd just melted. Without another word, she got to her feet and walked back to the house.

Lachlan watched her go, bemused. Obviously she'd been as surprised as he by the impact of their shared passion. He'd caught a brief glimpse of pain in her cerulean eyes before she narrowed them at him, and now she'd disappeared inside. He bent, gathered up the blanket she'd left behind, and began folding it, deciding he'd have to slow things down tonight when he arrived to escort her to the Upshaws' ball.

Charity had managed by sheer force of will to hold herself together until she made it inside the town house. Once there, she began trembling violently. She'd behaved like a besotted little fool! Her embarrassment acute, she chanced a look out the window and saw Lachlan calmly folding the blanket and then bending to pick up her book. Realizing it would be only moments before he came back into the house, she pushed away from the window and ran down the hall, looking for Amity, so she could relay what had happened.

She almost crashed into her sister, who was standing near the foot of the stairs talking quietly with Dr. Meadows. In her agitated state she didn't notice how closely the two stood, or how her sister colored gorgeously at being so unexpectedly interrupted.

"Amity, I can't explain here, but I need to talk to you. Quickly!" She tossed Dr. Meadows an apologetic look. "In the sitting room." She tugged on her twin's arm.

"Good heavens, Charity! What's got you so—?" She peered closely at her sister's face, saw tears brimming there, ready to fall, and turned back to Matthew.

"Go on," he prompted before she could say anything. "I'll just let myself out."

Amity gave him a grateful smile and then allowed herself to be pulled into the sitting room. Charity closed the doors and, her voice trembling with agitation, she began to explain why it would be necessary for her sister to attend a ball that evening with the Marquess of Asheburton.

Nine

Charity gave the bodice of her gown a critical look in the mirror. The amethyst frock set off her creamy complexion beautifully and did amazing things to both her eyes and her hair, but Charity could see nothing but flaws in the garment. The square neckline was demure, offering only the barest hint of the shadowy valley between her breasts. But was it still too much? She pressed her hand flat against the curving mounds, as if she could somehow make them disappear.

Amity, wearing the same dress in pale lilac, sighed. "Charity, the marquess has been waiting downstairs for nearly half an hour. He's bound to be getting impatient."

Her sister's face brightened with hope. "Maybe he'll become so annoyed he'll simply go away."

Amity laughed. "Your hair is perfect, your gown is perfect. You look beautiful." Her tone turned teasing. "If I didn't know better, I'd be inclined to think you were trying to look your very best for him."

"Quite the opposite," returned Charity tightly, in a voice laced with stress. "If I thought I could get away with it I'd go in a burlap sack." She gave her reflection a last rueful glance and then reluctantly followed her sister out.

They found Lachlan in the sitting room talking comfortably with Gareth. Both men instantly stood when the girls entered. Amity curtsied properly and smiled, but Charity stood, rooted in place, until her twin unobtrusively nudged her in the side. With a start, Charity bobbed a quick, half-hearted curtsy as well.

Lachlan smiled. "Good evening, ladies." He stepped forward and lifted Amity's hand for a kiss, immediately recognizing her by her less colorful attire and sweet demeanor. "You look lovely, Miss Ackerly," he said, his voice warm. "I shall be the envy of every man at the ball when I show up with such a beautiful young woman on my arm."

Amity blushed and withdrew her hand, then glanced uncertainly at Charity, who had yet to say a word. She suppressed a frown. Her fiery twin's moods and behavior had always been unpredictable, but she couldn't recall ever seeing her act quite this oddly.

When she realized her sister intended to remain silent, Amity spoke. "Thank you, my lord. I do hope you don't mind, but I've asked Charity to accompany us."

Lachlan did indeed mind. He'd hoped to find a quiet moment, perhaps on the ride home, to steal another kiss or two. He'd carried the memory of that morning's embrace with him throughout his busy day, and it had brought many a smile as he recalled Amity's unguarded ardor and her shy yet passionate response to his touch. With Charity along, a replay would be impossible. His polite smile faltered only slightly, however, before he recovered.

"In that case, the men will envy me all the more, for I shall arrive with the two loveliest women in all of London."

Charity, barely managing to suppress an indelicate snort, rolled her eyes. She looked at Lachlan, found him watching her, and offered up a sweet, saccharine smile. "You are too kind, my lord," she said softly, though her inclination was to tell him exactly what she thought of his, to her mind, insincere attempt at gallantry. For Amity's sake, she would hold her tongue for as long as she was forced to endure his company; then, when they reached the ball, she would gratefully disappear into the crowd.

She managed quite nicely during the short ride in his coach. Lachlan and Amity conversed quietly, leaving Charity to her thoughts, which, to her horror, kept returning to the kiss shared in the garden that morning. So caught up was she in her thoughts, she didn't even feel the coach come to a smooth stop and was startled when the footman opened the door.

Dutifully she allowed Lachlan to help her down and then placed her hand on the arm he offered. Amity took his other. The trio strolled inside, relinquished their wraps, and then joined the people waiting in queue for their names to be announced by the Upshaws' butler at the second-floor entrance to the ballroom.

Charity smiled a greeting at an acquaintance every now and then but remained mostly silent until after the servant had called their names into the crowded room and they had descended the ornate staircase. "I think I'll go look for some friends," she said, removing her gloved hand from Lachlan's arm as soon as her foot cleared the bottom step.

She'd given Amity a quick hug and took two steps away before Lachlan's voice stopped her in her tracks. "Charity."

She turned, one eyebrow raised in query, and waited.

"Try to stay out of trouble."

Charity's eyes widened, and she sucked in her breath. Of all the unmitigated gall! She opened her mouth to give him the blistering setdown he deserved, caught the pleading look on Amity's face, and closed it again with a snap. Without a word, she spun on her heel and disappeared into the crush.

Lachlan watched her go, and then turned back to Amity, who, relieved her twin had been willing to let the command go without making a scene, was now regarding him with a look of tolerant amusement. "I didn't handle that very well, did I?"

Amity laughed softly and shook her head.

"She's going to make me pay for it, isn't she?"

"I'd count on it, my lord."

He scanned the crowd, but Charity was long gone. "I'm not sure why your sister and I just don't seem to get along." He thought back to the first time they'd met, at Faith's wedding the previous year, and frowned. "I don't think she likes my teeth."

At that odd statement, Amity laughed aloud.

Those standing nearest the pair immediately noted that the Marquess of Asheburton, though so recently arrived in Town, already seemed quite comfortable with one of the Ackerly twins. Disappointed debutantes looked on in resignation, jettisoning their dreams of becoming a marchioness; the Ackerly sisters had, for two seasons running, captured the attention and the hands of Society's Most Eligible, and it appeared that this Season would be no different. The mamas, however, knew that until an engagement was actually announced, there was still a chance. They wasted no more time, hastening their young charges over to beg an introduction.

Lachlan handled it all with polite grace. Amity stood off quietly to the side, secretly grateful for the steady stream of blushing girls and their pushy mothers. She was even happier when a friend appeared.

"My goodness!" Amanda Lloyd eyed the gaggle of women surrounding Lachlan. "But didn't I see both you *and* Charity arrive with Asheburton?"

Amity nodded. "It looks as though my escort's dance card may be getting rather full, doesn't it?"

"But where's Charity?"

"She escaped as soon as we arrived." Amity glanced around the room but didn't see her sister. "I'm sure she's found some quiet corner in which to seethe."

"Seethe? Who made her angry this time?"

Amity pointed at Lachlan. "*He* told her to stay out of trouble."

"He did not!" Amanda looked highly entertained. She raked the besieged marquess with an assessing gaze. "He doesn't know her very well, does he?"

Lachlan chose that moment to glance over the heads of the women around him and offer Amity a warm, apologetic smile. She returned the expression. "He'll learn," she said.

"They don't even like each other. How is he going to learn?"

Amity's smiled softened, her eyes glowing at a memory. "When we were little girls, Charity had a friend named Robert Benton. If you chanced across us when we all played together, you'd have thought Charity *hated* Robert. She threw rocks at him, called him names, repeatedly chased him into a field that contained an angry bull, and once she even trapped him in our tree house by removing the steps of the ladder Papa had nailed to the tree trunk."

Amanda laughed. "That sounds just like something Charity would do. But what does that have to do with Lachlan Kimball?"

"Well, one day, when I was looking in our bedroom for a piece of paper on which I'd written some notes from a grammar lesson, I found instead a crumpled-up page torn from a journal Charity kept in the drawer beside her bed. When I opened it and smoothed it out, I saw that she had written 'Charity loves Robert' across it, over and over and over in big, loopy letters."

"So she was mean to him because she didn't know how to tell him she liked him," Amanda correctly surmised. "That's really a very dear story."

"I think she would have been content to eventually marry Robert, but he found another village girl who didn't plague him to death, and recently married her. Charity's too old for throwing rocks now, but because of the way she treated Robert, I'm not sure she dislikes the marquess as much as she wants all of us, herself included, to think."

As it turned out, Amity was wrong about her sister's whereabouts. She had not gone to seethe in a corner. She'd taken a few moments to calm down and was just on her way back to her sister's side, determined to keep her composure and to help her twin get through this evening as she'd promised. Beginning tomorrow, she decided, they would come up with a plan to rid themselves of the Marquess of Asheburton's unwanted attention.

She didn't get far, however. She stepped around a square pillar, glanced in the direction of the stairs, and stopped in her tracks. There, in the middle of a knot of fawning females, stood Lachlan Kimball. And he was completely ignoring Amity, who stood off to the side with Amanda Lloyd.

Infuriated again, Charity turned, leaned back against the pillar and closed her eyes. "Bloody wretch," she muttered under her breath, and then peeked around to see if anyone had heard. More hot words tumbled through her mind, all aching to slip past her tightly compressed lips and hurl themselves at the blackguard upon whom she could no longer rest her eyes. He was a cad, a bounder, a libertine. A . . . a . . . Her mind finally drew a blank, so she took a deep breath, struggled for control, and narrowed her eyes at the group near the stairs.

So, it was popularity he sought. Charity released her breath slowly and smiled. At that game, she could certainly best him.

She straightened her posture and glanced about the room until she saw a group of ladies separate themselves from the crowd and walk toward a hallway. Certain they were making for the ladies retiring room, Charity followed their lead. A moment to compose herself and freshen up would be just the thing.

A full thirty minutes of polite, perfunctory conversation passed before Lachlan was finally able to extricate himself. He exchanged a greeting with Amanda Lloyd, then bowed slightly from the waist and smiled at Amity. "If you can forgive my poor manners in neglecting you for such a span of time, I'd enjoy a dance, Miss Ackerly."

"Ah," she replied with a regal inclination of her head. "A pretty apology, my lord. Consider yourself forgiven, so long as you manage to conduct yourself as gracefully on the dance floor as you do in conversation."

Lachlan offered his arm. "I would, indeed, be less of a man if I were to back away from such a sweetly delivered challenge."

Behind his back, Amanda made a face, pretending to gag, and stuck her tongue out. Amity smiled serenely, placed her hand on the offered arm, and glided with him out onto the floor.

The Countess of Seth watched Amity and Lachlan for a few moments before deciding to look for Charity. With the exception of the conversation she'd just had with Amity, the ball thus far had been less than scintillating, and Amanda could think of no one better than the fierier Ackerly twin to enliven it.

She swept the room with her eyes, searching out her friend's distinctive strawberry blonde hair and brightly colored dress. The combination typically made her stand out in the endless sea of pastel-clad mousy brunettes and milquetoast blondes, but Amanda did not see the girl anywhere. What she did observe, however, was an unusually large number of pouting young women in the ballroom. They stood about in petulant little groups, whispering to one another and casting resentful looks at the wall of many-paned doors that opened out onto the terrace.

Amanda followed their eyes. There, framed by the wide open French doors, sat Charity on the railing of the marble balustrade, completely surrounded by men. Her color was high, her eyes were sparkling with fun, and her smile was vivacious and bright. The faces of the men surrounding her were no less animated, and as Amanda drew within earshot she began to understand why.

Charity was in her element, holding court, as it were, and her subjects were nothing less than utterly besotted. Snippets of the conversations began to float in through the open doors, so Amanda stopped and leaned against the frame, snapping open her fan and idly waving the air with it while she listened.

"You did *not* actually ride to the hounds, Miss Ackerly," said Lord Danforth in an incredulous voice.

"I most certainly did," responded Charity proudly. "My elder sister Patience caught me before too long, so I was unable to finish the hunt. I did, however, manage to keep up with the men from the village without anyone knowing I was a girl."

"But you could have been killed or maimed," protested another admirer from the outer edge of the ring.

Charity scoffed. "The danger was no worse for me than it was for any of the men on the hunt, my lord." She smiled and tossed the speaker a coquettish look. "Why, I'd imagine I'm in greater danger each time I step on the dance floor with one of you."

The men all laughed. Lord Pelligrew tentatively asked if he could refresh her beverage, and Charity willingly handed over her glass, causing the shy young man to blush furiously and scurry off. Amanda watched him go with a wry smile that changed to one of pleasure when she saw her husband making his way toward her.

"Jon! I thought you'd be off all evening, playing cards or whatever it is you gentlemen do when you're in your little man gatherings."

The Earl of Seth bent and placed a kiss on her offered cheek. "I missed your beautiful smile," he explained. "Now, what has you so amused?"

Amanda waved a hand in the direction of the terrace tableau. "Charity's entourage."

Jon frowned. "There must be thirty men out there." He glanced back into the ballroom and noted the angry gaggles of young women and their mothers. "Ashe won't like this," he predicted.

Amanda slanted him a look. "And what has he to say about it? He had at least this many young women surrounding him when they arrived. Amity was standing quite alone, off to the side when I spotted them." Her face lit up in comprehension. "Ahhh . . . that explains everything."

Jon raised his brow. "Care to elaborate?"

"According to Amity, Charity and Asheburton clashed earlier in the evening." Amanda laughed. "I'd wager she's out there giving him a taste of his own medicine. I've certainly never seen her intentionally court so much attention."

"She arrived with Ashe," Jon remarked, a note of disapproval creeping into his voice.

"He's escorting Amity. Charity should be able to spend time with whomever she wishes." But even as she said the words, Amanda knew this wasn't necessarily the way Society would see it. Just then, as if summoned, she saw Lachlan Kimball heading purposefully toward them, his eyes locked on the group around Charity.

"Uh oh," she said. "Looks like you were right."

Jon glanced over his shoulder and followed Lachlan's progress with a shake of his head. "You know, darling . . . it occurs to me that if you'd never befriended Grace Ackerly, my life would be a good deal less eventful."

His wife smiled up at him fondly, but that smile faded as Lachlan brushed past without seeing them and approached the group near the balustrade. Those on the perimeter caught his baleful expression and stopped talking. Charity's voice rang out quite clearly in the ensuing silence.

"Lord Bakersly, I'm not only quite sure that I could outrace you, if I were allowed to ride astride, but I'm also certain my younger sister Mercy could do so as well."

No one responded. Noting the sudden dearth of interaction, Charity looked around in confusion. Her eyes collided with the cold, flinty gray stare of the Marquess of Asheburton. "Oh, bloody hell," she muttered, and slid down from the marble rail upon which she'd been seated.

Lachlan flicked a glance at the silent men surrounding her. They promptly obeyed the unspoken command and scattered, some muttering quick good-byes on their way inside. Most simply disappeared, likely to spread the delicious bit of gossip they'd just witnessed.

Charity crossed her arms and lifted her chin, two bright spots of angry color flaring on her pallid face, but she said nothing.

Lachlan stared back a moment, then spoke. "While it is not my job to govern your behavior, Miss Ackerly, I feel duty-bound to do my best to protect your reputation, and, by extension, that of your sister, when you are in my company. I trust you'll manage to comport yourself with that in mind for the remainder of the evening." Without waiting for a response, he turned and strode back into the ballroom.

Jon sighed and followed suit. Amanda winced and gave Charity a sympathetic look. She walked over and placed a reassuring arm around her younger friend's shoulders. "Just forget that whole thing. Come back inside with me."

"I don't understand that man," Charity said.

Her voice was flat, and Amanda recalled what Amity had said about suspecting her twin's feelings for Lachlan ran deeper than they knew. She smiled wryly. "Men don't understand themselves. How can we be expected to do so?" She gave Charity's hand a gentle tug, and the two young women went back inside the ballroom.

When they entered, dozens of pairs of eyes swiveled to watch them and follow their progress through the room. Charity had never felt so dreadfully conspicuous. In hindsight she realized her behavior on the terrace had likely not been in her best interest, but she'd believed that, since it took place in full view of the assembled guests, it would be discussed and then dismissed in favor of the next pseudo scandal. Lachlan's actions, however, had turned it into a shameful act, adding fuel to the fires beneath the wagging tongues, and people would now imagine something deeper than harmless flirtation had occurred to make him step in.

For the remainder of the night, although Lachlan had apparently taken himself off to play cards in the drawing room or some other such male nonsense, Charity was studiously avoided. Nobody asked her to dance. Amity joined her and Amanda, having learned of the altercation, and the three girls stood on the periphery of the dance floor. Amanda and Amity did their best to improve Charity's mood.

The only male in attendance below the age of fifty who dared come near Charity was Anthony Iverson, who met with such polite disdain from Charity's companions that even he did not remain long. Thankfully, before too much more time passed, Lachlan reappeared. Amity sweetly asked if he would mind terribly taking them home. The marquess looked from Amity's open, earnest face to Amanda's disapproving one, and then at Charity, who refused to meet his eyes. Her expression was shuttered, icy, and distant.

"No, Miss Ackerly," he finally said. "I don't mind in the slightest."

"Charity?"

At the sound of her sister's soft voice, Charity dragged her unseeing gaze from the quiet street below. Amity stood in the doorway to the bathing chamber that connected their rooms, biting her lip with worry.

Charity smiled and walked over to the bed, waving her twin into the room. Amity broke into a relieved smile and met her there. They flopped across it like little girls, and both began speaking at once.

"I'm so sorr—" they said together; then each broke off with a laugh.

"I know you don't care for Lord Asheburton, Charity, and I'm very sorry about what happened, but I'm so grateful you went with me."

Charity flipped over onto her back and twirled a strand of hair around her finger. "You don't like him, either?" Her voice was deliberately offhand, but she held her breath, awaiting her sister's answer, unsure why it was so important to her.

Amity hesitated. "I'm sure he's quite nice, and he's certainly been kind to me. It's just that . . . well . . ." She paused, and then blurted, "I like somebody else."

Charity rolled to her side, propped her elbow on the bed, and cradled her head in her upraised hand, regarding her sister steadily. She tried to remember with whom she'd seen Amity dance besides the Marquess of Asheburton. "Lord Baker," she guessed. "No . . . that blond knight. Sir What's-His-Face?"

Amity laughed and knocked her sister's forearm so that her head fell back on the bed. "No, silly," she said. "It's . . . Matthew."

"Seriously?" A wide grin crossed Charity's face. "Dr. Meadows? Does he know?" She sat up and hugged her knees to her chest, completely adoring this new development. "Gracious, do Faith and Gareth know?"

"Hush, Charity!" Amity sat up, too, and grabbed a pillow. "Someone will hear you."

Charity snatched the pillow out of her twin's hands and shook it at her. "What did you think you were going to do with this? Smother me?" She laughed, more quietly this time. "Well, *does* he know?"

"No." Amity shook her head, then gave her sister a warning look. "And I don't want him to know, at least not until after the baby comes. No one should know. Faith doesn't need the excitement."

"So *that's* why you wanted me to tag along with you on your evening with that wretched man."

"Yes . . . and you must continue to do so, please. The marquess is the only one who actually calls on me. I haven't given him the slightest encouragement, and I don't want Matt, I mean *Dr. Meadows*"—she caught and corrected herself—"to think it's serious. I can't think of a single good reason to refuse to see the marquess that wouldn't look suspicious, since I haven't any other suitor."

Charity frowned. "I can think of at least a dozen reasons to kick him to the curb."

"No," said Amity firmly. "You can't. Not good reasons. Promise me you'll help me. Please."

Her twin sighed. "I suppose I can put up with him, especially since it means that, with any luck, he won't become my brother. We can hope he'll set his sights on some other unlucky family and cart some poor, unsuspecting girl off to the wilds of Scotland to waste away in his moldy old castle."

Amity held her tongue but watched her sister's face. *Charity doesn't even know she cares for him,* she realized with an inward smile.

Instead of articulating her thoughts, she reached over and gave her sister an impulsive hug. "I love you *so* much. You'll see. Soon enough you'll meet some young man you adore, and then we'll have the wedding we've dreamed about," she said, her face aglow. She climbed off the bed and headed for the door. "I'll see you in the morning."

Charity smiled in response, then crawled beneath the covers and reclined back against the pillows. As soon as she closed her eyes, however, an unbidden image of the Marquess of Asheburton's disapproving gray gaze popped into her head. "Go away," she muttered. But the command didn't work. Instead, those eyes softened to a glowing, molten silver. Exactly the way they'd looked just before he kissed her.

"I said go away," she told the eyes, then grabbed the pillow she'd taken from Amity and smashed it down over her face, forcing herself to think about place settings and all the other boring things she'd half learned in Madame Capdepon's Etiquette School. Left with no alternative, she finally found sleep.

Ten

Lachlan lifted a hand to knock on the door to the Lloyd town house, then hesitated and turned to face the street. Once he knocked, he'd be committed to not only enjoying Amity's company but also to enduring Charity's.

He began pulling off his gloves, one finger at a time, his thoughts on the events of the previous evening. There was no question in his mind that Amity Ackerly would make the perfect marchioness. She possessed the requisite poise and grace, as well as a quiet wit that was really quite charming. Her beauty, though not a requirement, was an additional boon, as were her impeccable background and connections through her sisters' marriages to nobility. There was also, of course, her connection to Charity.

He placed his gloves neatly together, palms touching, and began slapping them rhythmically into his palm. With a sigh of resignation, he reached up, raised the knocker and let it fall, then repeated the action once more. Marriage to Amity meant he'd be forced to spend more time than he cared to consider in her twin sister's company. It was plain the two girls were incredibly close. The fact that Amity had asked Charity to accompany them the evening last was one sign of that, but a more telling indicator was that Charity, despite her obvious dislike for him, had willingly tagged along.

Lachlan frowned at the still firmly closed door and rapped with his knuckles this time. While he waited, he weighed the relative merits of continuing his courtship of Amity against a lifetime of being thrust into social situations with Charity, and he considered both sides carefully. The all too brief moments he'd spent in the garden with Amity filtered into his mind. That kiss—an unbidden smile curved his lips when he thought of the kiss they'd shared, and he knew that his mind was made up. Her passion, though she had shown no outward evidence of it since that morning, had been deep and unmistakable.

Just as he raised his arm to knock again, the door was snatched open by Desmond, who managed—impossibly, given his shorter height—to glare down his nose at Lachlan. "It is not, my lord, at all necessary to beat upon the door in that fashion."

The marquess narrowed his eyes at the recalcitrant butler. He opened his mouth to give the man the blistering setdown he so richly deserved but closed it when he saw one of the Ackerly twins standing a few yards inward, her hand resting lightly on the banister of the sweeping staircase that led to the second floor. Her eyes met his, the expression in their green-blue depths inscrutable.

With an effort, Lachlan controlled his animosity and managed, in a relatively pleasant tone, to tell Desmond that he was here to visit Miss Amity Ackerly. Somewhat mollified, the butler opened the door wider and beckoned him inside. "I do hope she's expecting you, my lord," he said, his tone haughty and imperious. "Nobody told me to be prepared, you see, for visitors."

As Lachlan stepped inside, the girl at the foot of the stairs turned away and began the climb to the second floor. "I'll go let her know, Desmond," she said.

Charity looked more serene this morning, as though she had managed to find a way past her anger of the evening before, and Lachlan suppressed an urge to stop her and clear the tension that had arisen between them. Clad in a bottle green day dress that set off her bright hair and cerulean eyes, she was a striking presence in the dim foyer. The meager light filtering through the small panes of glass above the door managed to find and caress her features. He watched her disappear into the upper reaches of the house before Desmond ushered him into the sitting room to await Amity.

"That odious man has arrived."

Amity, seated on a low bench near the window, looked up from the linen collar she'd been embroidering. "Really, Charity, be fair. He's not odious."

"All right then," she amended. "He's rude, obnoxious, high-handed, and altogether egregious." Charity smiled, the expression an amusing contrast to her harsh words. "But I'm willing to agree that he's not odious."

Her twin sighed and set aside her needlework. She stood and shook the wrinkles out of her skirts, wishing Dr. Meadows had already come for his daily visit to check on Faith. "I don't suppose the marquess gave any indication as to the length of his visit?"

Charity shook her head. "I didn't actually speak to him, but I did see that he arrived in a phaeton."

Amity grimaced. "That must mean he intends to take me driving. You'll come along, won't you?"

"Not a chance." Charity backed toward the door, then stopped and scowled at the pleading look on her sister's face. "Can't you just tell him you don't wish to go?"

"We've already discussed this. Everyone will wonder why I'm turning away a man who is not only a wonderful matrimonial prospect, but who is also a great friend of the family."

"It's a two-seater," Charity pointed out, hoping logic would prevail.

"We're small. We'll fit." Amity slanted her sister a glance. "Or, if we don't fit, perhaps he'll simply visit here for a time and then leave."

"Oh, fine," Charity agreed, a bit crossly. "But I'm not speaking to him."

The periods of silence grew increasingly uncomfortable as the well-matched pair of grays stepped smartly through the park. Lachlan, crowded all the way to the left of the phaeton's high bench seat, guided them with an expert hand while he searched for a topic of conversation that would draw more than a short, polite response from the object of his affection. It was, however, difficult to think past the pulsing wave of animosity emanating from the obstinately silent form of Charity.

Amity, seated between them, seemed oblivious to both his discomfort and her sister's smoldering ire. That fact was the only thing that made Lachlan try to carry on with the conversation. "I thought the ball rather well attended last night, for an event held so early in the Season," he remarked.

"I agree," murmured Amity. Silence returned.

After a time, Lachlan tried again. "I wouldn't call it a crush, of course, but the company was good."

Hearing talk of the previous evening was too much for Charity to bear. Despite her resolve not to do so, she spoke up. "I wouldn't know. All company I might have enjoyed was frightened off."

Lachlan refused to rise to the bait. Instead, he changed the subject. "The Duke of Blackthorne tells me Pelthamshire is a picturesque little village about a half day's drive from London. Do you miss your home, Miss Ackerly?"

"I miss my family there, but Grace and Faith are here in London. Having come with Charity keeps me from feeling homesick, too, but I think we both look forward to going back home."

Lachlan waited for her to continue the proffered topic by asking him about his home. When she didn't, he sighed and again attempted to further the discussion. "I miss Scotland a great deal, although I come from a much smaller family," he said.

Charity leaned forward and looked around her sister. "Perhaps, Lord Asheburton, that is why you seem to have no idea how one should act in London." Her words were sweetly offered, and she smiled and batted her eyes a couple times for good measure. She sat back, satisfaction flooding warmly through her belly.

Lachlan, too, had finally had enough of her brooding animosity. "Would you mind telling me why you choose to be so continually contentious, Miss Ackerly?"

"Why, yes," returned Charity. "I do mind."

Between them, Amity shrank back.

"You're not angry with me," Lachlan mused after a thoughtful pause. "You're angry with yourself."

"Oh, quite the contrary, my lord. I am furious with you."

"Had I not stepped in, your reputation would be in tatters."

Charity snapped her head in his direction, but before she could speak she was forced to grab the edge of the seat to keep from being thrown off; he'd brought the vehicle sharply around to exit the park. "You did that on purpose!"

He smirked.

Charity glared at him. "Had you not stepped in," she retorted, "I'd have had a glorious time and nobody would have batted an eye. Instead, you called attention to a situation that was *not* a situation and turned me into a pariah!"

"There wasn't a suitable male in the group."

Charity gasped. "What? 'Suitable?' Now you're choosing my male acquaintances? Your high-handedness in areas that are none of your concern knows no bounds, my lord. Suitable for what, please?"

Lachlan belatedly remembered Amity, who sat quietly between them. A small smile played about the corners of her mouth, confusing and embarrassing him. He lapsed once again into silence.

Charity, however, wasn't nearly finished, her temper pushing her recklessly onward with the topic. "What, pray tell, is wrong with Lord Danforth, who merely wished to discuss horses?"

"He's broke and looking for an heiress," Lachlan replied evenly. Then he pointed out, "*Which* you are not."

Charity ignored that. "What about Pelligrew?"

Lachlan clenched his teeth. "He was a second in a recent duel."

"A second?" Charity's voice was laced with derision. "He wasn't even the person dueling, and now he's suddenly unsuitable?"

"He also doesn't sit a horse well," bit out the marquess.

Amity stifled a laugh and then quickly composed herself when they both looked at her. "Umm . . . the road, my lord." She pointed at the horses.

Cursing under his breath, Lachlan made a slight adjustment to allow another carriage to pass safely. He touched his hat in acknowledgment of the other vehicle's occupants. The twins both smiled brightly and waved.

After he executed the turn onto Upper Brook Street,

Charity's smile disappeared. She tossed out another name. "Lord Bakersly."

"Has been seen frequenting gambling hells. And the cut of his jacket is all wrong."

At that ludicrous reasoning, Charity narrowed her eyes. "Anthony Iverson," she said with deliberate intent.

"Stay away from him!" Lachlan growled in a low, dangerous voice. His eyes turned hard. Charity paled and grew silent, her anger finally taking her beyond the ability to speak. She stared resolutely forward for the remainder of the ride, her lips pressed into a tight little line.

Lachlan slowed the horses and turned to Amity, his voice softening. "I apologize, Miss Ackerly, for the unpleasant drive. May I escort you to the Danwells' ball this evening, to atone?"

Having believed herself all but forgotten, Amity was caught completely off guard and couldn't come up with a plausible excuse. "Th-that would be lovely," she stammered as the phaeton drew up before the Lloyd town house.

Charity hopped down between the wheels, not waiting for assistance, and she gained the ground without incident almost before the vehicle came to a complete stop. She shook out her skirts, tossed Lachlan a last venomous glare, and stormed up the steps, brushing past Matthew Meadows, who was just arriving. The doctor heard her mutter something about "That insufferable man," before she disappeared inside and slammed the door in his face.

The physician turned back to see the Marquess of Asheburton helping Amity down from his carriage, a smile on his face that was both fond and possessive. Out of nowhere, a surge of jealousy gripped Matthew, and he frowned. When, he wondered, had he developed these feelings for his wealthiest patient's sister? In consternation, he turned to go inside, only to be met with the solid, unyielding panel of oak.

Inwardly cursing Charity's temper and penchant for slamming doors, he politely turned and waited for the couple coming up the steps.

Eleven

"Good morning, Desmond."

The dour butler stopped and stared at the pleasant greeting from Charity, who had been particularly moody since the twins' arrival in London. So great was his surprise at the unusually affable salutation that, even though he'd only just shown Amity into the drawing room to attend a guest, he looked over his shoulder to be certain he hadn't confused their identities.

Charity laughed. "You look as though you've seen a ghost." Her eyes sparkled and she leaned toward him as if sharing a confidence, her voice a bit lowered. "Perhaps you should take a break. I've just come from the garden, and it's a beautiful day. I won't tell anyone."

Desmond recovered his composure and drew himself stiffly upright. "I'm sure I have far too many things I must attend, Miss Ackerly, for me to waste time cavorting in the garden.

"Suit yourself," returned Charity agreeably. "Have you seen Amity?"

"She's in the drawing room with his lordship, Miss. Perhaps you would be kind enough to go in there and inform Lord Roth that my wages do not cover doing *everything* in his home. Next he'll be wanting me to cook the meals and tidy the bedchambers." He turned away, muttering darkly under his breath, just loudly enough for Charity to hear, about it not being his job to manage the whereabouts of everyone in the ridiculously full household.

Charity watched him with a smile until he turned the corner, and then she set the book she was reading down on a table in the foyer. She glanced into the mirror above the table and tightened the bow on the aquamarine velvet ribbon holding back her strawberry blonde curls. Her color was high, her eyes sparkled with good humor, and her lips were curved in a smile she couldn't seem to dislodge.

After the debacle of her morning ride with Amity and the Marquess of Asheburton the previous day, Charity had gone straight to her room to take stock of the situation. She'd come to an almost immediate conclusion: nobody was going to ruin the Season for her. Especially not Lachlan Kimball. Her mind made up, she'd spent the rest of the day putting him out of her mind, and with firm resolve she'd confronted Amity about the ball that evening.

"I need to stay in tonight. Couldn't we ask Aunt Cleo to accompany you? She'd be an excellent buffer between you and the marquess."

Amity, after giving her sister a long assessing look, agreed. Together they composed a quick note to Cleo Egerton, carefully worded to keep the astute older lady from guessing there was anything afoot. Their eccentric aunt had replied almost immediately that she would be more than happy to act as chaperone, and Charity breathed a sigh of relief. She'd spent the evening quietly at home, visiting with Faith, who was tired of being confined to her bed and happy for the company. She'd gone to bed early and woke refreshed and ready to embrace the rest of her stay in London with a peaceful, tranquil heart.

Now, satisfied with her reflection in the foyer mirror,

Charity walked across the hall and quietly entered the drawing room so as not to interrupt the conversation between
her sister and Gareth, who was standing just inside the
doorway. Her sister was seated on a settee, her posture correct and primly erect.

Amity's eyes grew round when she saw Charity appear
behind her brother-in-law. Gareth spun to see what had
caused her expression to change, and when he moved aside,
Charity saw that they were not the only people in the
room. The Marquess of Asheburton sat there as well.

Charity felt a sudden spurt of annoyance. With an effort
she recalled her intention to not allow anyone, especially
this particular man, to spoil her Season. She pasted a pleasant smile on her face and greeted the marquess with a curtsy.
"Good morning, my lord. I didn't know you'd stopped in."

Lachlan stood and bowed politely. "Good morning, Miss
Ackerly. I hope you're feeling better today."

Despite her resolve, Charity narrowed her eyes, assum-
ing he was referring to her hasty exit from his vehicle. The
man had no couth at all. "Feeling better?"

Lachlan's smile faltered and he looked at Amity, who
stood as well. "Aunt Cleo mentioned your headache on the
ride to the ball last night," she said.

Charity counted to ten, her irritation now internally directed. "Desmond told me you were in here, Amity. I'll just
look for you after you've finished . . . um . . . entertaining
your guest."

She backed toward the door and, quite forgetting he
was there, bumped into Gareth. When she apologized and
glanced upward, her brother-in-law's golden brown eyes
twinkled down at her.

"Why don't you stay and talk a bit, Charity? I was just
leaving to check on Faith. Dr. Meadows should be here

momentarily, and this way we can be sure Ashe is"—he smirked—"entertained."

Trapped, Charity barely managed to keep from scowling. When the knocker sounded from out in the hall, nobody moved. It seemed an opportunity. "I-I could get the door," she stammered. "Desmond was going toward the kitchen a few moments ago and—"

"There is no need for you to do my job, Miss Ackerly," interrupted the butler from the foyer, his tone haughty and affronted. "Although I am impossibly overworked, I believe I still manage." He glided off toward the door with his nose in the air.

Lachlan looked astonished at the servant's audaciousness. "Honestly, Roth, I don't understand why you continue to employ that man."

Gareth grinned. "Desmond was a great favorite of my mother's," he explained. "My father consistently complained about him, but my mother was indulgent and talked the old earl out of firing him on multiple occasions. When they died and Jonathon became the Earl of Seth, he hired another man but kept Desmond as his under-butler, and when I eventually needed a butler, Jon was more than happy to send him over."

"Well, I like him," said Charity stoutly. "One shouldn't have to be constantly hushed simply because their behavior is deemed unseemly." She raised challenging eyebrows at Lachlan, as if daring him to disagree. He stared coolly back and didn't respond.

"Dr. Meadows, my lord," announced Desmond, who looked pointedly at the Marquess of Asheburton. "At least *he* was expected."

Charity snorted sharply with laughter. Amity gave her a hard look.

"Amity?" Faith's voice floated down from the balcony, where she was not supposed to be. "Do you have a moment?"

Charity's twin jumped up and left the room, followed closely by Gareth and Dr. Meadows, all three loudly admonishing Faith for being out of bed. Their voices faded into the second level of the house, leaving Lachlan, Charity, and Desmond alone in the drawing room. After a moment of awkward silence, the butler cleared his throat. "I suppose you'll be needing some sort of refreshment delivered, Miss Ackerly."

"No," said Charity.

"Yes," said Lachlan.

They stared at one another.

Desmond bowed. "As you wish, Miss Ackerly." He left the room without a sound.

Charity spoke first. "Do you always come into other people's homes and order their servants about?"

Lachlan ignored her. "Why are you so angry with me, Charity?"

The sound of her name on his lips washed over her warmly, and Charity blushed; the memory of the kiss they'd shared floated unbidden into her mind. "I'm not angry with you, my lord," she said in a low voice.

Mistaking her blush for an attempt to control her temper, the marquess persisted. "I wish you could see yourself, Charity. The look on your face, the way your fists are clenched at your sides . . . everything about you tells me you're vexed and trying to hide it. Why don't you just come out with whatever is on your mind? Get it out into the open so we can deal with it."

At that impossible suggestion, Charity panicked. Tell him she was remembering how it felt to be held in his arms, that she couldn't get the desire to feel his mouth on hers again to go away? Unthinkable. Unable to come up with a response, she crossed her arms and glared at him in renewed animosity.

Lachlan shook his head. "Someone should turn you over his knee and give you a sound spanking."

She sucked in her breath. "I dare you to try."

That was how Gareth and Matthew Meadows found them, returned from getting Faith settled back into bed: anger arced almost visibly between the two.

Gareth spoke first. "Amity asked me to let you know she's going to stay with Faith a while, and to thank you for the visit, Ashe."

His words broke the pervading air of conflict. In silence, Charity waited while Ashe took his leave, shame at losing her resolve stilling her tongue, then she left the room as well, murmuring something about the book she'd left on the table in the foyer.

Matthew and Gareth watched her leave. "That was interesting," said the latter.

Matthew recalled the look Lachlan had given Amity after their drive the day before and saw a sudden chance to keep his rival for her affections out of the Lloyd town house. He paused a moment and then took the plunge. "I hate to bring this up, because I know the marquess is your friend, but . . ." He allowed the sentence to trail off and waited.

Gareth eyed him curiously.

"Well, there just seems to be a lot of turmoil between him and Charity. I don't think the constant atmosphere of tension and excitement is good for Lady Roth's precarious condition."

Gareth's eyebrows beetled in a frown.

"I'd like to see her make it at least one more week before

the baby comes," Matthew continued, pressing his advantage. "I think it would make all the difference in the world for both Faith and the child."

The marquess paced a few steps, deep in thought. He knew that Ashe had an eye on Amity, quite possibly as a matrimonial prospect, and that Amity had neither voiced objection to his suit nor encouraged anyone else. Asking Ashe to stop courting her wouldn't be fair to either of them. He turned back to his friend and said, "You're right, of course."

Matthew silently congratulated himself . . . until Gareth's next words registered.

"I'll just have to send Charity to stay with Trevor and Grace for a while." He clapped Matthew on the back. "This is exactly why I wanted you to come into Town from Rothmere. Thank you, my friend. I'll just go up and discuss it with my wife. Can you see yourself out?"

"Of course," Matthew replied, stunned by how quickly his impromptu plan had backfired. He walked slowly to the door then turned to watch Gareth's back as the man made his way upstairs.

He retrieved his hat and coat from the stand, and then, feeling helpless, glanced toward the stairs, wishing he could take back the entire conversation. A soft smile worked its way across his face. Amity was making her way downward.

"Were you leaving so soon, Dr. Meadows?" she asked.

Was that a note of disappointment in her voice? Matthew hung his coat back on the hook, and then tried to do the same with his hat while still keeping an eye on Amity. He missed, and the object fell to the carpet with a soft thud.

"Oh, you dropped your hat," she said, and rushed forward to pick it up just as Matthew did the same. They bumped their heads together and straightened, laughing softly,

Amity with the hat in her hands. "Here you go," she said, holding it out. Suddenly shy, she couldn't look up to meet his eyes.

He reached out to take it. When his fingertips touched hers, he threw caution to the wind and took her hand instead. "Amity," he said.

Her heart pounding, Amity closed her eyes and bit her lip. "Yes?" Tingles worked their way up her arm, and she shivered delicately.

"Look at me, please."

Amity lifted her face, her eyes shimmering with newly awakening feelings. It was more than Matthew could take. Dropping his hat, he gathered her close and lowered his head to take her lips in a tender kiss.

"This is a disaster!" Charity swept into the room and threw herself across Amity's bed. Most of her curls had escaped the ribbon she'd used to tie them back that morning and now fell forward around her face, obscuring her view of Amity, who was seated on the window ledge. She impatiently pushed the hair back and peered at her twin.

Amity was staring off into space, wearing a dreamy expression. "He kissed me."

Despite her dramatic entrance, Charity felt herself soften. She pushed upright into a sitting position. "Dr. Meadows? Kissed you?" Her smile widened. "Well, gracious me. I didn't think he had it in him to make a move so soon."

Amity hugged her knees to her chest and blushed, then belatedly realized what Charity had said as she came in. "What's a disaster?"

Her sister blew at another errant curl. "Oh. Um." She looked sheepish. "I'm being sent off to Grace and Trevor's until after the baby comes."

Amity uncurled in alarm, her feet hitting the floor. She leaned forward, her eyes wide. "This *is* a disaster!"

"I know!"

The twins looked at each other for a long moment. Amity stood and started pacing between the window and the bed. "Well, I'll just have to spend a lot of time visiting you when Asheburton typically comes to call."

"Definitely," agreed Charity. "He doesn't know Trevor all that well, except through the Duke of Blackthorne, so it would look odd if he followed you there."

Amity sighed. "But if I'm over there too much, that means I won't get to spend much time with Matthew."

Both girls fell silent, Amity contemplating ways to maximize her encounters with Dr. Meadows while minimizing those with the Marquess of Asheburton. Charity, however, was thinking about kissing.

She slanted a glance at her sister's bemused profile. "What did it feel like?"

Distracted from her thoughts, Amity regarded her with confusion. "What did what feel like?"

"Kissing."

"Oh." She sat down next to Charity and squeezed her hands. "Like . . . warm and floaty. I can't find the right words, but it was the most wondrous thing I've ever experienced."

Charity nodded slowly, biting back questions. She wanted to ask if it felt like the floor had suddenly dropped out from beneath Amity's feet so that she had to hold on to Matthew for safety, or if her stomach felt as though stars had exploded into butterflies of light which then took flight to the most embarrassing places. She wanted to know if it felt the same way it had when Lachlan kissed her in the garden, but of course she couldn't bring that up.

Amity, though, guessed her sister's thoughts. "I'm sure that when you kiss someone you love it will be different than when Asheburton kissed you," she said gently.

Charity nodded. But inside her head, hidden even from the twin sister who was also her best friend, the same thought kept flashing.

What if I don't want it to be different?

Twelve

For the next several days, the plan worked beautifully. Amity left the Lloyd town house in the morning, just after breakfast, and she visited with Aunt Cleo or with Charity and Grace, avoiding the Marquess of Asheburton completely. She returned late in the afternoon and spent some time talking quietly with Faith, keeping her sister up to date on the happenings in town. Matthew adjusted his schedule to coincide with Amity's returns, and after he was finished with his patient they managed to snatch a few moments together before she had to begin preparations for her evening activities. Cleo and Charity would arrive together to pick her up, and they'd go as a group from function to function, the girls keeping an eye out for the marquess. On the odd occasion they did see Lachlan at a ball, they hastily gathered up their aunt and whisked her away to another event before he even had a chance to speak with them.

It worked splendidly until the day the baby came. Faith went into labor in the wee hours of the morning, prompting all the Ackerlys in London to arrive at the Lloyd town house to be there for the blessed event. Trevor Caldwell even came along with Grace to lend moral support to his good friend.

Hours passed with no word from Dr. Meadows or the midwife he'd brought along, and Gareth was becoming more and more agitated. By the time the clock in the hallway chimed the noon hour, he was beside himself. "I'm going up there," he announced.

"You most certainly will not, young man," barked Cleo Egerton.

"She's in good hands," said Grace, gently. "If you show up looking so concerned, you'll only make Faith worry about you. She needs to focus on delivering this baby." She gave Amity a pointed look.

Without a word, her sister nodded and left the room to go see if she could ascertain how things were progressing. Amity didn't make it past the foyer, though, because Desmond was just opening the door to the Marquess of Asheburton. Caught, she cast a longing glance between the stairs and the door to the sitting room, wishing she could escape up one or into the other, but he'd already seen her.

Left with no alternative, she walked to the door to politely greet Lachlan. "Good morning, my lord. I apologize, but things are rather busy here this morning." She smiled. "The baby has decided to come today."

"Well, that's wonderful news!" Lachlan stood uncertainly just inside the door, not wishing to intrude on a private event. "I'll just come and pay my respects another time." He turned to leave.

"Amity!"

Both looked to the stairway and saw Matthew Meadows coming down, his face glowing with happiness. Forgetting completely about the marquess, Amity met the physician at the foot of the stairs. "The baby's here?" He nodded, and they both went into the sitting room.

Desmond, tired of standing and waiting with the door open, closed it with a bang and strode off, leaving Lachlan standing awkwardly in the foyer with his hat in his hands.

A moment later he heard cheers and congratulations, and then he watched as Gareth sprinted from the sitting room and up the stairs.

Trevor Caldwell appeared in the doorway and spotted him. "Ashe!" He crossed the foyer, his hand outstretched.

Lachlan shook it. "I understand congratulations are in order."

Trevor nodded. "Gareth's just become the father of a little girl. Come on in!"

The marquess shook his head. "It's a family moment," he said. "I'd have left sooner, but that wretched butler Roth employs left me standing here. I'll just see myself out."

"Don't be ridiculous. You're Blackthorne's cousin, which makes you nearly family—or will, anyway, if little Mercy manages to bring him up to scratch." Trevor laughed and led Lachlan into the sitting room.

As soon as the two men appeared, Amity and Charity exchanged worried glances, and then both girls looked at Matthew, who grew notably grim.

Seated on the settee in the middle of the room, Cleo Egerton watched all three, and what she saw made her smile turn from happy to gleeful. She thumped her cane on the floor. "Well, Asheburton, I thought you'd forgotten all about our little Amity, here."

The room fell silent for a moment, and then everyone started talking at once in an effort to cover Cleo's embarrassing statement. Charity gasped, Amity blushed, and Lachlan looked even more uncomfortable than he already had. But Cleo wasn't finished. She could tell there was something going on between Asheburton, the handsome young doctor Gareth had brought from Rothmere, and the twins, and she was bound and determined to discover what it was.

She watched them a moment longer. Amity was looking

uncertainly toward Dr. Meadows, who raised his eyebrows at her. As if answering an unspoken question, she shook her head at him.

Charity, though, was the one who intrigued Cleo most. She was staring at Lachlan with an expression of such hopeless longing that Cleo was tempted to go over and thwap her in the head with her walking stick. Fortunately, nobody was paying attention.

She waited for the next lull in the conversation and then addressed Dr. Meadows directly. "I suppose you'll be happy to get back to Rothmere, young man," she said slyly, watching Amity out of the corner of her eye. Her niece's mouth formed an O of surprise.

Matthew hadn't thought that far ahead either, but he managed to maintain his composure. "I'll be in London for a few days yet at least, to make sure everything is going well with Lady Roth and the baby."

"Bah!" Cleo waved a hand. "That's what the midwife is here for, isn't it? I'm sure you're missed in that little village up there." She pushed herself up off the settee with the help of her cane. "Amity, I wish to go upstairs and see my new great-niece. Come, help me up the stairs."

Unable to protest without it appearing odd, Amity gave Charity a last look of despair and did as she'd been asked.

As they passed Trevor and Lachlan near the door, Cleo stopped. "You may resume your visits to Amity tomorrow, my lord," she said imperiously, as if informing him he had been invited to an audience with the Prince Regent himself.

Trevor grinned but then glanced at Grace. She narrowed her eyes at him, and he quickly composed himself. Lachlan, on the other hand, merely nodded. Amity kept her eyes carefully averted until Cleo began walking again and they left the room.

* * *

When Charity finally arrived at the Lloyd town house the following day, she was met by an extremely agitated Amity. "What took you so long?

Charity finished hanging up her pelisse. "Grace stopped by Amanda's before she dropped me here," she explained. "What happened?"

"Oh, *everything*." Amity twisted her hands together. "Nobody expected Matthew to stay after the baby came, especially since everyone just adores the midwife, so Gareth and Faith told him he's free to go back to Rothmere whenever he wants. And since he doesn't have any other patients in London, it would look ridiculous if he stayed."

"Well, okay." Charity remained calm. "So you'll ask Faith if you can go to Rothmere with them after the Season."

"I won't have to." Amity began pacing the foyer.

"Good gracious, will you please stay in one place so I can talk to you?" Charity put her hands on her sister's shoulders and stopped her perambulations. "Faith already asked you to come with her?"

"No."

"Then what is it?"

Amity touched her forehead to her sisters so they were eye to eye. "Matthew asked me to marry him," she whispered.

Charity's eyes widened. "Seriously?" She pushed her twin away and held her at arm's length, tilted her head, and then smiled. "You're serious."

Wordless, Amity nodded.

Charity glanced around the foyer, and though she didn't see anyone, tugged Amity into the sitting room and closed the door. "So, you said yes, of course." Amity nodded again. "And is he going to speak with Papa?" Amity shook her head. "With Gareth?" Again, Amity shook her head. "Oh, good Lord, you're eloping, aren't you?" Charity dropped into a chair and looked up at her twin.

Slowly, Amity nodded. "There's just so much going on with the baby here now." She looked down. "Matthew is worried that, because he is not titled, he won't be viewed as a suitable match for me, especially since Lord Asheburton has paid me such attention."

"But you know that's ridiculous," protested Charity. "Nobody cares about that. Papa would be happy for you to marry a pauper, if he knew you were loved."

"I know. I wish I could convince Matthew of that, but he's convinced he'll lose me if my family disagrees with the match."

Charity gave her sister a long look. "All right, out with it. What's the plan?"

Amity looked up in relief. "I *knew* you'd understand. We're going to need your help."

Charity gave her a dubious look.

Amity took a deep breath. "While you were being held captive at Amanda's, the Marquess of Asheburton stopped by."

Charity made a wry face. "Well, how could he not after Aunt Cleo practically ordered him to do so?"

"Exactly. And Gareth was upstairs with Faith and the baby, so it was up to me to entertain him, and of course he asked me to go to a ball with him tomorrow night."

"Of course."

"So, you know I can never think of a good reason to get out of something when I'm put on the spot like that. And then Matthew came in later and kissed me, and I told him he couldn't kiss me because I had to go to a ball with the marquess. He didn't like that at all and told me he'd be damned if he was going to stand around and watch while I glided out the door on Lord Asheburton's arm again. And that's when he asked me to marry him and we decided to elope." The torrent of words finally stopped pouring from her mouth, and she eyed her sister with guilty eyes. "Tomorrow night."

With sudden dread, Charity realized exactly what Amity needed her to do. "No way!" She stood up, and this time she started pacing. "I am not pretending to be you while being escorted by that . . . that . . . man." She spit out the last word like an epithet.

"It's the only way," pleaded Amity.

"I don't like him."

Amity bit her lip. "Actually, darling, I think you do." Charity stopped mid-pace and whipped her head around to stare at her sister, who stared back unwaveringly. "What's more, I think he cares for you as well." Her eyes were soft and understanding.

"You're wrong."

"Oh, Charity . . . not everything is a battle you must win at all costs. You spend so much time fighting everything, even yourself. Sometimes it's okay to just relax and let things happen around you." Amity paused, watching her twin struggle against her inner turmoil. "Think about his behavior at the ball that evening. Don't you think it was more the way a jealous man would act than a protective one?"

"I don't know," Charity muttered.

"Think about it," advised Amity. "Just do me a favor and think about it."

Thirteen

Charity wrinkled her nose as she surveyed the row of dresses in the wardrobe. Pale pink, pale lavender, pale blue, white, white, white. Every single frock was demure and correct and boring. And she had to choose one.

With a sigh she pulled out three of the brightest and spread them on the bed, finally choosing one in a mint green simply because it was the least fussy. Reflecting on the events of the day, she began getting dressed without waiting for Amity's maid to help her.

She'd traveled with Grace in the morning to visit Faith and the baby and then stayed, ostensibly to spend the afternoon with Amity before they both left to attend the ball that evening. By afternoon tea, both girls were jumpy and nervous while they waited for Matthew to come for his daily check on his London patients. So far, there had been three knocks on the door, all of them deliveries of more flowers to welcome little Imogen to the household.

At the fourth knock, Faith finally noted and remarked on it: "Goodness, Amity, you nearly jump out of your skin every time someone comes to the door. Are you feeling all right?"

Amity's eyes grew wide, so Charity hastily answered before her twin gave away the entire elopement plan, knowing her inability to skirt the truth when put on the spot. "I think she's just looking forward to seeing the Marquess of Asheburton again tonight."

Faith smiled and sipped her tea. "Gareth tells me he's been courting you since the Season began. I'm happy to see you return his interest. I understand he's rather well-regarded by Trevor, too."

Charity did her best not to snort and roll her eyes while Amity agreed that yes, he passed muster with many people of good standing and character within the *ton*. Fortunately, Desmond appeared in the doorway then and announced the arrival of Dr. Meadows.

All three girls stood. Faith excused herself and left the room to take Matthew upstairs. Amity and Charity followed her to the doorway and then peeked around the edge, silently following their progress with excited eyes until the pair disappeared down the corridor that housed both the master suite and the nursery.

"All right, they're gone." Charity reached out and grasped Amity's hand. "Let's go change."

Amity hesitated. "Do you think I'm doing the right thing?"

With a smile, Charity took her sister's face between her hands. "I think it doesn't matter what I think. The only thing you should be listening to right now is your heart . . . and Matthew."

Amity smiled back, a tremulous expression of thanks, and then she nodded firmly. Hand in hand, the girls ran up the stairs and down the hall to Amity's bedchamber.

By the time Matthew and Faith reappeared, smiling and talking about Imogen's good health, the girls were waiting together in the foyer. They exchanged greetings with the doctor, and then Amity, posing as Charity, turned to Faith. "Well, it's time to go back over to Grace's so I can get ready to go out this evening. May I send for someone to prepare a conveyance?"

Matthew spoke up. "There's no need for that, Miss Charity. I'm just leaving, and I'd be more than happy to drop you at Lord and Lady Huntwick's home."

Amity smiled. "That's very kind of you, Dr. Meadows. It is only a short way up the block, but these silly slippers, though fashionable, are certainly not meant for a great deal of walking."

"Yes," agreed Faith. "Thank you. That's a lovely offer." She gave Amity a hug then bent and kissed her on the forehead. "We miss having you and all your excitement around here, Charity. Now that Imogen has arrived, why don't you think about coming back to stay with Amity again?"

Amity gulped and nodded, not trusting herself to speak. Charity gave her a hard look from behind Faith's back and said, "Speak for yourself, Faith. Maybe I don't miss her all that much."

They all laughed, and then Amity and Matthew left, climbed into his curricle, and drove off down the street.

Charity watched them go, then took a deep breath and turned back to Faith. "I think I'll go read a bit before it's time to get dressed for the evening. Would you mind if I just took a light supper in my room instead of coming down for the meal?"

Faith tilted her head. Viewing her with assessing gray eyes she asked, "Are you sure you're feeling all right, Amity? Perhaps you should think about staying in."

"No, I'm fine," Charity hastily assured her, knowing that the more time she spent with her older sister, the sooner Faith would figure out that she and her twin had switched places. "I'm just really involved in this book and haven't had a great deal of time to read lately." She'd smiled disarmingly and walked away before Faith drew her into any more conversation.

And so here she was, dressed in Amity's mint green dress—she had to admit, it looked nicer than she'd thought it might—waiting for the Marquess of Asheburton to arrive.

As if summoned, she heard a vehicle pulling to a stop just outside the town house. Charity walked to the window and looked down. Lachlan Kimball was just stepping out of his coach, a bouquet of flowers in one hand and his hat in the other. He spoke to his footman a moment, and Charity rested her forehead on the cool glass, pondering what Amity had said about Lachlan having feelings for her. She chewed on her lower lip in consternation, her stomach doing odd little flip-flops as she watched him walk up the steps, placing his hat back on his head as he did, and then reaching for the knocker. She caught her breath. He was really very handsome.

The door opened, allowing light to spill out onto the steps below. Charity smiled to herself, hoping Desmond treated Lachlan with respect this one time. She'd made sure to tell the butler that the Marquess of Asheburton would be arriving that evening, in order to spare him the servant's typical indignation at unannounced visits. The last thing she needed was for the marquess to be in a poor frame of mind before she attempted to pull off the charade of being Amity.

A soft knock sounded on the door to the bedchamber, and a maid stuck her head inside. "Miss Amity, the Marquess of Asheburton has arrived."

"Thank you, Millie." Charity took a last deep breath and went down to begin her ordeal.

"You're awfully quiet."

Charity pulled her gaze from the row of opulent town houses passing at an astonishingly slow pace because of the evening traffic in this section of town. She sat with her hands folded primly in her lap, trying to distract herself from the knowledge that she was positioned across the coach from the one man who had the disconcerting ability to make her burn with both anger and yearning. She forced herself to smile and quietly replied, "I'm nursing a bit of a headache, my lord. I'm sure it won't trouble me the entire evening."

Lachlan leaned forward and covered her hands with his. "Would you prefer spending the evening in, Miss Ackerly? I can take you back home and we can see each other another night."

That was the last thing she wanted. There would be explanations to Gareth and Faith, and Charity was fairly certain she wouldn't get past the second sentence before her sister figured out that she wasn't Amity. She shook her head. "It's minor, my lord. Thank you so much, but I think it will fade within the hour." She turned back to the window, hoping he'd allow the silence until they reached the ball since she hadn't a clue how to go about having a simple, quiet conversation.

Lachlan sat back and regarded Amity's profile, trying to put his finger on the difference in her tonight. It was, to his recollection, the first time they'd been alone together since the morning in the garden when he kissed her. He smiled to himself at the memory.

"It's nice, Miss Ackerly, to spend a quiet spell with you in this manner. I know you enjoy having your sister along, but things are seldom calm when Charity is around. I confess to finding it a bit of a relief."

Stung, Charity bitterly recalled her sister's words. *What's more, I think he cares for you as well.* She blinked a couple times, angry to find herself on the verge of tears. *It's your own fault,* she silently chided herself, *for allowing such silly romantic notions to enter your head.* Instead of replying, she simply smiled and nodded, and then straightened in relief when she felt the coach pull into the small half-circle drive of the home hosting the ball they were to attend.

Inside, Lachlan placed his hands upon her shoulders. "I'm going to see if I can procure you some refreshment. Do you mind waiting for me here?"

Charity smiled and shook her head, still too angry to trust herself to speak. She watched the marquess walk away. His stride was fluid, reminding her of predatory cats about which she had read, and she shuddered slightly at the image. Such creatures were beautiful to observe, but only from a distance; up close they were deadly. She'd felt his gaze on her after their brief conversation in the coach and known she was in for a long night of trying to avoid situations in which they might find themselves alone.

Without warning, Lachlan appeared at her elbow and handed her a glass of lemonade. "I was going to bring you champagne, but thought it might intensify your headache."

"Thank you, my lord," she murmured, and took a sip.

"Would you care to dance right away, or would you rather look for some of your friends?"

Neither, thought Charity wryly. Aloud she said, "I think I'll find the ladies' retiring room and freshen up a bit."

Lachlan bowed and watched Charity go, his head tilted thoughtfully to the side. She seemed different than he remembered. The Amity Ackerly with whom he was familiar was quiet, yes, but poised and open and engaging. Tonight there was an air of nervous energy about her, even in the way she moved through the crowd, glancing about her as though expecting some sort of ambush. As though she were uncomfortable in her own skin. As though someone might know and reveal her secrets.

As the last phrase entered his head, several little inconsistencies clicked into place and he was suddenly overcome by a sense that the girl who accompanied him tonight was not Amity Ackerly. It was her twin sister. He was sure of it. But he had no idea why.

Setting his glass of champagne on a nearby table, Lachlan headed purposefully in the direction Charity had disappeared. He didn't want to spark a combative situation by openly questioning her. Instead, he would see if he could get her to reveal her identity on her own, and *then* he'd learn why. But the only way to learn what he must was if Charity spent the remainder of the evening at his side.

Unaware of her companion's resolve, inside the small room set aside for ladies to rest and repair their appearance, Charity sat quietly on a low stool and waited. She watched several groups come and go, and sighed when the last gaggle exited; a couple of the ladies had whispered to one another and then looked back in her direction. If she didn't go back out into the ballroom, rumors would fly that Amity Ackerly was secreting herself away from her escort for the evening.

She reluctantly rose and departed, but as soon as she exited the short hall off which the room was located, Lachlan appeared, pushing himself away from the wall and falling into step beside her. "Feeling better, Miss Ackerly?"

Startled, Charity almost dropped her fan. "W-why, yes," she stammered. "Sitting quietly for a few moments was just the thing." She had a moment of inspiration and handed him her empty glass. "And the lemonade really helped, I think." She smiled at him as brightly as she could. "I don't suppose you'd be a darling and go get me some more?"

The coquettish little smile and attempt to make sure they were in separate parts of the ballroom gave Lachlan even more reason to trust his instincts. He took the glass from her and smiled disarmingly. "Of course," he replied, but drew her hand through his arm. "Walk with me. I do so enjoy your company."

Charity kept the smile pinned to her face but looked away, pretending an absorbing interest in the other guests. She nodded at one or two acquaintances, then flipped open her fan and beat the air with it until they reached the refreshments table.

Securing two more glasses of lemonade, Lachlan guided her toward a small curtained alcove near the dance floor. Instant alarm set in. "Where are we going?" she asked, but then forced herself to calm down when she heard the breathy, urgent tone of her words.

"I thought it would be nice to sit and talk a few minutes," Lachlan replied. "Unless you'd rather dance?" He turned as though looking for a place to set down their glasses.

"No, the alcove is fine, my lord," she said. Numb, she wondered how early she could safely ask him to take her home without running the risk of encountering Faith and Gareth before they went to bed.

Lachlan made sure Charity was comfortably situated on a red brocade-upholstered sofa, and then handed her the lemonade. He sat beside her and sipped his own, watching her over the rim of his glass. Her misery was plain, despite the polite expression she was trying to maintain. He hid a smile, almost feeling sorry for her, then decided it was a perfect time to step up his game. "You seem . . . different."

Charity looked down and forced herself to count to ten. "Perhaps it is the headache, my lord."

He injected a note of worry into his voice. "Some air might do you good. Shall we take a turn on the terrace?"

"No!" Charity looked up, only to become lost in his inscrutable gray gaze. Her resolve softened, and she fought to keep her responses light. "I mean, no, thank you, my lord. I think a few moments of total silence would help me more than anything else."

"Total silence? At a ball?" His eyes turned teasing. "You ask much of me, Miss Ackerly. That sounds like something your *sister* would ask of an escort." He watched her closely. Charity's lips twitched, but she showed no other outward reaction to his words. Lachlan found himself grudgingly admiring the way she held up under assault.

Inside, Charity was seething with anger at his second negative reference to her that evening. She stood, abruptly deciding that if he was going to insist on remaining at her side the dance floor would be a much better place to be. At least there she could pretend not to hear anything he said.

She opened her mouth to belatedly accept his request for a dance but closed it again in horror when she heard the butler bellow out the very last two titles she wanted to hear announced as arrivals to the ball: *"The Earl and Countess of Huntwick!"*

Charity's eyes widened. In a near panic, she stepped over to the curtained opening and glanced at the curved staircase. Grace and Trevor were just descending, smiling and waving to friends and acquaintances. She turned back to Lachlan and smiled brightly. "You know, actually, I *do* think a walk on the terrace would be lovely."

Fourteen

Forcing herself to keep her eyes straight ahead, Charity strolled out onto the terrace with Lachlan, wishing he would pick up the pace a bit so that they would be away from the wall of windows and doors that afforded anyone who cared to glance in that direction a splendid view of those guests taking advantage of the temperate London evening. When he moved to the railing and seemed rather inclined to stay, she cast desperately about in her mind for an excuse to get him to go to one end of the terrace or the other. At the same time, she wondered if Lachlan had heard the butler announce the names of her sister and brother-in-law. She slanted a sideways glance up at him but couldn't tell from his profile as he stared out into the dark gardens.

She followed his gaze. The darkened gardens? Perfect.

Charity glanced back into the ballroom, hoping Grace would be waylaid by some of her many friends, and decided that spending some time alone with Lachlan was lesser of the two evils; her sister would discover her charade in a heartbeat. She let her hand slide from Lachlan's arm and backed toward the three shallow stairs that led to a dimly lit pathway. "Let's walk," she suggested. "We can get a bit farther away from the noise and heat of the crowd."

Lachlan almost smiled. *And from your sister,* he thought to himself. "Aren't you concerned about what people might think if they see you disappearing into the night with me?"

Clearly not grasping his meaning, Charity shook her head

and chanced another glance into the ballroom, checking if Grace's distinctive red-gold head was anywhere in sight. "Lots of people are going," she insisted, pointing at a couple descending before her. The furtive way they did so told Lachlan their intentions were definitely not chaste. Another perusal of Charity promised she had no idea why couples were slipping away.

He swept the terrace with a quick look. Few pairs remained outside, and those that did were engaged in conversation. If he was careful, he could shield Charity from them with his body until they reached the turn in the path that put them out of sight of the house. And then, while he had her alone, he could take the opportunity to shake her out of her charade.

"All right," he said, and moved around to her right side to quickly usher her down the steps and onto the cobbled path.

Charity was surprised but grateful at how quickly he was suddenly moving. Lachlan led her around a curve and shrugged out of his jacket. "The air is a bit chilly," he explained as he draped it over her shoulders. Instantly, his distinctive scent, an incredible, very male combination of leather, tobacco, and some elusive outdoorsy aroma she decided could only have come from Scotland, engulfed her. In one breath, Charity was carried back to that morning in the garden when he kissed her.

Lachlan didn't even notice the sudden dreamy look on her face. He'd covered her with his jacket, his main intention to hide as much of her pale green dress as possible, but voices were coming toward them down the path. For the moment the couple was absorbed with each other, but he knew if they walked past there would be no way to hide Charity's identity. Or, more correctly, Amity's, since she was the twin everyone assumed he'd escorted to the ball.

Quickly he tugged Charity off the walkway and behind a hedge, then stepped around and positioned himself so the only thing any passersby could see was his back.

"What are you doing?" Charity demanded.

"Shhh," said Lachlan, glancing over his shoulder.

"Don't shush me," she returned, and then gasped when he, realizing there was only one expeditious way to make her stop talking, pulled her suddenly against his chest. Without warning his lips descended on hers, stealing not only her words but her breath. Her eyes widened in shock for a moment, and she froze in his arms, desperately attempting to keep a firm grip on a reality quickly slipping from her grasp. His arms tightened around her, gathering her closer still. With a small surrendering whimper, she closed her eyes and melted against him.

Lachlan felt a strange surge of male triumph. Without thinking, he pressed his advantage and deepened the kiss, quite forgetting both his intention to keep her quiet and his earlier intention to force an admission that she was masquerading as her twin. He slanted his lips across hers and traced his mouth across her cheek to her earlobe, reveling in the sweetness of her ardor when she tilted her head to allow him access.

For Charity, at this moment in time, there was nothing else in the world except the two of them. Lachlan's hands, large, long-fingered, and strong, pressed into her back, cradling her against him. She felt safe, secure, and treasured. She felt the heat of his grip like a brand, even through the thick fabric of his coat and the thinner layers of her own garments, and she arched closer still, pressing her length against him, innocently stoking a fire entirely new to her.

"Yes," he whispered hoarsely into the shell of her ear,

stirring the tendrils of hair that curled there. "Just . . . like . . . that."

Before she could respond, he took her mouth again, drawing the plump morsel of her lower lip between his teeth and bearing lightly down until she caught her breath. Laughing softly, he turned so that his back was to the hedge, protecting her from the discomfort of the leaves and branches. His hand moved up her back to slide into the silky mass of her hair, each strand gliding through his fingers like liquid gold. He wanted nothing more than to bury his face in those fragrant tresses.

Utterly unable to form a coherent thought, Charity slid her palm up his torso to cup his cheek, opening her lips slightly in naive imitation of his actions. Her fingers followed the chiseled line of his jaw to the place their lips met. Lachlan growled and released her mouth, capturing her smallest finger between his teeth and then closing his lips around it to suckle gently before releasing it with a soft *pop*.

Charity buried her face in his chest, her humid breath escaping to bathe with warmth that hollow place between the twin planes of muscle. His fingers spread to cup her head and hold her there, his heart pounding against her cheek. With a tiny, whimpering sigh, she slipped both arms around his waist and stilled, more content than she'd ever felt in her entire life.

Lachlan, on the other hand, was coming to a swift, sobering realization. There was no doubt in his mind that the girl he'd just kissed was the same girl he'd kissed that morning at the Lloyd town house. There was also no doubt that this was Charity. *Not* her sister.

He closed his eyes a moment and then reached for Charity's shoulders, grasped them, and moved her so that a measure of space opened between them. Shaken from the spell that engulfed her, she raised passion-drunk eyes to Lachlan's. Her mouth fell open an instant before she allowed her face to fall into her hands.

"Oh my God," she muttered into her palms.

Lachlan waited for her to raise her head, searching for the words to tell her he knew the truth, that she didn't have to pretend anymore, but they wouldn't come. Warring with his need to protect and comfort her was the knowledge that she was likely just as upset by the fact that she'd melted into the arms of a man she didn't like as she was by the fact that she thought he didn't know her true identity. "Why didn't you tell me?" he finally asked.

She looked up. "Tell you what?"

The last thing he wanted was to accuse her and be wrong, so he kept silent, just looked at her steadily and waited for her to say something, *anything*, to help him out. She at last lifted her chin, straightened her shoulders and eyed him with the distant, regal hauteur he'd come to recognize. It was the way she looked each time they clashed, just before she shut down completely and froze him, and everybody else, out.

"I'd like to go home, please," she said.

The ride home was even more silent and awkward than the ride to the ball. Charity, instead of looking out the window this time, sat quietly and stared at her hands, unable to risk meeting his eyes, even momentarily. She was torn between anger with herself for again falling willingly into his arms when he thought she was his sister, and a heart-wrenching pain she didn't even begin to comprehend.

When the coach came to a stop before the Lloyd town house, she finally spoke. "I can see myself to the door, my lord."

Lachlan felt something twist in him at the flat quality of her voice. Everything about Charity was typically so vital, so alive; sometimes uncomfortably so. "I'm sure you can, but—"

She interrupted. "Please just let me go."

Utterly defeated by her distance, he sat back and watched. She climbed down with the assistance of his footman and then walked, head high, up the steps to the front door, and disappeared inside.

Charity flipped onto her stomach in Amity's bed and punched her pillow angrily as if it were at fault for her inability to find sleep. Unsatisfyingly, the pillow didn't fight back at all, not even when she completely lost patience and threw it across the room. It landed against the wall with a soft friendly thud that did nothing to quell her frustration. Every time she closed her eyes, she felt his hands upon her, saw his face descending toward hers, passionate intent smoldering in those silver eyes.

She finally sat up, swung her feet over the side of the bed, and padded across the room to pick up the pillow. No more, she decided. In the morning, after she'd dealt with the family learning of Amity's elopement, she would go back to Grace and Trevor's and embrace the Season properly. No more games, no more deception. Above all, no more Marquess of Asheburton.

Her mind made up, she climbed back into bed, rolled over, closed her eyes and finally fell into a fitful sleep.

Several blocks away, in his cousin's bed, Lachlan was having just as much trouble, but not because he couldn't get his feelings under control. Quite the contrary. He was trying to figure out how to stop seeing one twin and begin seeing the other—a daunting undertaking, indeed, since the sister he preferred couldn't stand being in the same room with him.

He linked his fingers behind his head and stretched out, smiling illogically up into the darkness. Twice now he'd kissed Charity Ackerly. Twice she'd shown a natural passion and sweet vulnerability that evoked protective feelings in him he hadn't anticipated. He didn't merely desire Charity. He wanted to take care of her. Forever.

His mind made up, he rolled over, closed his eyes, and finally fell into a blissful slumber.

Fifteen

"Good morning, my lord."

Gareth flicked a glance up at Charity before returning his attention to the newspaper he was reading while he ate his breakfast. "Good morning, Amity," he returned.

Charity took a deep breath. Matthew and her sister had been gone overnight now, and should now be well on their way to Scotland, so it was time to end the deception. "I'm not Amity," she said.

"Oh. Good morning, then, Charity." She watched her brother-in-law reach out, feel for his plate, and secure a slice of bacon. It disappeared behind the newspaper. "I didn't realize you were spending the night. Help yourself to some breakfast." His other hand popped out from behind the paper and pointed to the sideboard covered with breakfast dishes.

Charity filled a plate and sat down, feeling awkward. She buttered a piece of toast and regarded the open newspaper at the other end of the table, knowing she couldn't have a real conversation with her brother-in-law until he'd finished his meal and morning perusal of the *Times*. "Where's Faith?"

"Imogen had her up for feedings several times in the night. She's sleeping late."

They both fell silent, the only noises the occasional clinking of Charity's fork on her plate and the rustling of Gareth's newspaper. The longer they sat, the more nervous and miserable Charity became. She'd been prepared to face the music regarding Amity's elopement when she came down, and the waiting now felt interminable. She folded and placed her napkin on her nearly untouched plate of food and prepared to stand, intending to go wake Faith so she could tell her sister and get it over with, when they were interrupted by a sharp rapping on the door, followed immediately by excited voices.

Gareth laid his paper down in surprise. Charity, recognizing the nearly shrill voices of Aunt Cleo and Grace, gripped the edges of her chair. Belatedly she remembered that, in her agitation and subsequent preoccupation with Lachlan the evening before, she had completely forgotten to send word to the Huntwick town house that she wouldn't be returning home.

Grace swept into the room ahead of Cleo, Trevor, and Desmond, the butler chasing her at nearly a most undignified run. "My lady," he said in a labored, affronted voice, "you really *must* allow me to announce your entirely unexpected visit at this more than ridiculously early hour. You simply cannot be both unexpected *and* unannounced!"

Grace ignored him and came straight over. "Where's Charity?" she asked Charity.

"Relax," Gareth said in an amused drawl. "You're talking to her. I take it you didn't know she was spending the night."

Grace's face turned red, and she looked as though she might burst. Too angry to speak, she threw up her hands and turned to her husband, who, for once, looked grim instead of amused.

"No," Trevor said shortly. "She didn't tell us, nor did she bother sending a note around to keep us from worrying."

Cleo thunked her cane loudly on the floor and pointed it

at Charity. "Someone should turn you over his knee, young lady."

That particular phrase only reminded her that Lachlan had said much the same thing. She pressed her lips together and counted to ten, then took a deep breath and said evenly, "I can explain everything."

"I certainly hope so," Grace burst out, finally finding her voice.

"What's all the commotion?" Faith stood in the wide doorway, looking confused by the presence of nearly her entire London family in her breakfast room before ten o'clock in the morning. Her eyes settled on the one twin in the room. "Where's Charity?" she asked.

"Oh, bloody hell," Charity muttered. She'd finally had enough. "Why doesn't anyone ever ask where Amity is?"

"Because Amity is a dear sweet girl who would never stay out all night without letting someone know where she would be," said Cleo. She tilted her head to the side and watched Charity closely. "Or . . . would she?"

"She's probably sleeping late," said Trevor. "We saw her leaving a ball last night with Ashe not long after we arrived, and she didn't look as though she felt terribly well."

"Oh, no!" exclaimed Faith. "Maybe I should go check on her."

"No!"

They all eyed Charity in surprise.

Her heart leapt into her throat, and she swallowed hard, silently wishing she hadn't eaten those few bites of toast, since her stomach didn't seem at all interested in retaining them. "Perhaps if we all just sat down," she suggested. She stood and offered up her chair. "Aunt Cleo?"

While they all found places around the table, Charity walked to the doorway, nervously wringing her hands. She turned back to face her family and said, "Amity isn't exactly here for you to go check on, Faith."

"Well, that's just silly," her sister said. "I stuck my head in last night when Imogen was up, to be sure she . . ." Comprehension dawned. "Oh. You were in Amity's bed."

Charity bit her lip and nodded.

"Well," said Grace. "If she isn't exactly here, where exactly might she be?"

"She's run off with that handsome young doctor," Cleo announced. "I'd bet my last dime on it."

Gareth scoffed. "Meadows? Not a chance. Good man, good doctor."

Faith nodded in vigorous agreement.

"I'm so glad you feel that way," Charity said, her voice tentative, "Don't you think he'll make a good husband for Amity?" She winced, closed her eyes and waited for the verbal barrage. When she was met only with silence, she cautiously opened one eyelid and peeked at the table. Everyone was staring at her, a variety of expressions on their collective faces. Faith looked horrified, as did Grace. Gareth and Trevor looked amused. Aunt Cleo looked positively gleeful.

Feeling a desperate need to fill the sudden silence, she hastened to explain how the elopement had come about, her words tumbling over one another in her haste. "You see, Amity and Matthew fell in love almost as soon as they met, but he didn't know how to tell her because the Marquess of Asheburton was so persistent in his suit, but Amity didn't really like him, and who can blame her"—Charity paused and scowled—"since he's such a wretched bounder . . . and . . . and . . . a-a cad."

She waved her hands in the air in frustration, especially when she noted the broadening smiles on the men's faces.

Even Grace and Faith were trying to hide traces of amusement, but Charity plunged recklessly ahead. "Anyway, we
switched identities yesterday afternoon, and they're on
their way to Scotland, and they have enough of a head start
that nobody will catch them now, so we might as well all be
happy about it." She ended her rushed speech, took a deep
breath, and waited.

"Ashe *is* a cad," said Gareth after a long pause, his lips
twitching.

"And a bounder," Trevor agreed with sham solemnity.

Charity looked from one face to another in confusion.
"What is *wrong* with all of you?

Lachlan Kimball cleared his throat and stepped into the
room. Charity, who had her back to the arched entryway,
had been unable to see him appear just before her an-
nouncements, followed by Desmond, who looked less than
pleased at the arrival of yet another unexpected visitor.

Charity froze at the sound but didn't turn. There was no
need. She already knew who stood behind her.

"Perhaps, Miss Ackerly, you can force yourself to tolerate
my wretched presence long enough for a private word?"

Sixteen

Nobody moved. Charity refused to turn, refused to even answer. Instead, she just stood, rooted in place, a shuttered, icy expression on her features.

Aunt Cleo was the first to react. "Faith," she said, pushing herself up and out of her chair with her cane. "You haven't even offered me a single look at that baby, and I've been here for at least thirty minutes."

All at once everyone seized on the offered activity and began a mass exodus of the breakfast room. No one said anything. Faith and Grace each gave Charity a quick hug on the way past, while Gareth and Trevor each clapped Lachlan on the shoulder.

Aunt Cleo stopped in front of Charity, gave her a stern look, and then leaned around to include the marquess in her admonishment. "Don't you two go and mess up a perfectly good elopement." She patted Charity fondly on the cheek, then moved past to join the others, who had gone to the front sitting room to wait for Faith to bring Imogen down from the nursery.

Silence fell. Finally, Lachlan spoke. "Charity."

She turned, a brittle smile pasted upon her face, and politely asked, "Have you had breakfast, my lord?" She moved toward the sideboard as if intending to prepare a plate for him.

His heart wrenched. She looked small and fragile and pale, and he knew that a great deal more was weighing on her than her sister's elopement. "I've eaten, thank you," he replied.

At his gentle tone, Charity finally met his eyes. The protective look on his face was almost her undoing, but when he took a step toward her, she panicked and retreated to the other side of the breakfast table.

"I'm sorry you got caught up in our little family drama," she began, and then stopped, uncertain where to go with that line of thought. After all, he'd been a victim of deception at her hand, too. She looked down and scuffed one of her toes along a line in the pattern on the lush Aubusson carpet.

Warmth filled Lachlan at the self-conscious little gesture, at her large and wounded eyes, and he stifled the urge to laugh. Charity looked just like a little girl who'd been caught doing something forbidden, and he imagined she must have been quite a handful as a child. Goodness knew she'd already turned his life upside down in the few short weeks since the Season began.

He walked toward her, hoping she wouldn't look up and retreat again before he reached her. His luck held. He neared enough to reach for her chin, intending to tilt her face up to his, but she nearly jumped out of her skin and slapped his hand away.

"Good lord, Lachlan!" she exclaimed, taking a step back, not noticing in her agitation that she'd addressed him by his first name. "I see now why you reminded me of one of those predatory jungle cats I've read about."

A jungle cat? "Interesting," he said. "Would you like to know what *you* remind *me* of?"

"No," she said, cross, and turned her back on him to look out the window.

He stepped up behind her, placed his hands on her

shoulders and leaned down very close to her ear. "A kitten," he said. His warm breath tickled. "You remind me of a kitten that has been backed into a corner, ready to burst out, claws first, hissing and scratching."

She shrugged her shoulders, trying to shake off his hands. "Then stop backing me into corners."

They both stared out into the back garden in silence.

"I know it was you," Lachlan said.

Charity's stomach twisted. She knew he was referring to their first kiss, stolen in the very location at which they both stared, but she chose to purposely misinterpret. "Of course you do. I already admitted pretending to be Amity last night."

"I'm talking about the first time I kissed you, Charity. Right out on that lawn. That time I mistakenly assumed you were Amity, and I apologize for that."

"I don't know what you're talking about." Her voice was low, almost a whisper, and he had to lean close to understand.

It *had* been Charity. He was right. He was sure of it. "No more lies between us, kitten. I'd like to start with a clean slate."

"Start?" Charity tossed her head scornfully. "Start what? Have you suddenly decided that, since you can't have Amity, now you'll settle for me?"

Lachlan felt his patience begin to slip. "My courtship of Amity was based on a suggestion by Huntwick and on the memory of that first kiss—the kiss you deny we shared. Had you informed me of my mistake that morning, we'd likely never have come to this point."

Charity spun around, her eyes spitting blue sparks. "I haven't denied it." She tossed her head scornfully. "There's nothing to deny."

Eyes stormy, Lachlan's tenuous hold on his self-control abruptly snapped. Charity knew the instant it happened, and she gasped when she discerned his intent. Before she could move, he closed the distance between them in a single stride, snaked his arm around her waist, and hauled her against him. "Then deny *this*," he growled, taking her lips in a bruising, punishing kiss intended to remind her of all that had already passed between them.

She reached up with trembling hands and pushed at his shoulders in a desperate attempt to escape. Her struggles were ineffective against both his strength and the burning glow of desire that began the instant their mouths touched. That warmth spread throughout her body, engulfing her with tingling, aching sensation. With a small sigh, she again gave up and melted against him.

Lachlan's brief anger dissolved. Exerting supreme effort, he forced himself to let go of her, placed both of his hands on her rib cage until he was sure she was steady on her feet, and then he broke off the kiss, his heart pounding with the physical need he felt. He stepped away from her.

As Charity felt the warmth of his hands on her sides fall away and his lips leave hers, her eyes flew open. "No," she whispered, "not yet." She stood on tiptoe, took his face between her hands and renewed the kiss.

"Oh . . . *God*. Charity." Lachlan struggled against the incoming tide of his arousal, trying to take another step away, but she followed his movement. He groaned and surrendered, suddenly slanting his mouth across hers, tracing the line between her lips with his tongue. She opened her mouth, tried to catch her breath, and he took full advantage, deepening their embrace.

For Charity, the world felt as though it had suddenly tipped sideways. She slipped her arms around his waist and held on for dear life, shyly mimicking the movements of his tongue with her own. Her fingers spread on his back, the taut muscles there rippling beneath her palms, and when he began thrusting his tongue into her mouth in an ageless if primitive suggestion, she clenched her fingers and dug them into the thick material of his jacket.

"So sweet," he murmured against her lips, and then slid his mouth down the plane of her neck to nibble the thin layer of skin above her pounding pulse. His hand moved up her rib cage to settle on the soft mound of a breast, and he felt himself stir and harden when his palm again encountered the stiff little nubbin that told him of her equal arousal.

When she slipped her hand around and tucked it inside his jacket, he realized that if he didn't stop this now he would take her here on the floor of her brother-in-law's breakfast room while her family waited just down the hall. "Stop," he said, capturing her wandering hand in his own.

She lifted her lips again, seeking another kiss, and he pushed her gently back against the wall and then braced his hands on either side of her. Locking his elbows, he forced himself to maintain some space between their bodies. He rested his forehead on the wall next to her face.

"You have no idea what you do to me, kitten," he said.

Hot shame flooded Charity as she realized how wantonly she had just thrown herself at him even after he tried to stop her. For a second time. "Oh, God," she said in a broken voice. She covered her mouth with her hand and ducked under his arm, walked a few steps away and then stopped. She stared blindly out the window until the beauty of the garden scene blurred. Angrily, with her back to him so he couldn't see, she wiped away the tear.

"Charity." Lachlan took a single step forward and then stopped. He couldn't trust himself to touch her again.

"Just go, please."

"We should . . ."

She turned to stare at him once more, her chin lifted and her eyes cold. "No. We definitely should not. Please go."

He searched her face for a second but then without another word spun on his heel and left the room, his long strides echoing sharply up the corridor. A scant moment later, Charity flinched as she heard the front door slam.

Seventeen

"But I don't *like* him."

Charity tossed that statement over her shoulder at Aunt Cleo as she climbed out of the Huntwick coach and walked toward the town house steps. The rest of its occupants followed suit. Everyone stepped inside and surrendered their wraps.

"I think you do," the old woman said.

Charity sighed. Too much had happened in too short a time for her to even muster the energy to be angry with her wily old relative. She eyed the stairs, contemplating hiding in her room to escape the conversation, but knew it would just be waiting another time. "I'm sure he's a good man, and that he will make some very fortunate girl a lovely husband. But I'm not that girl."

Cleo snorted and went into the front sitting room, her cane hitting the floor with more force than necessary to punctuate her next words. "You certainly looked like that girl after your little talk in the breakfast room."

Charity sucked in her breath, her face draining of color.

They all sat down, Grace taking a seat next to her younger sister on a green-striped settee. "Aunt Cleo!" She shot her aunt an exasperated look and put an arm around her sibling's shoulders. "Whether the events of the past two days have been wrong or right, they are water under the bridge and we'll deal with them as a family. If Charity does not wish to continue an acquaintance with the Marquess of Asheburton, she does not have to do so."

Charity gave her a grateful smile.

"Well, if that's the case and she doesn't like the man, she shouldn't come out of a private meeting with him looking like she's been thoroughly kissed!"

Trevor laughed and then quickly tried to cover it with a cough. His wife glared at him.

"She's right," said Charity in a small voice. "He did kiss me. He kissed me and I liked it, and I *hate* that I liked it."

Grace patted her knee. "You'll find someone else you like to kiss." She turned to her husband. "Won't she?"

He looked startled at being addressed. "Oh, of course," he agreed. "Although, I will point out that you weren't very happy about kissing me, at first, and you have yet to find someone else."

Grace narrowed her eyes. "*Yet,*" she said, warningly.

Trevor just grinned.

"I'd really just like to put it all behind me," said Charity wearily. She stood. "I think I'll go lie down for a bit. I didn't sleep at all well last night."

The assembled company watched her go. When she was out of earshot Cleo said, "I'll take her to the Rutherfords' ball with me tonight. Asheburton is probably still smarting from whatever Charity said to make him leave so abruptly, and will likely spend the evening playing cards, or whatever it is you men do when you can't handle your women."

Grace shook a finger at her. "Promise me you won't interfere. I think we all need to stay out of this."

Trevor snorted, making no attempt to hide his disbelief. "Since when did you learn what it means to not interfere? Your entire family thrives on interference." He stopped speaking when he saw his wife's face darken. Realizing he might actually have gone too far, he tossed Cleo a jaunty salute, pressed a kiss on Grace's cheek, and beat a wise and hasty retreat to his study.

Lachlan Kimball swept into the study at his cousin's town house and headed straight for the well-stocked liquor cabinet. Above a sideboard laden with neat rows of crystal he upended a glass, found the decanter of brandy, and poured himself a generous helping. After a couple of rejuvenating swallows, he sat down on the edge of a burgundy leather upholstered club chair and considered the events of the morning.

The entire situation with the Ackerly twins had been a debacle from beginning to end. He should have listened to Sebastian's warning about becoming involved with any of the sisters in that family. Taking another slow swallow, he leaned back. He had options. Entire ballrooms full of options. After all, London was positively teeming with marital prospects.

It was time, he decided, to just choose one of the more pleasant girls the mamas of the *ton* were continually parading past him like cattle. He would simply use the process of elimination. He'd dance and converse with them until he found one reasonably well spoken, not opposed to living in Scotland, and who, most importantly, utterly lacked a taste for drama.

He stood and walked to the desk. A stack of invitations to events taking place that evening sat neatly in the center, awaiting his perusal. He picked them up, perched a hip on the ornately carved edge of the two-hundred-year old piece of furniture, and fanned them out. After a moment's trepidation he decided it didn't really matter which he chose; he doubted, after what had transpired between Charity and himself over the past twenty-four hours, that she would be in the mood to leave her sister's home this evening. Choosing an invitation at random, he tossed the rest into the rubbish bin.

Just before he stood, his eyes fell on another piece of paper in the bin next to the desk. Struck by a sense of familiarity, he bent and plucked it out. It was the list of potential marital prospects he, Thorne, Hunt, and the Lloyd brothers had created the day he arrived in London. He scanned the list until he came to the last name: Lucinda Harcourt. He tried to remember what his friends had said about her but drew a complete blank. Fairly certain he'd remember any mention of bad qualities, he decided to take a chance. He jotted a quick note and then took it into the hall. His burly valet, Niles, was just coming down the stairs.

"Oh, good." Lachlan handed him the folded note. "Would you have a footman deliver this note to . . ." He paused as he tried to remember the young lady's name.

Niles glanced at the name Lachlan had written on the outside. "Lucinda Harcourt, my lord?"

The valet's gravelly voice was just as rough as his appearance. Lachlan had first encountered him in one of the dark alleys of London, defending a woman of the streets from a group of drunken men bent on obtaining her services for free. He'd prepared to step in and help but soon realized it wouldn't be necessary. While he watched, Niles broke one man's jaw, another man's collarbone, and several ribs on a third. The rest ran off, including the prostitute, leaving Niles abandoned to the young Marquess of Asheburton. Upon learning the honorable pugilist was out of work and homeless, Lachlan had taken him to Asheburton Keep and offered him a position as his valet, despite his lack of experience.

"Milord?"

Startled out of his memories, Lachlan stared blankly at his valet before recalling the topic at hand. The servant had unfolded the missive and read it without asking permission. "Oh. Yes. Her."

Niles offered him a long look and then grinned, his craggy face splitting oddly as he did. "Do you mind me asking why you're taking a girl you don't know to one of your fancy parties? Did that lassie you were after toss you over?"

Lachlan just turned toward the stairs, clapping the valet on the shoulder. "I don't mind you *asking,*" he said, and then offered nothing further.

Niles watched his master go, glanced down at the note in his hand, and headed off in search of a footman. He hoped the marquess managed to find a wife soon so they could get back to Scotland. Although the city had once been his home, London, with its noises and smells and lack of room to breathe was not at *all* to his liking anymore.

Eighteen

It took Lachlan less than five minutes in Lucinda Harcourt's company to recall precisely how his cousin had described her: *A complete henwit. Attractive, but no substance.*

She certainly was attractive. Seated across from him in the coach beside her silent duenna, she was the picture of quiet, pale blonde sophistication. Her hair was elegantly coiffed, her gown exquisitely crafted, her beauty of the sort that soothed one's eyes and brought a smile to one's face. Then she opened her mouth and attempted to follow a conversational lead. Within seconds, it become evident she had the intellectual capacity of a porcelain figurine. Even when he suggested the weather was unusually balmy, she'd blinked in confusion and asked, "You mean outside?"

By the third vapid response, Lachlan simply nodded and gave up. After they arrived at the ball and she began to socialize she would surely manage to become interesting.

He hoped.

Cleo frowned and watched Charity smile and sweetly decline yet another request to dance. She was beginning to think talking her niece into an evening out in an effort to help her forget the events of the morning was a mistake. Although from all outward appearances Charity appeared to be having a marvelous time, Cleo knew her well enough to see her smile was forced and overly bright, and that it did not reach her eyes.

She sighed and peered around, hoping to spot Amanda Lloyd or some of Charity's other young friends; standing about with an elderly aunt wasn't going to put the sparkle back in the girl's eyes. But she saw nobody with whom Charity had become friendly in Town, so she decided it was likely best to call it a night.

She'd just laid a hand on Charity's arm when her eyes fell upon a couple at the top of the stairs. She sucked in a shocked breath.

Charity glanced over in surprise. "What is it, Aunt Cleo?" The older lady's sudden pallor and stunned expression caused her to follow the direction of her stare, and she felt the blood drain from her own face. The Marquess of Asheburton was descending the ornately carved staircase, and he had a young woman on his arm.

"Who is *that?*" she hissed.

Startled, Cleo dragged her gaze from the unexpected arrivals, glanced at her niece and then smiled. The withdrawn young woman she'd brought to the ball was gone, replaced by vintage Charity, full of life, brimming with energy, ready to spit fire.

"Oh, that?" Cleo feigned innocence. "That is the Marquess of Asheburton."

Charity narrowed her eyes and crossed her arms.

"Oh! You meant the girl with him, of course. Silly of me. Of course you know Asheburton," stalled Cleo. "Rather well, I believe," she added. Slanting a glance at her niece, she noted the girl's visible impatience and reluctantly acquiesced. "Her name is Lucinda Harcourt, and it's her third season out. Her parents are modest landowners and have some connection with the Earl of Tallimon, who has apparently spent a pretty penny sponsoring and outfitting the girl each Season."

"She's really quite beautiful," said Charity thoughtfully.

"Yes. She is." Cleo watched her closely. "They make a rather nice couple, don't they?"

Charity looked away. "They do, at that. Will you excuse me a moment, Aunt? I think I'll go freshen up a bit." She snatched a glass of champagne off the tray of a passing waiter and swept off without awaiting any response.

Cleo followed her niece's progress, a path leading her right in front of the main staircase. She glided under the nose of Lachlan Kimball without giving the slightest indication that she knew he was there. Had she been able to do so without calling attention to herself, Cleo would have clapped her hands with pride at the girl's performance. Instead, she watched Lachlan nearly miss the last step down into the ballroom as he caught sight of Charity's distinctive strawberry blonde head. Cleo stifled a laugh, thunked her cane on the floor in satisfaction, and turned to go find her friends.

Charity reached the ladies retiring room, in which she found herself blissfully alone. She looked down at the glass of champagne in her hand, then tilted back her head and drank it in three long swallows. Done, she set the glass on a table and turned to face herself in the mirror. The young lady in the reflection gazed back with a serene expression, which was puzzling; apparently she felt a good deal angrier than she looked.

Charity turned, paced a few steps back, and then closed her eyes, but that was no good either. She recalled the way he'd looked while casually descending the ornate staircase, his dark good looks a perfect foil for the stunning, sophisticated blonde on his arm. Charity's stomach clenched into a tight little knot of—

Of what?

Of *nothing*, she decided firmly. Resolute, she reopened her eyes, spun around, and faced her reflection again.

He had a lot of nerve, kissing and holding her the way he had just that morning, when he had to have known he'd be spending the evening with another woman entirely. Well, the wretch could just enjoy himself with whomever he pleased, she decided. And she would do precisely the same. She tossed her reflection a bright, brittle smile, and ventured from the retiring room back out into the crowd.

The next two hours flew by; Charity laughed through them. She flirted, she danced, and not once did she so much as glance in Lachlan Kimball's direction. Cleo watched both parties in delight, although much of her focus was on Lachlan. The man quite literally resembled a thundercloud. Lucinda Harcourt clung to his arm, seemingly oblivious to the fact that he was paying no attention to her, toting him from group to group, chattering away like a brainless magpie, unable to see past her own frivolous existence and note the developing storm.

The dowager glanced at Charity again, who was accepting yet another glass of champagne from one of her many admirers. Cleo watched with satisfaction for a few minutes before glancing away, but when she looked back, she gasped and nearly jumped out of her skin. The Marquess of Asheburton was standing right in front of her, without his date, his expression positively murderous. "How long, my lady, do you intend to allow this?"

Cleo straightened her shoulders and eyed him with icy regality. "Allow what, my lord?"

"Charity's behavior."

The dowager raised disdainful brows. "Just what business is it of yours? She appears to be having a grand time, doing exactly what all the other young ladies of her class do at such events. She's dancing, my lord, and socializing, and enjoying a great popularity."

"She's drinking, Lady Egerton. She's drinking quite a bit. It's not normal behavior for Charity. Perhaps, as her relative and chaperone, you would have noted it if you hadn't been so busy watching me."

Cleo's eyes widened and she banged her cane on the floor. "Mind the way you speak to me, young man! Given your behavior with regard to both of my nieces and the company you've chosen this evening, I'd say you have no leg to stand on."

"Please forgive me if I have offended you, Lady Egerton." He gave her a pointed look. "But given your unassailable chaperoning skills, it must have caught your notice that Anthony Iverson has been hovering in her vicinity for the past hour."

Startled, Cleo glanced again in Charity's direction. Her niece was gone.

"Oh, dear," she said, quite forgetting her ire. "Charity knows better than to associate with the likes of that man."

"Charity has a tendency to do precisely what she should *not* when she's under the influence of her rather formidable temper. I cannot imagine being under the influence of several glasses of champagne in addition will help in the least." Lachlan swept the room with his eyes, seeking not only Charity's bright hair and attire but Iverson. When he found neither, he laid a hand on the old lady's shoulder. "Wait here," he instructed. Then he strode off in the direction of the doors to the terrace.

Stepping outside, Lachlan looked to the right and the left, hoping he'd see Charity talking and laughing in one of the small groups that had moved outside to escape the crowd and the noise within. She was nowhere to be found. His eyes roved the garden, delving into each shadowy nook. It was, by the *ton's* standards, a rather spare garden with open expanses of beautifully manicured lawn rolling between small, well-tended beds of foliage. There were gaslights lining a footpath of neatly spaced flagstones, making it difficult for a couple to slip away for a dark tryst.

Satisfied that Charity wasn't out here, Lachlan turned and walked back into the ballroom. He caught Cleo's anxious eye and shook his head slightly to indicate he hadn't found her, but unable to shake a feeling of urgent dread, he located Lucinda and politely extracted her from gossiping with a group of her equally vapid friends. "Let's take a turn around the room, shall we?"

Lucinda dimpled and placed her hand on his arm. "I thought you'd abandoned me, my lord," she said, her eyes as wide and guileless as those of a china doll. Lachlan gave her a distracted smile and led her toward the steps, skirting the dance floor and keeping to the room's perimeter, his eyes alert for any sign of his quarry.

Her fingers were tingly. Charity giggled and held them up in front of her, then thrust them toward Anthony Iverson's face and wiggled them. "They feel like they should sparkle," she said in a wondrous tone.

Anthony glanced over his shoulder and then smiled down disarmingly at her. "Do you think you can walk very quickly and quietly with me to that gate over there?" He pointed across a short expanse of lawn to a narrow, wrought iron entry set into the side wall of the garden.

"'Course I can," said Charity cheerfully. "I can do *lots* of things." She started to take a step in that direction but was brought up short by her companion.

"Not just yet," he said. "We're playing a game, sort of

like hide and go seek. Did you ever play that when you were a little girl?"

She nodded quickly but then blinked when the action made her dizzy. She reached out and clutched his sleeve to maintain her balance. "My head feels all sparkly, too," she said, swaying slightly.

Anthony grimaced. If he was going to get her out of here, it would have to be soon, while she could still walk. He looked toward the terrace one more time and then emerged from the shadows at the side of the house, tugging Charity along behind him. She stumbled in his wake, somehow managed to keep her footing, and giggled again.

"Shh," he hissed.

They reached the gate, which he opened quickly, wincing at the sharp metallic clang. He wanted their absence to be noted, but needed time to get her away from the ball first. He pushed Charity ahead and then slipped out just behind her.

Charity leaned up against the garden wall, lifted her skirts slightly and looked down at her feet. They appeared to be right where they belonged, but, oddly, she couldn't feel them. She looked at Anthony in mute appeal.

He chuckled. "You're going to be just fine," he said, and then bent and swept her effortlessly into his arms.

"Oh, thank you," she said with a musical giggle, punctuated by a hiccough. "Where are we going?"

"To my coach."

"Why are we going to your coach? Aunt Cleo will wonder where I've gone." A tiny little thread of alarm rendered Charity momentarily sober, but it was dispelled when Anthony said, "I told her I would see you home."

"Well, that was very nice of you," she pronounced. Her eyes felt suddenly heavy, and she rested her head on his shoulder. "No reason for her to leave early if she's not sleepy too," she murmured into his cravat.

Yes, thought Iverson. *That was very nice of me.* He sneered. Certain families had recently snubbed him and given him the cut direct one too many times. He now had a plan to avenge himself on their hypocrisy, to perhaps earn the reputation he'd been unfairly given. Every breath of scandal that touched the Caldwell and Lloyd families was either ignored or brushed away because of their prominent places in Society. Not this time. Tonight he'd keep Charity away long enough to ensure her reputation was beyond redemption.

He looked down at the beautiful girl who had passed out in his arms and smiled with anticipation. While he was at it, he saw no reason why he shouldn't sample the goods . . . and by doing so, further ruin any future chance of a noble match.

Beyond worried now, Lachlan mentally ticked off the minutes since he'd last seen either Charity or Iverson. It had been at least half an hour. Short of questioning everyone with whom she socialized during the ball, or searching the entire town house, either of which would raise eyebrows and threaten Charity's reputation, he had no idea what to do. He'd circled the entire room and already convinced Lucinda she needed a moment in the ladies room, after which he'd carefully questioned her about the occupants, feeling slightly guilty that he was using the unsuspecting girl in such a manner. He stood now near the terrace doors and racked his brain, fighting the impulse to leave and begin a search that was sure to be fruitless. Cleo remained where he'd left her, and even across the room he could see her signs of strain.

Lucinda, who had stepped away to talk with a wildly

gesturing group of young women, returned to his side. "Goodness," she said in a breathy little voice, "Papa is always afraid I'll do something stupid and get myself in trouble, but I never really knew what he meant until now!"

Distracted, Lachlan flicked her a glance. It was all the encouragement she needed.

"Therese Thomasson-Sinclair just told me that she saw one of those bothersome Ackerly twins sneaking across the lawn and out the gate with Anthony Iverson!" She paused to take a breath and then plunged onward, flushed with pleasure and acutely aware of the fact that she had finally managed to garner some interest from her escort. Lachlan's former guilt evaporated when he realized she had been gleefully gossiping about the very girl whose reputation he was attempting to save. "I didn't think much of it until Therese said it was high time one of those girls got herself in trouble since they keep marrying all the best men." Lucinda nodded at this proffered wisdom, her blonde curls bobbing cheerfully.

"Miss Harcourt."

She glanced up to see Lachlan watching her in a way that made her quite uncomfortable. "My lord?"

"Did Therese say when she saw them?"

"N-no," she stammered. "I could go ask."

"That won't be necessary," said Lachlan. He took her arm and led her over to Cleo. "Lady Egerton, permit me to introduce Miss Lucinda Harcourt."

Lucinda bobbed a pretty curtsy but then jumped when the older lady poked Lachlan in the chest with her cane, ignoring the introduction. "Where is my niece?"

"Miss Harcourt will explain while you take her home. After that, go tell Huntwick I've gone after her and will send word if I need his assistance." Cleo opened her mouth to ask questions, but Lachlan cut her off. "Go now. There's no time. Word is already spreading through this ballroom and will make it to others. *Go.*"

He spun and took a couple of steps before turning back. "I will find her, Lady Egerton," he promised, his voice fierce.

Wordlessly she nodded and watched him go.

Nineteen

By the time Marquess of Asheburton's coach finally rumbled northward out of London, it was over two hours since he'd last seen Charity and his fears ran in a thousand directions.

"Head for Scotland," he ordered his coachman, praying that Iverson's intent was at least that noble. "Stop at every inn along the way, even those you deem unsuitable places for me to stay. I'll make a quick inquiry, and, if need be, we'll continue on."

Three times they stopped, and all three times he learned nothing. Just outside the city the condition of the roads and the darkness made it necessary to travel more slowly, which gave Lachlan far too much time to think. What if the pair had headed straight for Scotland without stopping, and he was wasting time? Or what if they'd gone in the other direction? He pinched the bridge of his nose and shook his head. He clenched his teeth, fighting against the rage just thinking that man's name incited. It would take every ounce of control he possessed to leave Iverson's throat intact once he found them.

The coach slowed. Lachlan pushed the curtain aside and looked out the window. They were approaching a large inn on the outskirts of a village. As soon as the vehicle came to a stop, he disembarked and swept inside. He found the innkeeper straightening chairs and wiping tables in the dining area.

"I'm looking for a couple, possibly traveling as man and wife, who may have stopped here within the past two hours," Lachlan announced.

The man rubbed his forehead. "Didn't see no couple *walk* in. Young man said his wife was sleepin' in the coach. Cook saw him carry her in. Dressed like you, he was, all fancy like from some big party."

"Did the young lady have hair of a rather unique shade? Somewhere between blonde and red?"

"I'd have to wake Cook and ask." The innkeeper hesitated. "Why yer so interested?"

"The young woman is *not* his wife, and she's here against her will. Please wake the cook." When the man looked skeptical Lachlan added, "I'll pay you three times the normal price for a room in addition to what the young man has already paid."

Making a mental note to charge the insistent nobleman four times the going rate, the innkeeper hastened off to wake the cook, although he was already fairly certain the rich gentleman had indeed found the couple he sought. Members of the Quality didn't just appear in the middle of the night very often, especially so close to London. They either arrived early enough for dinner or continued onward.

By the time he returned, he could see that the visitor had come to the same conclusion. When the sleepy cook confirmed that, yes, indeed, the young lady's hair was reddish-blonde, both men stepped back from the look of rage suddenly emanating from their questioner's eyes. "Show me," the man ordered. "Quickly."

The innkeeper grabbed a candleholder with a sputtering stub of a candle and led Lachlan up a narrow flight of stairs to a long corridor on the second level. He pointed down the hall. "Last room on the left," he said, then gave Lachlan the candle and turned to go back downstairs. "Doors only lock from the inside," he said on his way down. "If you break anything, you're paying for it."

Lachlan stalked down the hall, setting the candleholder on a table he passed. As he reached the end of the corridor, he heard a scuffling from inside the indicated room, punctuated by agitated voices. He turned the knob and pushed, then threw his shoulder against the panel when it wouldn't budge. The cheap wood gave way instantly, and he entered the room with a crash.

In the space of two seconds, he saw all he needed to see. Iverson had Charity backed into a corner, where she was holding him off with a chipped porcelain bowl and pitcher. Before either party could react, Lachlan was across the room and had Anthony by the throat, lifting him and pressing him against the wall with one hand. "I should kill you right here!" he thundered.

Eyes bulging, Anthony brought both hands up to Lachlan's wrist, scratching, clawing, and pushing in an effort to drag some air through his constricted windpipe. He braced his feet against the wall and shoved with all his might, fighting to stay alive. Charity slid down in her corner, the bowl and pitcher hitting the floor with harmless thuds as her hands fell to her sides.

Lachlan glanced down at her, and she looked back up at him in mute appeal, her dress torn and her hair a rat's nest of pins and sapphires. She needed him far more than he needed to exact justice right this moment, so he reluctantly relaxed his hold on Iverson's throat and allowed the cad to slide down the wall until his feet touched the floor.

"You're not worth it," he muttered, dropping his hand and stepping back. "Get out of here. I'll deal with you later."

Lachlan watched him scurry from the room and then turned back to Charity. He knelt and reached for the hand clenched around the handle of the pitcher. "Let me take that, kitten," he said, his tone gentle.

She looked through him, her eyes glassy and wounded, either unwilling or unable to comply with his request to let go of her makeshift weapons. Carefully he pried her fingers open, one at a time, until he could take the items from her and set them back behind him, out of her reach. The bowl was easier, and once they'd both been safely moved, he tilted his head to catch her eye.

"Charity. Look at me."

Tears spilled from beneath her eyelids as she stared down, so horribly ashamed of herself that she was unable to meet his eyes. "I'm so sorry," she said brokenly, and took a quivering breath. "I don't know how I got here."

Lachlan's heart wrenched, and all residual anger he might have had with her instantly dissolved. In spite of the behavior that had placed her in this situation, the fact remained that she had been through a great difficulty, and he ached beyond all else to take away the guilt and pain.

"You're not accustomed to champagne, little cat." He sat down beside her, unsure whether she'd accept comfort from him, though he ached to hold her and to provide solace in his arms. To his surprise, she lifted her head, shifted her weight, and settled against his side with a whimper. Tenderness swept through him. He opened his arms, pulled her more snugly against him, then lifted her altogether and settled her into his lap.

"So tired," she murmured. Her hand fell softly on his chest. She flattened it for a moment and spread her fingers. Lachlan covered it with his own and held it there, and at last he felt her fingers relax and curl into his palm as sleep overtook her. They sat like that for a while, Lachlan's mind spinning with the magnitude of what now had to happen, and with the steps he needed to take to set things in motion.

When Charity's breathing was deep and even, he stood up, lifting her with him, and carried her carefully to the bed. He turned down the covers with one hand, then gently settled her onto the sheets and removed her shoes. When he'd placed them neatly beside the bed, he tucked the covers around her shoulders and brushed a lock of her disheveled hair from her forehead. She looked so young, so vulnerable. And now it would be his job to protect her for the rest of his life.

After he was sure she wouldn't wake—he dreaded the idea of her finding herself alone—he left her there and made his way downstairs. The innkeeper was nowhere to be found, but Lachlan found an inkwell and some paper in a desk near the entry. Hastily he scrawled two notes, walking outside and blowing on the ink so that it would dry faster. Having failed to give his coachman any instructions, he found the conveyance was right where he'd left it. The footman looked startled when his employer suddenly appeared, but snapped to attention right away.

"Go inside and up the stairs and wait for me outside the last room on the left. There is a young lady asleep in that room and, as its door has met a rather unfortunate end, I'd like for you to stand guard."

The man bowed and rushed off, and Lachlan next motioned for his coachman to join him. He handed the man the two notes. "Take one to the Marquess of Roth, and the other to the Earl of Huntwick. After that, go to my cousin's town house, wake Niles, and have him quickly pack what he can while you get fresh horses and return. We'll leave midafternoon tomorrow, so you can get some rest."

"Yes, my lord." The coachman watched as the marquess turned and began to walk back into the inn. "My lord?" Lachlan turned back, eyebrow raised in inquiry. "Where are we going?"

Lachlan paused a moment, as if he felt saying the words out loud would somehow make his decision all too real, but then he said with finality, "Home."

Twenty

It felt as though her blanket had somehow managed to work its way into her mouth. Charity slowly opened one eye and then hastily closed it again when light rushed in and began physically pounding at her head from the inside. She groaned.

"There is a glass of water on the table next to you. And some toast. You'll feel better once you've eaten and had a good deal of water."

At the unexpected sound of a male voice, Charity sat bolt upright, her eyes flying open without regard for her headache. "Sweet mother of mercy, what are *you* doing in my bedchamber?" She clutched the blankets to her chest and looked around.

Lachlan watched the outraged look on her face change to one of confusion when she realized she was still wearing her clothing from the previous evening. He suppressed a smile. "This is not your bedchamber, Charity. Do you have any memory of last night?"

"Oh. *God.*" The confusion was rapidly changing to horror. "I mean, yes, I remember some of . . . wait, you were there with that insipid woman who looks like a porcelain doll. And how in the *world* did we end up here?" She stopped and looked up him, noted the sober look on his face. "Where is here?" she asked.

Lachlan sat down on the edge of the bed, picked up a piece of toast and a glass of water. He urged them on her.

"I'll tell you everything if you'll just eat and drink a bit. You don't want to ride in the coach when you're feeling this way."

With an unusual show of obedience, Charity accepted the toast and dutifully took a bite. It was dry and cold. She made a face and swallowed a gulp of the water. "Champagne is far lovelier while one is drinking it than it is the next day," she remarked wryly, and took another bite of toast.

Lachlan smiled. "A little lesson in moderation, kitten." His smile faded. She had no idea, yet, of just how big a lesson it had become.

Charity watched his expression change and took another sip of the water. "I can see from your face that things are not good. Tell me what happened, please," she said after she'd swallowed. She put the toast back on the plate and focused her attention on him. "Where are we, how did we get here, and"—her eyes widened—"oh my goodness, my sisters! My family must be frantic."

"They know you're fine and that you're with me."

She looked around the room again. Images kept flipping into her mind. Laughter. Music. The garden gate. "I don't remember leaving the ball," she said slowly. "Were you in the garden with me?"

"No, kitten." He watched her carefully. "You were in the garden with Anthony Iverson."

"We were hiding," she agreed. "And then everything began to go all tingly."

Lachlan felt his rage at Iverson begin to build again, and deliberately he fought to remain calm. The last thing he needed just now was for Charity to become freakishly uncooperative.

"You were seen leaving the ball through the side garden gate by a young woman named Therese."

Alarm bells went off inside her head. "Therese Thomasson-Sinclair?"

"I don't know her, but I believe that was the name given."

Charity bit her lip, feeling suddenly sick. If Therese had seen her, that meant this was all over the *ton*. She closed her eyes. "I've ruined everything, haven't I?"

"Don't do this to yourself, Charity. While things are bad—"

She opened her eyes and regarded him with a miserable expression. "Tell me the rest."

"From what I've guessed, Iverson somehow talked you into leaving with him and brought you here, to an inn on the outskirts of London. When I found you, he had you backed into a corner and you were holding him off with a bowl and pitcher." His lips twitched a tiny bit. Although the situation was dire, he didn't think he would ever forget the sight of tiny little Charity and her porcelain weaponry, the pitcher outthrust like a sword, the bowl held back protectively like a shield. "He and I discussed the situation, came to an agreeable alternative arrangement to his plan, and he left."

An agreeable alternative. That seemed somewhat odd. "He simply left? Why didn't you take me back to London at that time?"

"Because," said Lachlan, then stopped, glancing at the bowl and pitcher to make sure they were still well out of her reach. He was trying to think of a good way to tell her that she really couldn't go back unmarried; her reputation would be in shambles. "Because you're not going to London," he said, stalling to give himself time.

It was all too much for Charity's befuddled brain to handle. She rubbed her forehead and asked, "And now you will be taking me back to Pelthamshire?"

"No."

"My lord, please. I know I've done a terrible thing, and I'm quite sure there will be consequences, but if you could just see your way to getting me back to my family, I would very much appreciate it."

"I *am* your family, kitten." His tone was suddenly gentle.

Charity felt a momentary rush of warmth, which made no sense, before his words set in. "What do you mean?"

Lachlan considered his options. He could tell her . . . or he could *ask* her, hoping she would be so stunned by his proposal that she would agree before her temper ignited. He took her hands in his and said, "Charity, I know that we have had our difficulties, but I think with time and work, we could really have something . . . special." He swallowed hard, feeling suddenly awkward and oddly vulnerable. He ruthlessly buried the sensation and continued. "There is a great deal of passion and feeling between us, which gives me hope that we would get on well together as—"

Before he could finish, Charity guessed at the direction he was taking and jerked her hands free. "Stop!" She pushed at the covers and scrambled out from beneath them, then rolled away from him to get out on the far side of the bed. "Where are my shoes?"

"Listen to me, Charity."

"No, thank you," she replied, her voice deceptively sweet. She gave a polite little smile, bent and looked beneath the bed. Her footwear was on the other side, neatly placed near his feet. "I will not listen to you. And I would like my shoes, please."

He looked down and saw them. "Where do you think you're going to go if I give you these?"

She crossed her arms and glared. "You said we're on the outskirts of London. I . . . I'll get a ride to Grace's house . . .

no, to Faith's." Grace was liable to react more strongly than Faith, she realized. Her heart was pounding so hard she was sure he could hear it across the room.

"Marry me, kitten."

Charity threw up her hands and scowled. "Oh, bloody hell, did you have to *say* it?"

He stood and walked slowly around the bed, his gaze locked on her horrified face. Her eyes widened with each step he took, and she looked frantically toward the door, but there was nowhere for her to flee in stockings and a badly rumpled dress from the night before.

"Marry me," he said again, his voice tender and cajoling. She chanced a glance into his eyes and felt her heart begin to pound harder. Quickly she looked down and scuffed her toe along a crack in the hardwood floor.

Lachlan closed the distance between them and pressed his advantage. "If you would please marry me," he continued, his voice husky, a trace of the Scots accent woven into his words, "I wouldn't have to spend the rest of my life wishing I could do this again." He crooked a finger under her stubborn little chin and lifted her face to his. His lips neared hers.

"Don't," she whispered just as their mouths met, and then he robbed her of the ability to speak and to breathe, took away all her senses with a mere brush of their lips.

"Go ahead, kitten," he said, lifting his mouth. "Tell me not to kiss you."

"Don't kiss me," she said in an aching voice—and then stood on tiptoe to press her lips back to his.

With a little moan, she uncrossed her arms and slid them around his waist. Lachlan felt his control begin to slip. He caught the back of her head in his hands, felt the tangled silk of her hair slide between his fingers. His lips slanted softly against hers and he molded her mouth to his, but then with supreme effort he forced himself to end the kiss and simply hold her there, nose to nose, his forehead resting against hers.

"Tell me you don't want to marry me," he demanded hoarsely.

Charity bit her lip. "I don't—"

That was all Lachlan allowed, taking her lips this time with a ferocity that shook her to the core. She clung to him and gasped when the hand in her hair tightened into a fist. He took full advantage of her parted lips, deepening the kiss to taste and tease her, and Charity was lost—lost in his scent and his strength and in the promise of everything yet to come. She couldn't think of anything except being held by him, which suddenly felt safe and peaceful and right.

Lachlan knew the instant she gave in, felt it to his very soul. Understanding washed over him, blanketing him with warmth and a feeling of belonging he hadn't known existed. Was it possible to have found his way home in the arms of this small, infuriating English girl? He almost laughed inside at the romantic turn his thoughts were taking. He lifted his head and demanded, "Say yes."

Charity tried, but her voice didn't seem to work. She nodded instead and buried her face in his chest. Lachlan wrapped his arms around her and held her close.

"Good girl," he said, and pressed a kiss to the top of her head. "Now let's get you fed, into some comfortable traveling clothes, and we'll be on our way."

"Traveling clothes?" Charity pulled back and looked around. There were two large carpetbags near the door, which she just noticed was hanging half off its hinges. "Oh," was all she could manage.

"I sent word when I found you, kitten," Lachlan explained. "Grace sent those, along with this note." He handed her a folded piece of parchment. "I'll go down and order a luncheon and have the coach prepared while you change."

Her head reeling, Charity took the note and watched him leave. Slowly she opened the parchment and read the few words scribbled therein:

Trust yourself, Charity. And trust him. We love you very much.

With tears in her eyes, she refolded the note, squared her shoulders, and reached for one of the bags.

Twenty-one

"How much longer before we reach Scotland, my lord?"

Lachlan looked up from the investment proposal he was reading and smiled, just as if she hadn't asked him the same question half a dozen times already. They were well into the fifth day of travel and would reach Asheburton Keep by nightfall, after they stopped at the border and took care of the business of becoming married. "We should be in Scotland within the hour, I'd imagine."

He returned his attention to the papers in his lap. It had been a very long few days.

The first, which was really just a half day, had been the easiest. Charity, still exhausted from the excesses of the evening before, had curled up like a child on the seat across from him and slept. Lachlan spent the time watching her and wondering what sort of reception they would receive when they reached his home. There was no doubt in his mind that his mother would be a problem. Then again, his mother had never met someone like Charity. He smiled ruefully. They'd spent the night at a small inn where Lachlan was able to secure two rooms, which Charity did not question.

The next couple days were uneventful as well. Charity was obviously a bit uncomfortable and likely embarrassed by her behavior. Rather than continue to cause her discomfort, Lachlan decided to leave her alone in the coach to sort out her thoughts while he rode along on one of the outrider's horses. She seemed to have settled by the time they stopped for the night. They'd enjoyed a quiet dinner and then re-tired, again to separate rooms.

Today started out well enough. Charity was well rested, wide awake, and in astonishingly good humor. She'd re-marked on the passing scenery for a bit and then fallen si-lent. Lachlan put on his spectacles and began reading. But after a while, he'd noticed she was fidgeting.

"What's wrong?"

"Not a thing," she'd said with a bright smile, stilling herself.

Silence reigned again for a bit. He could feel her looking in his direction, but whenever he looked back at her, she turned away to stare out the window or down at her hands. Finally he removed his spectacles and set aside his reading material. "Charity, what has you so unsettled?"

She looked, for all the world, like a little girl who knew she'd done something wrong and was now trying to keep from getting caught. "Well, it's just that . . ." she started to say, paused, and then began again. "I mean, we're going to get married today, but I don't really know anything about you."

A very true statement. He didn't know her particularly well, either. Lachlan considered a moment and then re-marked, "But isn't that the way marriages typically work in Society? The participants seldom know much about the other. Sometimes they haven't even met before they marry."

"I have never wanted a marriage like that," Charity said. "My sisters don't have that. Even Amity married for . . ." She stopped and bit her lip, wondering if Amity were al-ready married and on her way back to London, if perhaps, they had even passed one another on their journey.

"For love?" He watched her closely.

Charity flushed uncomfortably and then nodded.

Lachlan contemplated that. While he had never really witnessed a loving relationship between a married couple, and had given no consideration to matters of the heart when he'd decided to take a wife, it was the only thing to which Charity was conditioned. Huntwick and Roth both adored their wives, and, although the Ackerly girls had been raised mostly motherless, he strongly suspected their household was governed with love and laughter. The contrast to his own upbringing was likely startling. Of course she would want love. And it was the one thing he wasn't sure he could give her.

"Hmm. You make a very good point, kitten."

Charmed by the nickname he'd begun using with increasing frequency, Charity tilted her head inquisitively to the side, a small smile quirking up the corners of her mouth. "Kitten?" she repeated.

Lachlan nodded. "Yes. You are very small and have sharp little claws. I've learned to keep that fact rather prominently in mind when dealing with you."

He picked up his papers and spectacles from the seat beside him and slid them into the satchel he'd brought into the coach with him that morning. If his soon-to-be wife wanted to know about the man she was about to marry, it was a trifling wish, one he could easily grant. "Come over here. I'll tell you anything you wish to know about me."

For a few moments Charity looked at the hand he held out, but then she placed her own in it and allowed him to draw her to his side of the coach. "I'm not sure what to ask you," she admitted as he settled her comfortably against his side, draped his arm around her shoulders and waited. She thought a few moments, and then hesitantly queried, "Were you a happy child?"

"Hmm." Lachlan idly stroked her hair with one hand, his mind wandering back into a past he seldom visited. "I had happy moments. Mine was, I'd wager, very different from your childhood."

She tilted her head back until she could see his face. He wasn't smiling, but he didn't seem angry, either. "Would you rather not talk about it?"

He shrugged. "It's fine. There are things about me that I'd like for you to know from the outset."

Things? That sounded mysterious and intriguing. Charity straightened and turned so she sat facing him, her legs curled beneath her on the seat, prepared to give him her complete and utter attention.

Lachlan smiled wryly at her expectant look, took a breath and decided to gamble on her trustworthiness, just as he was gambling on her suitability as a wife. His friends had married Ackerly girls and none seemed the worse for it. Then again, none of them were bastards who currently held titles rightfully belonging to a half brother

"It isn't a pretty story, Charity," he warned. "To begin with, I am not the legitimate heir of the Marquess of Asheburton. That honor actually belongs to my younger brother, and my mother is none too pleased about it."

He watched her carefully, trying to gauge her reaction. Charity didn't seem at all shocked by the fact he'd admitted to being a bastard. Quite the contrary. If anything, she looked even more fascinated.

"Sebastian Tremaine is actually my first cousin," he continued, "my *only* cousin, to my knowledge. Our fathers were brothers cut off and disinherited by our grandfather, the previous Duke of Blackthorne, for a variety of sins, none of which truly bears repeating other than to note that they certainly had such a punishment coming. The old duke eventually had a change of heart, mainly because he wished to pass the title to a direct heir.

"He hired men to investigate what became of both of his sons. Sebastian's father married, impregnated, and quickly deserted a girl in England, not far at all from Blackthorne Manor. Upon discovering the existence of his grandson, the duke wasn't as focused on his search. Instead, he contacted Sebastian's mother, revealed his identity, and made her an offer of financial support. The girl, young, frightened, and hurt by her husband's disappearance, agreed only on the condition that Blackthorne not take Sebastian away from her. So my cousin received an education befitting a duke's grandson, although he knew nothing of his lineage until a few years ago when Blackthorne became ill.

"My father, on the other hand, didn't bother marrying my mother." Lachlan's face turned hard as he thought of his own lot. He glanced down, startled, when he felt Charity slip her small hand into his. His heart warmed at the little gesture. He gave her a smile, squeezed her hand in acknowledgment, and went on with his story. "By the time Blackthorne's investigators found my father's trail, my mother had married the Marquess of Asheburton, who agreed to claim me as his own."

Lachlan's voice was gruff with obvious affection when he spoke of his stepfather. "Andrew Kimball was an awkward, shy, unattractive man, but he was kind and generous to a fault. All he asked was that my mother keep her secret and bear him a son of his own, after which he would leave her alone. My mother vehemently denied any relationship with my father when Grandfather's investigators came, but one of the men saw me and instantly noted my resemblance to members of the Tremaine family. And so, despite my mother's protests, they sent word back that I was another grandson."

He stopped and eyed Charity to assess her reaction. She

seemed enthralled but not unhappy, and crowed, "I *knew* you and Blackthorne were closely related from the first time I saw the two of you together. At Faith's wedding."

Lachlan raised his eyebrows, a glimmer of humor filling him. "You did, hm? As I recall, you seemed rather focused on my teeth and whether or not I had warts. I'm surprised you even noticed the resemblance."

She wrinkled her nose at him but smiled. "Go on, please. This is your lineage, not your childhood."

"My grandfather's investigators' reports were thorough. They meticulously detailed everything about my existence for the duke, right down to the foods I ate and the child-hood games I played. The debt was staggering, as it turned out, on the estate I would someday inherit. Asheburton Keep was not self-sustaining, and the rents from the village did not nearly compensate for the cost of the upkeep. The marquess, though kind, did not have a head for numbers, and the marriage between my mother and himself could best be described as estranged. As a result there were no tutors for me or my brother, and, since my mother fancied herself far above the villagers, she refused to send us to their rather primitive school."

"But you're incredibly bright, my lord," said Charity. The loneliness he must have felt as a boy nearly broke her heart. "And you're successful. Everyone says so."

"Everyone?" His voice was teasing. "Before today, I was of the impression that you had no interest in hearing anything about me, Miss Ackerly. Perhaps even now you're simply humoring me and don't really want to hear the rest of the story."

Charity didn't answer the accusation. Instead, she leaned forward, braced a hand on his chest, and pressed a soft, shy little kiss to his cheek. "I'm sorry I was so wretched to you, my lord." Her tone was contrite, and when she pulled back to look into his eyes, Lachlan saw twin pools of sincerity tinged with a shadow of regret.

"I know you are, kitten," he said. "There's no need to apologize. We were both rather wretched to one another." He slipped a hand into the silky curls at the nape of her neck and pulled her close, taking her lips slowly, caressing them with his own until she sighed against his mouth.

"Where was I?" he asked.

"Kissing me," she replied in a dreamy voice.

He chuckled. "You'd better turn back around before I am unable to *stop* kissing you. There's a good deal more to tell, if you're interested, and I can't stay focused when you look at me like that."

Surprised by his admission, Charity happily complied, turning so that she leaned back against him, nestled snugly into the curve of his arm. When she was comfortable, he resumed his tale.

"Upon learning of the fact that I was to be the next Marquess of Asheburton, the Duke of Blackthorne decided against coming forward to claim a relationship. He already had an heir in Sebastian, and, since it appeared everyone had long accepted me as Andrew Kimball's son he turned his attention to finding a way to facilitate my education, since my mother refused to allow him to help in any way. Sending a professional tutor was impossible, given the circumstances, so he did the next best thing. He sent an old and trusted friend who at one time studied to become a member of the clergy."

Charity scowled in confusion. "But how would that not also raise suspicion?"

"Gregory was an old man, and he took the time to integrate himself with the Scottish locals before he got to know me. He showed up one day when I was about five years old and asked my father if he could rent a cottage in the hills near the keep. Gregory kept mostly to himself, although I would occasionally see him when I was playing out that way. And then one day we came face to face, struck up a conversation, and that was that. I followed him back to his cottage and we talked for hours. I was almost ten by that time, and quite a lonely young boy. I had no playmates except my younger brother, and my mother often denied me even his company. Finding someone who would actually spend time with and talk to me was like finding a treasure, and I quite lost track of time. When night approached, he pointed it out and walked me back home.

"The following day I returned to his cabin, bright and early, for what was to become a daily visit. He was easily the most patient man I have ever encountered. He knew how to do everything, and took the time to teach me as well. He hunted only with quiet weapons, and with surprising success, despite his age. More than once I saw him catch small prey with his bare hands. His cottage was filled with books, and while I enjoyed the time we spent together outdoors, my favorite occupation was to sit and read and learn from those books. It completely escaped my notice that everything he taught would someday contribute to my ability to successfully run an estate or uphold the responsibilities of my title."

Charity tilted her head back and looked at him, a troubled expression on her gamine face. "What is it, love?" he asked.

"I was just thinking about how difficult it must have been for the old Duke of Blackthorne to have not only lost his sons, but to be denied the opportunity to know his grandsons."

"We all make choices, Charity. He chose to—understandably—disinherit his sons."

"I know. It just makes me sad."

Lachlan squeezed her shoulders. "If it makes you feel better, the fact that he placed Gregory in my life, and that he left Sebastian with his mother, were both unselfish choices that likely allowed us to grow up unencumbered by the material wealth that spoiled our fathers."

She smiled. "Will I get to meet Gregory, my lord?"

He shook his head. "No. He fell ill when I was about fifteen. He told me good-bye, gave me all of his books, and returned to England to live out his final days there. Suddenly left with a great deal of time, I began noticing things around the estate that could be improved. I made some tentative suggestions to my father, which he then implemented. Before long we were working together, making investments with the profits from the improvements. The investments continued to pay off, and soon we were able to begin improving the village. For the first time since he became the Marquess of Asheburton, my father actually enjoyed a good relationship with the villagers—which did *not* please my mother at all."

The bitterness in his voice did not escape Charity, especially in contrast to the warmth she heard when he spoke of his home, his stepfather and his brother. "You've barely mentioned your mother," she said cautiously. "And when you do, your voice turns cold."

Lachlan sighed. "I suppose it's not very fair of me. My mother is a difficult topic. I have very few good things to say about her, and I'm reluctant to color your opinion before you meet her. My brother Lewiston adores her, but then she has always doted on him.

"I don't mind so much that she ignored me for most of my childhood." He paused for a long moment, and Charity waited, too, wondering at his silence but sensing he wasn't having emotional difficulty. Rather, it seemed he was choosing his words carefully. Finally, he said, "What I *will* do is warn you that my mother will likely not welcome you with open arms, but that it has nothing to do with who you are. She does not wish for me or for any child that might come of my marriage to hold the title and lands."

"Because you're not a true Kimball?"

Lachlan shook his head. "I can't imagine that part of it even matters to her. No, it is the way I look. Apparently, my resemblance to my real father is startling."

"But that's not your fault," protested Charity. She pushed away from his chest and sat up straight, her arms crossed in indignation. "That's horrible!"

Lachlan gave her a fond smile, charmed by her fierce loyalty and the fact that she was apparently prepared to do battle for the man she'd considered her foe only a few short days ago. "It's all right, kitten. I've become accustomed to it. She's the reason I traveled to London to find a wife. She sabotaged the only relationship I ever began at home, one with a pretty young girl from the village who certainly did not deserve the interference. My mother does not want me to marry, and she definitely does not want me to have a child. Especially not now."

"Why do you say that?"

"Because when my father died, none of us were aware that he'd drawn up a new will. Everyone always knew that the title, the keep, and the entailed lands would go to me in the event of his death, but according to the will he'd executed when he married my mother, a large portion of his estate was to go to her. For some inexplicable reason, a very short time before he died, he changed it. He left everything, including control of my mother's portion, to me."

Charity sat silently chewing on her lower lip. Lachlan allowed her a few moments with her thoughts. When she finally looked up, her face was carefully blank. "Do you still love her?"

"My mother? Of course I love her. But I don't *like* her very much."

She fidgeted. "No," she clarified. "I meant 'the pretty young girl from the village.'"

A slow grin broke over Lachlan's face. When she saw it, she scowled.

"Are you jealous?" he asked.

Charity colored. "No."

He crooked a finger under her chin and tilted her face up. "You are. You're jealous."

She swatted his hand away. "I am *not* jealous!"

Lachlan laughed and scooped her up from the seat beside him, pulling her over and onto his lap. He leaned down and whispered in her ear, his warm breath stirring the tendrils of hair that curled there. "I think you're adorable when you're jealous, my lady."

His voice crept deliciously through her mind, low and tender, and she quite forgot that she was annoyed with him. She nuzzled her face into his neck and kissed him there, breathing in his scent, reveling in the scratchiness of a growth of beard against her cheek. It took a moment for what he'd called her to register. With a start, she realized that in a very short time that's what she would be: a lady.

Before she could fully process that reality, the coach pulled to a smooth stop. Charity lifted her head and looked around.

"We're here," said Lachlan. "Are you ready?"

Twenty-two

"Charity?"

Lachlan's voice came to her as if from a distance, and Charity reacted slowly. She felt numb and disconnected from reality. On some level, she knew what was happening around her; she was simply unable to cognitively participate.

When her eyes met his in a blank stare, Lachlan abruptly decided she'd had enough for one day. Instead of putting her back into the coach and continuing another hour to Asheburton Keep, he decided to take them a room in Gretna Green. Meeting his mother was the last thing he wished to thrust upon his wife now.

It had started when they first emerged from the coach into the late afternoon sunshine. The easy conversation they'd shared up to that point had abruptly evaporated, and he sensed her drawing away into herself. She followed him into the blacksmith's shop and repeated her vows with his footmen as their witnesses, but her voice lacked its characteristic spirit and the life had drained from her cerulean eyes.

She'd sat quietly through the dinner he ordered and ate little. When he addressed her, she smiled and responded but her words were few and softly uttered. His concern mounting, he led her to the rooms he'd taken for the night.

"I'll be right nearby," he said, and pointed at the door connecting their chambers. "If you'd like, I'll leave the door open."

"That would be fine, my lord," she replied, and then sat down on the edge of the bed to stare off into space. After a long, worried look, he left her there and went into his own room to get ready for bed.

Two hours passed and he heard nothing from her room. No rustling of bedclothes, none of the sounds that would normally accompany a person preparing to retire for the night. He'd completed his own preparations and climbed into bed, stretched out on his back with his hands propped behind his head, his mind too occupied with Charity's odd withdrawal to sleep.

It couldn't be that she feared the wedding night. He'd gotten them two rooms and been very clear about it. His logic was the same as it was the entire trip north: he did not intend to consummate his marriage until he could do so at home, in his own bed. There were both emotional and practical reasons for this decision. From a practical standpoint, he wanted no question as to the legitimacy of the child. Unfairly coloring her son's child as a bastard was not beyond Eloise, he was sad to say, and he would take every step to avoid such accusations. The emotional reasons for waiting were much simpler. He wanted her virgin's blood on his sheets, in his home, not spilled on the bedclothes of some inn on the road between London and Asheburton Keep.

Given Charity's odd descent into silence, he now wondered if he should have taken a single room and spent the night trying to draw her out or comfort and reassure her. She was a strong-minded and strong-willed young lady, but the events of the past few days would have shaken a woman twice her age with ten times her experience. Instead of taking care of her, he'd left her alone on her wedding night in a strange country, abandoned her to understand and deal in solitude with a future that held only questions.

Cursing, Lachlan sat up and swung his legs out of bed to sit on its edge, staring through the darkness toward the open door between their chambers. With a sigh he stood, pulled on a pair of trousers, crossed through and then stood beside Charity's bed, staring down at the small English girl he'd married.

She was curled atop the coverlet, still clad in the dress she'd worn all day—her wedding dress, as it turned out. Lachlan felt another small twinge of guilt. She should have been courted and coddled and danced attendance upon in the weeks leading up to their marriage. Instead, they'd spent most of their short acquaintance sparring with one another. She should have had a lavish London wedding in a church before everyone she loved, with glowing descriptions of the glittering reception that followed printed in all the newspapers the next morning. Instead, she'd been married in a blacksmith's shop with only his servants to witness, her dress crushed and wrinkled from several days' travel.

The moonlight streamed in through the room's lone window to caress her face, peaceful in sleep, with a gentle glow. Her features were delicate and fine, and though Lachlan knew all too well her stubborn resilience, he couldn't help but think that she looked like a fragile doll tossed in the center of the large bed, broken and discarded.

Something wrenched inside him, and he reached down to smooth her tousled curls, washed nearly blonde by silver moonbeams. At his touch she stirred and he straightened, watching as her eyelids began to flutter open. With a little sigh, she stretched and then looked around the room in momentary confusion. Her eyes settled on him, and she pushed herself to a sitting position.

"We're married," she said in a voice thick with sleep.

Lachlan nodded, a small ironic smile briefly touching his lips.

Her gaze dropped from his face and traveled down the bare expanse of his chest. Somewhere deep inside herself, she knew she should register shock at being alone in a room with a half-dressed man, even if that man was now her husband, but she couldn't take her eyes from him. "You're beautiful," she breathed. Unable to stop herself, she reached out to touch the hard, flat plane of his stomach.

Lachlan caught her hand with his own before she touched him, before her innocent caress was his undoing. "Charity," he said hoarsely, "I don't know what I'll do if you touch me there."

Her eyes, wide and utterly without guile, lifted again to his and she shook her head. "But I thought you came to do what wives do with husbands."

Oh. God. How he wanted to.

"Is that what was bothering you earlier?" He sat down beside her, more as a means of hiding his growing arousal than in an effort to be closer.

Her face clouded, and she withdrew her hand from his. "No, my lord," she answered quietly. "It's that you *had* to marry me. You did it to protect me, because you're friends with the men who married my sisters . . . I'm so sorry I put you in that position." She raised eyes brimming with un-shed tears to his. "Amity and I were going to get married together and live near one another in Pelthamshire. It was what we always planned."

"Oh, little kitten." He scooted across the bed, pulled her into his lap and softly kissed the top of her head, reveling in the fact that, no matter how he held her, she always fit perfectly against him, every single time. "Listen to me and know that I've never been more serious in my entire life than I am right now: You did not put me in this position. I am here with you entirely by choice and completely because of my own actions. Do you believe that?"

"But if I hadn't—"

He cut her off. "If you hadn't, this is still exactly where we would have ended up. I'm sure of it."

Charity closed her eyes, wanting with all her heart to believe, but she held her tongue, afraid to say the words she felt fluttering around inside her chest.

When she rubbed her cheek against his chest, Lachlan groaned and tried to ignore the way his body responded to her innocent movement. "We got here together, love. Believe me when I tell you I have never been more aware of a woman in all my life, from the very moment we met."

He paused, and when he spoke again, she could hear a smile in his voice. "I remember the day I first saw you so clearly. Do you remember it? In Hunt's foyer?"

She nodded.

"We both tried to fight it, and we each had our reasons. But time and again, we have ended up right where we are now: in one another's arms. There must be a reason for that."

She finally spoke, her voice so low that he had to tilt an ear to catch it. "I like it when you kiss me, my lord."

Lachlan's heart slammed into his ribs. Although he knew he was starting something he did not want to finish here, in this inn, on this night, he slid down in the bed, taking her with him. Ignoring the warning bells going off in his mind, he turned her in his arms and took her lips in a kiss.

Instant fire erupted between them, and their embrace was anything but gentle. Charity, fueled by longings he'd awakened in the past, didn't hold back any longer. She kissed him with all the fervor and eagerness she'd kept in check before. This time, she cupped his face in her hands, pressed herself close, and touched her tongue to the crease between *his* lips. This time, *she* tasted and coaxed until he moaned and opened. And, when she tentatively teased the edges of his teeth with the pointed tip of her tongue, he did the same, slanting his mouth across hers until she whimpered and willingly surrendered ownership of the kiss.

Lachlan forced himself to lift his lips from hers but pulled her fiercely against him. "Do you have any idea how rare this is, kitten?" His voice was gruff, tight, and he fought to control the urge to take her and make her his in every imaginable way.

"No," she answered honestly.

It hit him, then. She really did not know, had no idea of the power she held within her delicate hands.

"No, I suppose you don't," he said ruefully, staring over her head into the darkness, wondering how much she knew about the acts performed in the marital bed. He sat up, gave her a quick kiss on the forehead, and pushed her off his lap.

She laughed a little. "Watch it there!" Rolling off the bed, she shook out her skirts, which had become all twisted around her legs, then climbed back on.

Lachlan grinned. "Would you like me to stay here with you for the rest of the night, or go back into the other room?"

"I was actually wondering why you did get another room, my lord. This bed is awfully large, and I know you can afford it but the expense is entirely unnecessary and I don't mind sharing and . . ." She eyed the comical expression on his face. "Why are you looking at me like that?"

It was becoming increasingly evident that she had no idea of the more intimate pleasures in store for them. "Did your sisters ever talk to you about marriage and children?"

She furrowed her brow. "Well, I assumed we would have some children. But since Amity and I didn't really give them a chance to talk to us about marriage before we each ran off to get married, it hadn't really come up."

Lachlan looked uncomfortable. "So you have no idea how we would"—he cleared his throat— "*obtain* those children?"

She narrowed her eyes. "Why are you asking me this?"

He watched her carefully. "Because husbands and wives typically go about the business of creating a baby together, in bed. And it involves a lot of kissing and touching and cuddling." His body tightened at even the thought. Ruthlessly, he continued. "What you need to know is that I do not want it to happen *here*. So, no more kisses tonight. If you don't think you can stop kissing me, I'll go into the other room."

Charity sat down and contemplated that. "So . . . we've already started making a baby?"

"Well, yes," he answered. "In some ways, we have. And I promise to tell you everything that is going to happen before it does so that you are not frightened or surprised."

"All right." She shook her head in mystification and then bit her lip. "Will it be hard to sleep in here and not kiss me?" The look on her face was a beguiling combination of earnest sincerity and confusion, and it was in that instant, in the darkest hours of his unconsummated wedding night, that Lachlan realized a truth, one he'd thought only hours before might be an impossibility for him: he was in love with Charity.

"It will be difficult in some ways, kitten," he answered honestly, "but I've never been one to back away from a challenge." He held open his arms. "Come here."

She smiled, crawled across the bed, turned her back to

her husband, and nestled warmly into his arms. Within moments, she was asleep.

It took Lachlan a little longer. He wrestled with the recognition of his feelings, wondered if she felt the same, if she even had the ability to fall in love with him after their brief, eventful acquaintance. Unable to find a solution to that particular problem, he turned his thoughts to a more pressing problem: his mother. There was no putting it off beyond tomorrow; when they woke they'd make the short trip to Asheburton Keep, where his mother was certain to do her level best to undermine and ruin the delicate, tentative bond he'd began to form with Charity. It would be a fight from which he would be mostly removed, except where he needed to step in to protect his wife. He was determined to allow Charity latitude to find her own way to deal with Eloise Kimball. He'd support her in every way, but the battle would be between two indomitable women. He had no idea who would prevail.

Twenty-three

Absolutely not."

Charity stood by the steps of the coach and considered her options. Only days before she would have responded with stubborn insistence, but in the aftermath of their discussion the evening before, and in the spirit of the warmth that had arisen between them, she found herself oddly loath to take her usual confrontational path.

For that reason, she lifted her eyes and stared at Lachlan in mute appeal. "But it's so small. And helpless."

Lachlan found he was not proof against such an expression, against the hope shining in the not-quite-green depths of his wife's gaze. He remembered what she had said about her plans to live in Pelthamshire near her twin after she married, and he felt his heart softening. He was taking her so far from her family. How could he possibly deny her the companionship of a pet? He regarded the animal and almost quirked a smile at the irony. A *kitten*. Charity had found a kitten and wanted to bring it home with them.

As if it knew an improvement in its circumstances was imminent, the tiny creature lifted its head from his wife's bosom and gave him a look of pleading identical to the one on his wife's face. Except—Lachlan looked more closely— was that a shade of smug satisfaction in its golden eyes?

"No," he said, and turned to get into the coach.

Charity didn't follow. She cuddled the miniature black cat, kissed the top of its head and then stared once more at her husband, who firmly shook his head. The look on her face turned mutinous, so he decided he had better explain.

"There is nowhere in the vehicle for the animal to relieve itself. It isn't trained."

Her face brightened. If Lachlan was willing to discuss it, she was sure she could convince him. "You said it was a very short drive to Asheburton Keep." She held the kitten under its front legs, her hands spanning its tiny rib cage, and thrust it out. "And he looks smart. See? I bet he'll wait and let us *know* if he needs to go out."

"She," her husband said wryly. The way she was holding the kitten, with its back paws dangling freely, gave him the perspective to easily determine that it was definitely not male.

"She, then." Charity nodded agreeably. "Even better." She gifted him with a cajoling smile.

"My mother," he warned, "has two enormous wolfhounds that rarely leave her side." He disappeared into the coach. "That animal will be an appetizer for one of them."

Charity followed, the kitten tucked into the crook of her arm. "I'll take care of her. I promise." She smiled happily.

Lachlan glowered. "Not if you are their main course," he warned darkly.

Charity laughed. At the musical sound, it was all Lachlan could do to maintain the scowl he'd pasted to his face. "It will be fine," she assured him. She plunked the kitten into her lap and tilted her head to look down at the creature. "What shall I name you?"

The kitten, jet black with big golden eyes, stared back at her but said nothing.

"What do you think, my lord?"

"I think it would be a shame to waste the name, since she's going to be mauled the second you take your eyes off her."

Charity narrowed her eyes at her husband and then smiled down at her new friend. As the coach began moving, the kitten yawned and raised a paw to give it a half-hearted lick. "She's very brave," Charity remarked. "Most cats dislike traveling."

"Mm. Yes. Stalwart."

As if in response to Lachlan's sardonic assessment, the kitten leaped across the space between the seats and sat, regally erect, beside the marquess. He reached down to scratch her head and then hastily pulled back his hand when she hissed at him.

Charity laughed. "Serves you right."

Her husband raised his eyebrows. "That animal has the haughty bearing of a Roman goddess."

"Then we shall call her Minerva." Charity smiled with delight, and even the newly named kitten seemed inclined to agree with her choice. Lachlan just shook his head and stared out the window. The road was beginning to smooth, and familiar landmarks were cropping up with regularity.

Soon enough, the coach rounded a bend. Lachlan rapped on the roof three times and waited for the vehicle to stop. When a footman opened the door and put down the steps, he disembarked and then reached back to offer a hand to his wife. "Come see your new home, my lady."

Charity stepped out into the crisp air of a bright midmorning, her eyes glowing with surprise and delight. Even before she looked in the direction her husband was pointing, she was entranced. The colors here seemed somehow brighter, more vibrant and alive. There were enormous stones, light gray against the rolling emerald hills. The vegetation was lush and full and . . . and . . . her mind spun, trying to find the right word. *Sharp,* she decided. Everything was clearly defined and sharp.

Lachlan placed his hands on her shoulders and turned her around, pointing down the road that followed a gentle grade into a valley. Nestled into the valley was a small, picturesque village.

"Oh, my lord," Charity breathed. "I want Amity to see this. It's absolutely lovely." She peeked up at him, her eyes turning that odd shade that wasn't quite blue but was definitely not green. "That is Ashton?"

He nodded and smiled. "And that, my lady, is Asheburton Keep."

Charity's eyes climbed the hill behind the village. About halfway up was a large stone fortress, its medium gray walls a stark contrast to the bright green hillside and the thatched cottages of the village below. It was square and rather imposing, with low towers at each corner, the parapets crowned with flags she assumed bore the family crest flying in the gentle breeze. She leaned back against Lachlan and felt his arms slip around her waist.

"So the rumors were true," she said, a smile in her words.

"Rumors?"

"You *do* live in a castle."

Lachlan laughed. "Hardly. It's a bit too small to be considered a castle." He gave her a squeeze. "But you can pretend you're a princess if you like."

Minerva chose that moment to jump out of the coach and wind herself around their ankles. She mewed and looked up at Charity, who bent and picked her up. The kitten climbed up onto her shoulder, where she perched, stared up at Lachlan, and hissed.

He hissed back.

Laughing, he and Charity climbed back into the coach to complete their journey.

*   *   *

"There is a coach coming up from the village, my lady."

Lady Eloise Kimball, Dowager Marchioness of Asheburton, raised her perfectly shaped eyebrows in an expression of bored disdain. "Already? The Season isn't even half over yet." She looked toward the window, although it didn't afford her a view of the road that led to the keep. Silence fell. The footman bowed and backed out of the solar when it became apparent she would require nothing further of him.

Her eldest son's quick return from London meant that he'd likely decided against finding a wife in the glittering pool of Season debutantes, which was good news. It also meant he'd be back in residence, undermining her authority in the running of the household. She loathed the frugality with which he managed the estate, even though she recognized that it was the very quality which had afforded them the means to live so comfortably. She dropped a hand to the head of Belle, one of her beloved pet wolfhounds. The other canine, Boris, who was curled up near her feet, lifted his head and growled low in his throat. The two dogs were in constant competition for her affection, something Eloise fostered and encouraged.

Lewiston Kimball watched his mother for a moment. When she made no move to get up, he stood and walked over to the window and looked down just in time to see the coach cross the drawbridge and disappear from view. A few seconds later it emerged into the courtyard, pulled around the short, half-circle drive and rolled to a smooth stop before the shallow steps that led up to the enormous front doors. He watched a footman lower the steps and open the door. A moment later his brother stepped out, then turned and reached back into the vehicle.

Lewiston's eyes widened. Stepping out of the coach and into his brother's arms was a petite young woman, her strawberry blonde hair glinting in the late morning sunlight. Bemused, he turned back toward his mother.

"Shall we go down and greet Lachlan?"

Eloise waved a dismissive hand. "No, indeed. He can come up here if he wishes to see me. You go."

Lewiston chanced another glance outside. The young lady was just reaching back into the coach for something. He couldn't quite make it out, though it appeared to be a small black bundle. He grinned widely. "Suit yourself, Mother." He walked over to her chair, bent, and pressed a kiss to the cheek she raised toward him. "I'll pass along a greeting to them from you."

Eloise watched him leave the room. He looked so much like his father, though he wasn't increasing in the midsection the way Andrew Kimball had in his later years. Still, she thought, it was unfortunate neither of her sons had inherited her blonde good looks. She would have to make sure Lewiston married a pretty girl so that there was a decent chance of attractive grandchildren. And a girl with an outgoing disposition to overcome his occasional reclusiveness.

She frowned, bothered by something she'd missed, and thought back over the last few moments. Grandchildren. Lewiston. Lachlan . . . *Them?* Her eyes narrowed. Lewiston had said he would pass along a greeting from her to *them.* She sucked in her breath in sudden understanding.

In a single motion she threw off her lap robe and stood, gathered her skirts in one hand, and left the room. Belle and Boris trotted along after her, curious about where she was going in such a furious rush. She swept down the stairs and through the great hall.

"Lewis!"

He stopped midstride and turned back, an amused look on his face.

"You said 'them.' " Eloise's voice was modulated, but her son could sense the rage, simmering just below the surface, that frequently kept the household on edge. The only person who seemed immune to it was Lachlan, which always served to enrage his mother even more.

"Why, yes. I did," he replied.

Eloise caught up to him. "He's brought a . . . friend?" She placed an emphasis on the last word, hoping against hope that whoever accompanied her eldest child was not a woman.

Lewiston hesitated and then nodded, deciding not to tell her exactly what he'd seen. She'd learn for herself soon enough. Sure enough, voices drifted down the corridor from the entryway. One was distinctly female.

He gave his mother a steady look and held out an arm. "Shall we?"

Eloise scowled but placed a hand on the offered arm and lifted her head, her expression turning icy, regal and distant. They walked out to the entryway together with Belle and Boris following, the dogs' nails clicking on the cold gray stone floor.

The newly arrived couple stood near the open doors. Lachlan was in the act of introducing the young lady to Phillips, their butler, a proud, possessive smile lighting his face. He looked over when he heard his family approach, and his smile faded. He waited for Charity to finish speaking to Phillips and then placed a hand at the small of her back.

She smiled up at him, noted his expression, and followed the direction of his gaze. Her heart gave a nervous little lurch and began pounding nervously, but she pasted on an open, engaging smile and stepped toward her new in-laws, the hand not cuddling Minerva to her chest extended in friendly greeting.

The dogs and the kitten became aware of each other at precisely the same moment, and instant pandemonium erupted. Minerva hissed low in her throat, her ears flattening. Before Charity could stop her, the small bundle of fur wriggled and jumped from the protection of her arms to land softly on the stone floor. She arched her back and bared her tiny, sharp teeth in the direction of the advancing, barking dogs.

"Minerva . . . no!" Charity bent to try and scoop up her pet before the dogs got to her, but the kitten skittered out of reach, right toward the snapping jaws of Boris. Charity raised her eyes to Eloise in mute appeal but was met with a distant, glacial glare.

Lewiston reacted instead, stepping forward and grasping Belle's collar. He hauled her back and away but couldn't get to Boris before the dog reached Minerva. The group watched in horror as the huge wolfhound snarled and tensed, preparing to attack the small intruder to his home. Charity gaped in horrified fear, squeezed her eyes closed, and then turned and pressed her face into her husband's chest.

It was over in a matter of seconds. Boris jumped forward, barking loudly, then yelped in sudden, unexpected pain and backed away, whining piteously. Cautious, Charity peeled an eyelid open and chanced a look. The wolfhound had retreated to a safe distance. A long scratch on his muzzle was oozing a small amount of blood. He eyed Minerva, who was crouched and alert, ready to spring into an attack if necessary. The cat inched forward, hissing, her little tail puffed to an astonishing thickness, and then stopped when Boris whimpered and hid his face beneath one of his massive paws. She tilted her head to the side inquisitively.

Belle barked and lunged, pulling against Lewiston's hold on her collar, but Minerva paid no attention to her. The kitten instead watched as Boris extended his tongue out of his mouth and swiped it across the scratch. He whined again and settled down, resting his head on his paws in a pose that was unmistakably submissive.

At that, Minerva completely relaxed. With a sweet little mew, she walked up to Boris, rubbed the side of her face on one of his paws and began licking at the cut on his nose, as if offering an apology. Belle seemed calmed by this, sat down next to Lewiston and watched, her tail thumping on the floor. It was the strangest thing any of them had seen in some time.

"Well, would you look at that?" remarked Lewiston, a slow grin dawning on his face. Cautiously, he let go of Belle's collar. The dog didn't move.

Eloise looked far less pleased. "Why is this creature in my home?"

Lachlan raised a brow. "It is *our* home, Mother, and 'that creature' belongs to my wife." He watched Eloise's face pale, and felt an unexpected surge of satisfaction sweep through him. He placed his hands lightly on Charity's shoulders, and his bride looked up from watching the animals to offer a slightly more tentative smile of greeting than her first.

"Mother . . . Lewiston . . ." Lachlan said. "Please meet the new Marchioness of Asheburton, Charity Ackerly Kimball."

Anthony Iverson looked up from the dance card upon which he'd just scrawled his name and saw the Duke of Blackthorne heading purposefully in his direction. "Perhaps another time," he murmured to the seemingly disappointed young lady. He glanced toward the doors that led to the terrace, decided he'd be better off inside the crowded ballroom, and turned to flee the approaching nobleman. He drew up short when he saw Gareth and Jonathon Lloyd coming toward him from that quarter. Turning in a third direction, he immediately bumped into Trevor Caldwell.

"Bloody hell," he muttered.

"Going somewhere, Iverson?" Trevor pulled a watch out of his waistcoat pocket and glanced at it. "It's early yet."

Anthony looked distinctly uncomfortable as the other men converged around him. His colorful garb stood out, a garish splash of satin in the knot of dark-coated gentlemen. He looked from one to the other, and wisely held his tongue.

"Do you enjoy gambling, Iverson?" Gareth Lloyd's tone was pleasant, which drew a startled look from the cornered young rake. "You must, although I can't imagine you're very good at it. You had to have known that showing up at any social event for the remainder of the Season was a poor bet."

Anthony finally found his voice and played the only card he thought he held. "If you intend to make a scene, you'll do as much damage to Charity's reputation as she might have done herself."

Gareth turned to his brother, nodding and holding a hand out in Iverson's direction. "Did you hear that, Jon? This just proves he is a very poor gambler." He turned back to Anthony. "If you're going to bluff, you should first ensure your opponents don't know you hold nothing in your hand. In this case, we all know that that is precisely what you have. Nothing."

"People saw Miss Ackerly leave the ball with me," the young man protested.

"And that's where you're wrong." Gareth slung an arm

casually across Anthony's shoulders and began strolling toward the door with him, the other men following. The pleasant look faded from Gareth's face and his eyes turned from chocolate to glittering obsidian. "People saw my sister, the new Marchioness of Asheburton, leave with you."

"My sister," added Trevor.

"And mine," put in Jon. They all looked at him. "Well. Quite nearly."

Anthony's eyes widened in sudden understanding as they reached the foot of the stairs. Sebastian stepped forward. "And now that she has married my cousin, she is a member of my family as well." His golden gaze caught and held Iverson's until the young man looked away. "Lord Asheburton sends his regrets," continued the duke. "He wanted to handle this in person." He looked pointedly up the stairs. "Leave. Leave now."

"Th-the ball?" Anthony looked around the room, noting for the first time that the environs had become noticeably quieter as the people nearest his group had stopped to watch the developing drama.

"Leave London." Jon's voice was clipped.

"You might consider leaving England," Trevor added in a helpful tone. "I understand the Colonies afford exciting new opportunities to start again."

"Opportunities," echoed Anthony weakly.

"The opportunity, at the very least, to remain alive," whispered Gareth.

"Intact," added Sebastian, to clarify. "I'm sure we understand one another."

Iverson processed the angry faces of the men who represented some of the most powerful families in England, nodded tightly, and started up the stairs. Halfway up, however, he looked out over the sea of guests and then back at the men who stood in a row at the foot of the staircase.

"This isn't over," he warned. "Someday, you'll all pay for this. Especially that damned Scot." Before they could respond or come after him, he turned, swiftly completed his ascent, and left the ball.

Twenty-four

Eloise paced the upstairs solar like a caged lion, waiting for Lewiston to conclude his conversation with Lachlan and his new bride, irritated by the fact that he was taking so long. He *knew* she was waiting.

She stopped in midstride, listened for a moment, and then walked to the window where she stood, staring out over the beautiful rolling hills into which the village of her childhood was tucked, her face pensive. Lachlan had married far too quickly for it to have been anything other than a union of convenience. There hadn't even been enough time for the girl to be pregnant, forcing his hand by that method. More than likely she had simply maneuvered him into a compromising situation, and her family, jumping on the chance to claim a connection to a peer of the realm, had insisted he do right by her.

Eloise eyed a ribbon of smoke rising from a building in the distance, recognized that it came from the blacksmith's shop, and smiled a slow, calculating smile. Beth Gilweather, she thought to herself. Lachlan had not so long ago fancied himself in love with the pretty little blonde. The girl was far too beneath the lofty Kimball family to be at all considered as a marital prospect, and because of that Eloise had ruthlessly destroyed the relationship by convincing Beth that Lachlan planned to abdicate to Lewiston—a dream that had actually come true when Lachlan learned the truth of his parentage. Lewiston had been too weak to take him up on it, however.

Now, however, the blacksmith's girl might be actually useful. It was too late to keep Lachlan's marriage from happening, but not too late to undermine it. Eloise had no choice. The only way she would ever see Lewiston become the Marquess of Asheburton—as was his right—was to pray Lachlan did not produce an heir. That way, if Lachlan suddenly died, Lewiston would be forced to take his birthright. She'd have to explain why her prediction of her elder son's abdication hadn't come to pass, but then she could convince Beth that the old flame could yet be salvaged. She could depend on the girl's self-serving instincts.

Eloise heard her younger son's footsteps on the stairs to the solar and turned away from the window, for the moment putting Lachlan's first love out of her mind. The instant Lewiston entered the room she began peppering him with questions: "Tell me about the girl. How did she manage to trap Lachlan? Does she even have a clue what it means to be a marchioness? Tell me she at *least* has some ability to converse properly. Lord above, with hair that color one really must wonder if she's just some doxy from the streets of London."

Well used to her typical overreactions, Lewiston waited patiently for his mother to reach the end of her tirade. When it appeared she was finished, he spoke. "You can set your mind at ease regarding her background. Her father is a scholar as well as a large landholder in a village called Pelthamshire a few hours out of London."

"But he is *not* nobility." Eloise looked smug.

"Neither were you, Mother," Lewiston pointed out in a reasonable voice. "However, Charity does have very close connections to some of the most important families in England. One sister is married to the Earl of Huntwick, another has married the Marquess of Roth, and her aunt is the Dowager Countess of Egerton." He paused a moment, anticipating her reaction to his next words. "And they are all very close friends of the current Duke of Blackthorne."

Eloise pressed her lips together, fighting the tide of resentment that rose within her. *Blackthorne.* No matter how she tried to ignore them, her ties to the Tremaine family always managed to chafe. "Where is the happy couple now?" she asked.

"Lachlan's giving Charity a tour of the keep and introducing her to the staff." Lewiston gave his mother a stern look. "Give the girl a chance, Mother. She's really quite a lovely little thing, and Lachlan seems terribly fond of her."

Eloise turned back to the window, effectively dismissing her younger son. "Lachlan is a fool and has surely been taken in by this young woman. Don't make the mistake of falling into the same trap."

"And this"—Lachlan opened a set of double doors on the right side of a long, lushly carpeted corridor with a flourish, bowed from the waist, and indicated she should precede him—"is your chamber, my lady."

Charity smiled at his dramatic gesture and slipped past, laying a hand briefly on his cheek as she did. He reached up, caught it in his larger hand, and entered the room beside her so that he could fully enjoy his bride's gasp of awed surprise. She did not disappoint.

"Oh, my lord," she breathed. "It's beautiful!"

And it truly was. Decorated in shades of rose and plum, the room exuded a sense of warmth and comfort that engulfed Charity like a warm fleece on a cold day. The tour of the rest of the castle had taken all afternoon, and she had found the ancient structure, at times, rather cold and un-welcoming. Her husband's love for his home, however, was obvious, so she kept her reactions to herself except when they were positive.

By contrast, this room was completely modern, inviting, and comfortable. The bed, across from and to the right of the entrance, was its focal point, set into a corner framed by tall windows affording a beautiful view of the hills on both sides. It was covered in a sumptuous rose silk with matching curtains caught up and tied to the posts with ropes of bur-gundy satin. Yards and yards of soft Aubusson carpet in a muted mauve covered the floor, and the mahogany furni-ture glowed with attention and coats of painstakingly ap-plied wax.

Lachlan brought the hand he held to his lips, softly kissed the backs of her fingers, and then pointed at the doors to their left. "Through there is a bathing chamber, completely modernized, a dressing room, and connecting doors to my bedchamber. I'd like, if it is something with which you are comfortable, to leave both sets of doors ei-ther unlocked or open."

Charity bit her lip and dipped her head, a small smile tugging at the corners of her mouth. She had wondered what the sleeping arrangements would be, now that they were married, and found she was suddenly shy about asking the question that was foremost in her mind. Both of her el-der sisters slept in the same bedchamber as their husbands, and while she knew that was not the normal practice for married couples of their class, she hoped her husband would be open to such an option. There was, she had discovered, something amazingly comforting about sleeping with some-one so much larger, someone who held her through the night. She'd felt safe, and warm, and coveted. She sighed happily. Really, she just wanted to be near him.

Lachlan took in her silence as she looked down at the floor, wondered if she were uncomfortable with his suggestion, or if she simply didn't want to tell him she hated the idea of being so accessible to him. He waited until he could no longer stand it and then reached under her chin to lift her face to his. What he saw made his breath catch.

Charity's eyes were glowing with warmth, their clear aquamarine depths shining with happiness, and Lachlan fell into her entrancing gaze, the world receding until nothing else existed. Her lips curved in a winsome smile.

"My lord?" she whispered, and stepped closer.

"It's Lachlan, kitten." His voice was gruff. "Call me by my name, please. I love it when you say my name."

"Lachlan," she corrected without hesitation. His name came easily to her, and she said it once more, allowing the two syllables to roll slowly off her tongue and cling quivering to her lips, as if reluctant to fall away into the charged air between them. "W-would it be all right if . . ." She stopped, and he watched as a pink blush stole across her cheeks, brightening her already glorious color.

"If?" he prompted, holding his breath.

"Well, I just enjoyed the way things were at the inn last night. You know, when you held me and we fell asleep . . . t-together," she stammered.

Lachlan's heart slammed into his ribs. Was she asking what he thought she was asking? Did she mean that she wanted to sleep with him, to be held in his arms at night, to share his chamber? He searched her face. Her eyes looked wide and utterly without guile.

Charity waited for him to respond to her hesitant statement, hoping he would ask what she was afraid to put into
words. When the silence between them grew, she felt her
heart begin pounding. Perhaps she should have waited—

Without warning, he scooped her up into his arms and
strode across the room. Charity caught glimpses of marble
and pewter as they swept through the bathing chamber.

"Lachlan!" she laughed. "What are you doing?"

"Hush," he said, shifting her weight effortlessly to one
arm so that he could free a hand to open the double doors.

"I will not," she protested, though there was a smile in
her voice. Crushed against her husband's chest, she tilted
her head back and to the side so that she could see where he
was taking her. The first thing she noticed was the enormous bed on a raised platform in the far corner. Lachlan
was heading straight for it.

Sudden panic hit her, unexpected and inexplicable, and
she began struggling to get down.

"Wait," she said, pushing against his chest. He let her slide
down and set her gently on her feet. She shook out her skirts
self-consciously, took a couple steps away from him and
looked around the enormous chamber.

The last rays of light from the setting sun filtered through
the tall windows that dominated an entire wall. Rich velvet
draperies in a deep navy blue framed them, caught and
pulled aside by twisted silk ropes of the same shade, waiting to be drawn for the evening. On the wall opposite the
windows, logs lay neatly in the fireplace, ready to roar to
life should the need to warm the room arise, and two chairs
upholstered in a buttery-soft burgundy leather flanked the
hearth.

Charity took a step toward this cozy seating arrangement. "Would you like to sit and talk, my lord, until it is

time to go down to supper?" She fixed him with a bright smile, trying to hide the fact that she felt an odd fluttering in her stomach she did not understand. After all, it was not as though she had never been alone in a bedroom with her husband, she reasoned to herself.

Lachlan watched her closely, utterly enchanted by the little gestures and expressions that revealed the nervousness Charity was feeling. He reveled in it, knowing it was the first and last time he would have the opportunity to enjoy her thus. After tonight, her eyes would be open and knowing, the mysteries of intimacy between a man and a woman removed. After tonight, they could spend the rest of their lives learning to enjoy one another in new and beautiful ways. But tonight, just tonight, he could tenderly guide her through the unknown and awaken the natural sensuality she'd already shown every time they had kissed.

He smiled warmly, his gray eyes a molten, simmering silver. "Are you hungry, kitten?"

Charity stopped in her tracks. "Hungry?" she asked uncertainly, completely forgetting that she'd been the one to broach the topic of the evening meal. "Is Cook ready for dinner?" His deep voice had sent chills skittering down her spine. She looked uncertainly toward the club chairs, and then back at her husband, who hadn't answered. The bed loomed large in the background and she felt her heartbeat quicken. "No, my lord," she murmured. "I'm not hungry."

Lachlan followed her eyes and turned in a circle, his arms spread to take in the whole room around them. "What do you think, love? Can you be comfortable in here, or would you rather spend your evenings in your own chamber and occasionally visit me in mine?"

Charity's thoughts returned to the time she'd fallen

asleep in his arms, to the comfort and warmth and sense of belonging she'd felt. Her face softened and she took an inadvertent step toward him. "Here, please," she said in an aching voice, her face glowing with unconscious longing.

Lachlan closed the distance between them in a single step. He lifted a hand, tucked a wayward curl behind her ear, and then crooked a finger beneath her chin to tilt her face up to his. "Remember that I promised you I would tell you everything that will happen between us, so that you have nothing about which to worry, nothing to fear?"

Wordless, her eyes huge, she nodded.

"Well, I want a promise from you as well, kitten. Promise me that you will always ask any question that comes into your mind, that if there is something about which you are uncomfortable, you will stop me and tell me." He cupped her cheek in his palm, his smoldering pewter gaze holding hers. "I don't ever want there to be anything misunderstood between us. I do not intend to hold back with you. I hope you won't hold back from me."

Charity's heart lurched a bit. Her lips curved in a winsome little smile. "I *do* have a question, my lord."

Lachlan's heart sank a little at her continued use of the formal address instead of using his name. "Ask," he said evenly.

She bit her lip. "Well, I was just wondering . . ." She stopped and looked down, then squared her shoulders as if gathering courage, and raised eyes glowing with promise to his. "I was wondering," she repeated, "if you were going to kiss me now, or if you intended to wait until after—"

She didn't get a chance to finish her sentence. Warm, possessive pride flooding through his veins, Lachlan kissed her, drawing her plump lower lip between his, tasting her sweet surrender as she melted into his arms with a contented little sigh. He lifted his mouth from hers and chuckled low in his throat when her eyes flew open in protest.

"Shhh," he crooned, and pressed a soft kiss to each eyelid so that she closed them again. "There's no rush." He kissed the tip of her upturned nose.

Charity slipped her arms around his waist and held on, lifting her lips to his for another kiss. Instead, he brushed his lips on her cheek and trailed over across her cheek until he reached her ear. She gasped and then moaned when he took her earlobe between his lips, wondering at the curious glow that was building within her and slowly spreading outward in warm, tingling swirls. When he began nibbling on her ear, the glow exploded.

Her knees went weak. She cried out his name and clutched handfuls of his jacket in her fists. "Hold me," she breathed, and he did, taking her face between his hands and kissing her with all the passion he'd fought to control over the past three days.

"You should have had a lady's maid to prepare you for this night, kitten," he said against her mouth, when he finally stopped kissing her to catch his breath.

"Why?" she asked, her mouth seeking his to perhaps coax another kiss.

"Because," he said wryly. "We are both entirely too dressed for this sort of thing."

He watched her delicate brows draw together and pulled her head to his chest. "We've been married for over twenty-four hours, love, but tonight is our wedding night." He tugged at a trailing end of the ribbon she'd used to tie back her curls that morning. "Your maid should be removing all the silly pins and clips and such you used to hold up your beautiful hair." The ribbon pulled loose and fluttered to the floor. Lachlan buried his hands in those curls and kissed her again, a long, slow, drugging kiss that stoked again the warmth inside her.

"Do I *have* a maid?" she asked when he raised his head, her voice sensual and low-pitched.

"Not yet." Lachlan smiled. "She'd have helped you out of your complicated gown." They looked down at the mostly unadorned blue frock and both laughed.

"I suppose I don't follow the fashions very well," Charity said, and then looked up into his eyes. "*You* be my maid, darling."

Twenty-five

Lachlan's heart almost stopped. Charity was asking him, innocence glowing in those amazing eyes, to undress her. "I'm not sure I know how to do it right," he said. "Perhaps you could coach me."

She smiled. "What would you normally be doing while my maid was helping me?"

"Waiting impatiently."

Charity laughed. "Surely you would have some preparations of your own. Do you have a valet?"

Lachlan nodded. "He's on his way from London after wrapping up a few of my affairs. But I tend to prefer doing my own dressing and undressing. He's not a very conventional valet, I suppose, though he does keep track of my garments and see that they are cleaned and pressed."

Charity was intrigued. "Not conventional? In what way?"

The last thing Lachlan wanted to do at the moment was get into a discussion of his staff. "You'll understand when you meet him," he said. "Why don't we just forget about maids and valets and . . ." He stopped when Charity tilted her head to the side and stared at his chest. "What are you doing?"

She reached out and fingered one of his shirt studs. "So you have a valet but you dress yourself, and I am to have a maid although I've always managed quite well alone. And now we are to forget about them both? Seems a shame to put perfectly good people out of work." She laughed softly.

Lachlan stared at the tip of her finger, suddenly jealous of the shirt stud. His heartbeat increasing, he ached for her to reach out to him like that, to touch him with no prompting, and he wanted her to ache with the need to touch him utterly of her own accord. He stared down at her, his gray eyes smoldering.

"Darling?" he said.

In that instant, although she was in uncharted waters, Charity unconsciously sensed her feminine power for the first time. Following an instinct she didn't know she possessed, she let her finger slip from the shirt stud to draw circles upon the fabric around it.

Lachlan swallowed hard and caught her maddening finger in his hand. He brought it to his lips. "Your maid would undoubtedly have laid out some ridiculously beautiful nightgown with a matching frilly dressing gown, garments which, though pretty, would serve absolutely no purpose whatsoever. Not tonight."

She inched closer and inhaled deeply, utterly enjoying his distinctive scent. Closing her eyes she asked, "Why would they serve no purpose?"

"Because you wouldn't be wearing them for very long."

Her eyes flew open. Despite the momentary rush of bravery she'd just enjoyed, a blush stole across Charity's face and her eyes narrowed suspiciously. "What do you mean?" she said, her initial trepidation returning.

"Although we are married, I haven't really made you my wife, kitten. I intend to rectify that tonight." He watched her chew on her lower lip a moment, her even white teeth sinking deliciously into the plump bit of flesh. "Look at me, Charity." His voice was firm but gentle, and she raised her eyes to his. He cupped her face in his hands and kissed her softly. "Beginning tonight, there will be no need for secrets between us. Nothing to hide, nothing to fear."

"I already have nothing to hide from you," she said quietly.

"Then come to bed. Let me make love to you, and teach you how to make love to me."

He shrugged out of his jacket, let it fall to the floor and then took her hand and led her toward the dais. Charity's heart was pounding, but she allowed herself to be pulled along. They climbed the three shallow steps together and stood next to the enormous bed.

Twilight had come without either of them noticing, and the room had grown darker. Light from the rising moon streamed in through the tall windows and fell diagonally across the mattress. It was into one of these moonbeams that Charity had stepped, and the sight of his wife made Lachlan catch his breath. She looked tiny and impossibly fragile in the near darkness, her skin pale in a face dominated by her large, wary eyes. He unclasped and removed the studs from the wrists of his shirt, seeking a way to make her feel as if she had a modicum of control in a situation she didn't understand.

He cupped the studs in his hand, and then took a step back to place them on the nightstand. "Would you like to help me get ready for bed?"

Wordless with uncertainty, Charity nodded. Lachlan smiled encouragement, took her hands in his and then brought them to the studs that held his shirt together in the front. Feeling shy, her fingers fumbled with the first until it fell open. Charity handed both pieces to Lachlan, and then began working on the second. It came apart, exposing an expanse of his skin to her view, and she blushed but continued working. By the time she had finished, his shirt had fallen completely open, revealing his firm, muscular chest with its light covering of crisp, dark hair. Tentatively she reached out a hand but stopped and looked up at him, an unspoken question in her eyes.

"Yes," he answered, his voice hoarse. "You can touch me. *Please* touch me."

Her courage buoyed by the need in his voice, Charity's fingertips found the skin just over his heart. His pectoral muscle twitched in response when she touched it, and she drew back for a bare instant then flattened both hands on his chest. Without thinking, she stepped closer and pressed a kiss into the hollow spot over his sternum.

Lachlan groaned, buried his hands in her hair, and held his wife there, cradling her head against his chest, her natural sensuality once again surprising him. Her inexperience was evident and intoxicating, as was the eagerness with which she embraced new experiences despite her fear.

His hands drifted down her back to the short row of buttons that held her simple, high-waisted dress closed, and Charity tensed when she felt his fingers working at the closure and then forced herself to relax.

"This undressing," she asked, her voice a little breathless. She felt the bodice of her dress loosen. "It is part of lovemaking?" She slipped her arms around his waist and rubbed her cheek on his chest.

"It is." Lachlan's voice was warm. "Some people have difficulty with that, or suffer from insecurity." When Charity pulled back to look up at him, her eyes wide, he assured her, "There is no reason for any of that. Not between us."

He slipped the dress off her shoulders. Charity felt the cornflower silk slither down her body and pool around her feet but kept her eyes on her husband's face. Now clad only in her chemise, she smiled briefly and reached for his shoulders, pushing his shirt back and off, unconsciously mimicking his movements with her.

Lachlan let the garment fall past his fingertips to join his wife's dress on the floor, remembering the last time she had seen him shirtless, in the inn on their way to Scotland. That time she had told him he was beautiful. This time she said nothing, but her eyes glowed with newly awakening feelings, and he found he loved her eloquent silence as much as he'd loved her words.

He pointed to a spot on the bed, indicating she should sit on the edge. Trustingly she complied, and when she did, he knelt and began removing her stockings and shoes. Charity looked down at the top of his head and found she was unable to resist sinking her fingers into the dark, thick waves. At her touch, he turned his head and pressed a kiss through the thin material of her chemise into the soft flesh of her thigh. Charity gasped, her skin tingling where his lips lingered. She felt as though all strength had left her limbs, though her fingers unconsciously tightened in his hair. When she felt his hands close around her ankles and begin sliding up her legs, she moaned.

Lachlan enjoyed every sound, every tiny wriggle of reaction. His wife's skin felt like silk beneath his fingers as he pushed her chemise up her calves. He stopped at her knees. "Stand up for me, kitten."

Without a word she complied, and he rose with her, lifting the chemise up and over her head. She lifted her arms to help him and then looked down, watching as the snow-white garment landed on the steps of the dais. Her stomach did a little flip-flop, and she felt self-conscious at being naked for the first time with her husband, despite his assurances that she should not.

He stepped around her and pulled down the covers on

the bed. Grateful, she slipped beneath the sheets, pulled the blankets up to her chin and then lay there blinking up at him.

Lachlan almost laughed. "You're adorable, Lady Asheburton." He reached for the button on his trousers and watched as she shyly averted her eyes. Quickly he divested himself of his remaining attire and climbed into the bed.

His wife shifted to make room for him. When she'd settled, Lachlan turned on his side, propped his head on a hand and regarded her steadily, waiting for her to say whatever she had on her mind. Charity bit her lip and finally said in a whisper, "Tell me again why we are naked."

Lachlan's lips twitched, but he managed to remain solemn. "Well, there are several reasons," he replied. "From a practical standpoint, clothing would only get in the way. Lovemaking is about creating children, after all, and the physical act of joining our bodies is best done without encumbrance."

Charity frowned, as if she were trying to imagine how that would take place, but she didn't interrupt.

"Another reason is symbolic, indicating that a man and his wife are of one mind, with no barriers between them." Her expression didn't change, so he continued. "For some couples it ends right there. But not for us."

"Why not for us?" Charity's eyes were huge, glowing in the dim lighting. Lachlan felt as though he were drowning in them. She still had the covers pulled up under her pert little nose, but she no longer looked frightened or wary. Instead she looked intrigued, hopeful, and a little bit vulnerable.

"Because," he began, but his voice caught. He cleared his throat and tried once more. "Because every time I touch you, it feels like magic. Every . . . single . . . time."

Charity's grip on the blanket loosened a bit.

"When I kiss you, the world stops. When I hold your hand in mine and feel how small it is, all I want to do for the rest of my life is protect you and keep you close to me, where I know you're safe and happy."

Charity turned on her side to face him, the sheet slipping down slightly to drape across her chest, offering him a tantalizing glimpse of the shadowy valley between her breasts. "It's the same for me," she whispered shyly. "I didn't understand why or what it is."

"It's rare, kitten." His gray eyes found hers again, drew her in. She stared back. "And so, for us, I can only imagine that the more intimately we touch, the more amazing it will become."

Her last fears melting away at his words, Charity tilted her face up to his for another kiss. "Teach me."

It was all Lachlan needed to hear. Almost before the words left her mouth, while they still trembled in the air between them, he kissed her. Gone was the tender, tentative lover. This time he kissed her with all the pent-up passion and ardor that had been building from the first moment his lips touched hers.

Charity followed his lead. She didn't notice when the sheet slipped from her upper body to drape across her hips. She kissed him back, her hands cupping his face. When his lips left her mouth to rain kisses over her chin and down her throat, she tilted her head back, offering him unlimited access to that slender column, his name slipping off her tongue in a whispered sigh.

Lachlan felt as though he were drowning. Her scent assailed him, intoxicated him with its sweetness. He trailed a hand down her side, lightly brushing along her rib cage, leaving her skin tingling. It settled softly on her hip before drifting back over the gentle curve to settle into the indention of her waistline.

"So soft," he murmured, and then cupped the soft fullness of her breast in his palm. He raised passion-drunk eyes to hers, not to seek permission but to ensure that she was still with him.

He dipped his head again and drew her dusky pink nipple into his mouth. Tiny jolts of pleasure curled outward from her breast. Charity arched her back and cried out, her hands sliding into his thick dark hair, clenching into fists when the sensation swirled through her midsection to heat her most secret, sensitive place. Lachlan laved her sensitive nipple with long, flat strokes of his tongue, then closed his mouth and suckled until she writhed beneath him. He growled low in his throat and pushed her fully onto her back, his mouth never leaving her breast.

She tasted sweet and fresh and distinctly feminine, and Lachlan drank in his wife's responsiveness like the headiest of wines. He felt her fingers uncurl and then tighten again, digging slightly into his scalp as she pressed herself upward against his mouth as if she wanted to be closer still. Still suckling, he cupped her other breast, catching her nipple between his first two fingers and squeezing slightly, applying pressure until her moan became a gasp. When he heard that, he released her nipple and moved swiftly to give her other breast equal attention.

Charity thought she would go mad—mad from what he was doing to her with his hands, mad from what he was doing to her with his mouth, mad from her inability to reciprocate. Her hands and mouth felt oddly empty, a feeling which warred with the aching heat that was making her feel slick and full at her core. Driven by need, she slid her hands from his hair down the sides of his face and onto his upper back, and then dug her heels into the bed to slide further beneath him. Her unexpected movement tugged her nipple from his mouth. She kissed him before he could protest.

Surprised, Lachlan laughed against her mouth and playfully nipped at her lower lip. "Kitten wants to play, hmm?"

Charity didn't answer, just pressed herself against him. She ran her tongue along the crease between his lips. Her wriggling and kissing was almost too much for Lachlan, and when she wrapped her slender legs around one of his, he abruptly lost control.

"Charity," he said, his voice urgent. "Look at me."

She kept kissing him. "Mmhmm?" she purred, and he knew she wasn't listening, that she was lost in the haze of passion that was overwhelming them both. He gave up trying to slow her down and with deliberate intent moved the leg she had caught between hers until it pressed against her heated center.

That got her attention. "Oh," she breathed.

"Yes," he returned. One hand found the plump flesh of her buttocks, cupped it and then pulled her toward him, causing her to rub herself along his thigh.

"Lachlan!" Her husband's name ended in a moan. Her eyes fluttered closed and she buried her face in his chest. She'd never done anything so wanton and uninhibited, and, God help her, she wanted more.

Lachlan held perfectly still, held even his breath, and waited. But then, on a surrendering outward breath she caught one of his hardened nipples between her lips and began suckling him as he had her, flexed her hips so that she moved against him exactly the way he'd just taught her, driving herself toward something she surely felt she needed but could not identify.

"God, Charity, yes." He caught his wife's face in his hands and forced her to meet his eyes. "You're driving me insane. Listen to me." He knew he wouldn't be able to wait much longer, and he wanted to make sure she was ready.

Charity stopped moving and blinked slowly, trying to focus on what her husband was saying. Her body was languid, saturated with desire, and she'd never felt quite so alive.

He kissed her. "In a few moments, I'm going to make love to you, kitten. It might hurt a little at first." He kissed her again, as if to lessen any fears she might have.

"How?" The single word was soft, hesitant.

Lachlan took her hand in his and brought it to his chest. "I can hear your heart pounding, love. Can you feel mine?"

She nodded, wordless, her eyes huge.

"We make each other feel this way, make each other feel things. Strong, beautiful things, and we are fortunate that we are able to enjoy those feelings. Our bodies are made for expressing this beauty in the most intimate way, and the things we have been doing—kissing, touching, tasting— prepares us for lovemaking." He drew her hand down his chest and then across her abdomen while he spoke. When he continued lower, she gasped in shock and tried to pull away.

"Don't, love. Please don't," he said in an aching voice. "Please trust me."

Charity remembered the words of the note Grace had sent from London. *Trust him, trust yourself.* She stared into his eyes for a long moment, as if seeking an answer to an unspoken question. Finding what she sought in their molten silver depths, she nodded, bit her lip, and relaxed her hand.

Lachlan's heart swelled with love at her bravery, and he continued. He brought her hand between her legs and covered it with his own. "There is no shame, love, in know-ing our bodies." Charity blushed despite his words when she felt her own moist heat on her fingers, but she did not pull free this time. "You are slick here, darling, because your body is preparing itself to join with mine."

His voice was hypnotic, soothing, and she nodded, caught in the spell he was weaving around them. He parted her cupped fingers, slid one of his own between them, hesi-tated a moment, his eyes on hers, and then began slowly easing it inside her. As he did, Charity gasped and arched her back.

"Lachlan," she whimpered, her voice caught somewhere between a choke and a sigh. Waves of pleasure streaked outward from that slowly invading finger, and she closed her eyes, giving herself over to his caresses.

"That's right, love . . . let it happen." He stroked her, his finger moving in timeless rhythm until her eyes flew open and her mouth formed a silent O of surprise. Swiftly he took her mouth in a kiss, matching the thrusts of his tongue with the strokes of his hand until she cried out into his mouth and convulsed around him.

Lachlan propped himself on an elbow and watched his wife slowly return to awareness. She lay quietly within his arms, her breathing slowly becoming even again. When her eyes fluttered open, he kissed the tip of her nose.

"W-what . . . what was that?" Her voice was thick with residual warmth of her completion.

"That, my beautiful girl, is the gift of which I spoke."

"You felt it, too?" She placed her hand on his chest and turned more completely into his arms, snuggling against him as a tingling glow began to steal across her skin. She giggled.

"Not yet, kitten," he answered. "Why are you laughing?"

"It tickles," she said, a small smile playing about her lips. "All over. It is more lovely, even, than champagne."

Wonder filled Lachlan, and he caught her up against him, stroking a hand tenderly down her side. He had been right about her from the first when he'd sensed the depths of her passion after their first kiss. She was a natural seductress, charming and sensual, beautifully responsive to his touch.

She traced a finger around the flat male nipple that had so recently been in her mouth. "Lachlan?"

"Mm?"

"What did you mean when you said 'not yet'?"

Her sweetness was intoxicating. "I'm being patient, love. When I feel the way we discussed, my body will be deep inside yours." He stroked the hair from her forehead and then kissed the spot he had exposed.

"How?" she persisted. "Should I touch you the way you touched me?"

Her question was so innocent and yet so unbelievably provocative. Lachlan found himself momentarily unable to answer. He swallowed hard, nodded once and then groaned when he felt her hand touch the taut plane of his stomach and then hesitantly begin to slide lower. "Charity," he finally breathed, and caught her wrist in his hand.

"Am I doing it wrong?" Her eyes were huge in the semi-darkness.

"God, no," he said. "There is no wrong way for you to touch me. You're doing everything right. I just didn't want you to be . . . startled." He released her wrist and watched her closely. When her fingers found him, her eyes widened, though not with fear. With wonder.

She closed her fingers around him, sudden understanding. "This part of you will . . ." She stopped and blushed, unable to bring herself to actually say what she imagined.

Lachlan covered her hand with his. "This part of me was made to fit inside you." His voice was thick with need and with the effort to keep from spilling himself into her hand; he couldn't wait much longer. Gently he eased her onto her back, kissed her softly, and nudged her legs apart with one of his. He knelt there between them, poised at her entrance, and looked down at the woman he was about to make his in every way.

What he saw made his breath catch in awe. Charity was looking up at him with eyes filled with love, tenderness, and the promise of forever, and he thought he might drown in them. Her hair was tossed in artful disarray on the white linens, her skin a dusky pale peach in the near darkness.

"You are unbelievably beautiful, Lady Asheburton," he said, his voice hoarse with passion. *"Charity."*

She smiled tremulously, reached up and cupped his cheek in her hand. He caught a fingertip in his mouth and then released it. Charity's eyes drifted lower, past the muscles of his abdomen, delving into that shadowy place where his body would join hers. Swiftly, she looked up and met his eyes again.

Lachlan leaned forward, laced his fingers with hers and braced their interlocked hands on the bed. Slowly, he began easing himself into her tight, slick passage. Charity held her breath in wonder at the sensation of being filled for the first time. Heat blossomed from her core, and she wriggled her hips a little, following an instinct to push back against him.

"God—*don't.* Charity."

She stopped instantly, her eyes locked on his face.

He held perfectly still, just barely inside her. He had hoped it would be easy, but that hope died when he nudged up against the barrier that proclaimed her innocence. When she began wriggling, it took every ounce of his self-control not to push forward and make her completely his. He closed his eyes and waited, silently willing her to do the same.

After a moment, he gave a tiny new push but stopped when her eyes widened in surprise. He leaned forward, his fingers still laced with hers. "Kiss me, kitten," he whispered against her lips, and when she complied, he surged into her, breaking the barrier, taking her small cry of pain into his mouth. He held still once again, buried deep within her moist heat, fighting the urge to move until she stirred beneath him.

Charity shifted her hips slightly, the pain already subsiding, replaced by the most curious stretching sensation. She broke off the kiss and buried her face in Lachlan's neck. Slowly he pulled back. Thinking he was stopping because he'd hurt her, Charity wrapped her legs around him to keep him there. "No! Don't go, please. I-I'm okay."

Lachlan half groaned, half chuckled. "I couldn't go anywhere if I wanted to. Trust me on this. Follow my lead. Your body knows what to do," he whispered, and began moving within her again.

Charity watched his face, awed by the expression of sublime pleasure on his handsome features, but a moment later she was ensnared by the sensual web he wove and closed her eyes. He began to pick up the rhythm. She caught her breath and then began moving against him, trying to imitate what he was doing, trying to help, timing the motions of her hips to meet his thrusts.

"Yes, love, that's it." His voice was taut, strained with the effort he was exerting to hold back his own pleasure until she found hers. "Let it come to you," he added. And then the world spun away and there was nothing but his body and her body and their quickening heartbeats.

Charity's hands roved her husband's flesh, touching him

anywhere they could reach, drinking in the feel of his muscles through her palms and fingertips, the fine sheen of perspiration making her hands glide without effort over the rippling valleys and planes. Lachlan sighed and whispered in the shell of her ear, words that weren't words, words that somehow made perfect sense, and she responded with moans and mews, her body and eyes begging him to take her to a place she could not name. And then, at last, she crested that peak, threw her head back, and cried out her completion.

When her body contracted around him, Lachlan scooped Charity up from the bed and pulled her into him, her back arched over his forearms as she rode the crest of her pleasure. He drove into her again and again, and she writhed, her hips clearly moving of their own accord, her thighs gripping his hips, until at last he cried out her name, thrust one final time and fell forward, carrying her with him, spilling himself deep within her womb.

They lay there, legs tangled, bodies connected for some time while their heartbeats slowed, neither wanting to break the spell with words. Lachlan opened his eyes and pushed himself up on one arm. The exquisite girl in his arms stirred, too, but her eyes remained closed. Her russet lashes lay like dark fans on her pale cheeks, and while he watched, a single tear slipped from beneath one eyelid. It rolled slowly down her cheek.

Lachlan caught it with his tongue. "Charity," he said. "Look at me." She opened her eyes and he caught his breath. All the love in the world was right there in those cerulean depths.

Charity smiled, but the words she wanted to say to her husband got caught in her throat, lodged there in the thick swell of emotion that engulfed her. There was no need to say them, though. Lachlan knew. "I love you, too," he whispered, then rolled onto his back, Charity held securely in his arms.

He settled her astride his hips, and then began teaching her all the ways they could learn to please each other.

Twenty-six

"Good morning, my lord."

At the sound of his younger brother's voice, Lachlan looked up in surprise from saddling Apollo. Typically he was the only member of the family out and about this early in the day.

"Good morning, Lewiston," he replied with a smile. "So formal. Since when did you start 'my lording' your big brother?"

Lewiston grinned. "Mother hates it. I think it's good to occasionally remind her that you're not the only one who can push back." He tilted his head toward the horse. "Resuming your rituals, I see."

Lachlan nodded. "Yes. I find I've missed my morning rides more than I realized."

"So much that you left the bed of your charming bride so soon?"

Lachlan raised a brow but did not stop preparing his mount. "Charity was sound asleep when I left and will likely remain so for hours."

They had been up most of the night, laughing and talking and making love. Charity had finally fallen asleep in his arms near dawn. With all the events of the past few days crowding his mind, Lachlan had found it impossible to sleep. When the sun began to paint the morning sky with the pinks and oranges that heralded a new day, he gave up, kissed the top of his wife's curly head and slipped from the bed. Quietly he'd dressed in riding clothes, pulled the drapes closed so she wouldn't be awakened by the morning sun, and left the room. The hills were calling him.

He finished saddling Apollo and led him out into the paddock. Lewiston followed.

"Speaking of mother," the young man began, but then he stopped with a grimace.

"She's unhappy. I know. She is always unhappy with me. I wasn't suffering under the delusion that she would feel any differently about my marriage." Lachlan gave his brother an assessing look. "Why? What has she said?"

"Very little, once I set her straight about Charity's background and family." Lewiston watched his brother swing up into the saddle. "She's taking a trip into the village this morning. Said something about obtaining a proper lady's maid."

"For Charity?" Lachlan's voice registered surprise. "What an uncharacteristic thing for her to do." Apollo danced sideways, eager to get out and run free after weeks in the paddock. The marquess stroked his neck soothingly.

"I think she means to find one for herself," Lewiston clarified, his tone wry. "She's never had one in all the time we've known her, but now that you've brought an English lady into the house who is accustomed to such a luxury I suppose she intends to do whatever she can to appear less provincial."

"Ah. That makes more sense." Lachlan nodded at his brother and tugged on Apollo's right rein, pointing the horse toward the gate. "Ironically, the only time Charity has ever had a maid was during her very short time in London this Season. And I believe she shared the maid with her twin sister." He grinned and dug his heels into the stallion's flanks. "Have a good morning," he tossed back over his shoulder.

*   *   *

A rustling punctuated by occasional bumps and knocks slowly penetrated Charity's consciousness. She woke slowly and opened her eyes to the gloom of a dark, unfamiliar room. When she heard the sound of a drawer being quietly opened and then closed again, she pushed herself to a sitting position, clutched the bedclothes to her chest, and scraped tangled curls from her face.

After she registered the fact that she was alone in the most enormous bed she'd ever occupied, it took a few seconds for the events of the previous evening to come flooding back. She blushed a little, and then a slow smile spread across Charity's face. She stretched one arm upward, yawned hugely, and tilted her head back, reveling in the sensation of her hair swishing across her shoulders and the decadent feeling of her naked legs against the soft sheets. With a happy sigh she plunked back down into the soft pile of pillows, snatched one up, and hugged it to her chest. There was, she decided, a very naughty sort of beauty to waking up nude in her husband's bed. She doubted she would ever sleep clothed again.

Expecting to find Lachlan near the wardrobe getting dressed for the day, she glanced toward the source of the noise. Instead, she saw a short, burly man she didn't recognize rifling through the contents of her husband's drawers, his back turned to her. With a quickly stifled gasp of alarm, she sat up, tugged the sheet from where it was tucked at the end of the bed and gathered it around her body in a silent, desperate attempt to cover herself.

Keeping an eye on the intruder, she scooted, as quietly as possible, toward the side of the bed nearest the doors to the bathing chamber. Without warning, the bed creaked. Loudly. Charity froze. The man straightened and turned toward her. His face was lined, craggy, and distinctly menacing.

His dark eyes locked on hers, surprise evident in their glittering depths. When he took a step forward, Charity scrambled into action, calling out, "Don't make another move!" She gathered the sheet more securely around her body. "My husband will be home soon," she warned. "Any minute now he'll be back."

The man stopped in his tracks and stood frozen, watching her warily. Charity slid down from the bed, taking her makeshift dressing gown with her, and sidled toward the fireplace, hoping to secure one of the long iron tools from the stand to use as a weapon.

The man followed her progress and, realizing her intention, hastened to reassure her. "My lady, I mean you no harm. I simply did not realize you were in the bed." He smiled but was utterly unaware that his effort to be charming only made him look even more frightening. "I'll just go on downstairs—"

Charity lunged the last few steps to the fireplace. "You'll do no such thing!" She grabbed the poker and spun around, brandishing it like a sword. "I'm not afraid to use this!"

With her head high, her chin outthrust, and her eyes spitting blue sparks, she looked absolutely glorious, even clad only in a wrinkled bedsheet. The man's smile broadened into a grin, and he held up a placating hand. "I believe you!" He chuckled. "Aye, his lordship must have his hands full with you, lass. I am Niles, my lady. Your husband's valet."

Charity lowered the poker a fraction of an inch and glared down its length. "You don't look like a valet," she accused.

"Well, begging your pardon, love, but you don't look much like a marchioness."

She narrowed her eyes at his audacity.

Niles chuckled. "I believe I like you, my lady. What do

you say we drop the animosity and begin again?" His voice held only the slightest trace of a Scottish accent, and his words were cultured and intelligent, in startling contrast to his rough appearance.

Charity cautiously lowered her arm, which had begun to ache with the effort of holding up the long piece of heavy metal. With a toss of her reddish-gold head, she drew herself up as tall as possible and gifted him with a withering stare. "If you would be so kind, I'd like for you to leave."

She tightened her grip on the sheet that served as her only covering as Niles nodded and glanced at the scattered scraps of clothing she had worn the previous day, now littering the floor beside the bed. Color flooded her cheeks.

"I brought your things from London, if you'd care for something fresh," he announced. "The trunks have already been taken to your chamber." He gave the fire poker a last rueful glance and then bowed and left.

The second the door closed behind him, Charity dropped the poker and fled through the bathing chamber to the safety of her own room.

"Ah, Niles. You've arrived sooner than I'd expected."

The valet looked up from his task of putting away the things he'd brought with him from London, a gruesome smile on his craggy face. "Aye, my lord. We made good time by traveling at night and stopping only long enough to rest the horses." He reached into a pocket and withdrew a folded piece of paper, which he handed to his employer. "This is from the Duke of Blackthorne, my lord. His grace was of the opinion that you would need me here as soon as possible, so he told me to hurry."

He glanced toward the doors that connected to the marchioness's chamber. "Now that I've met your young lady, I imagine he thought you'd need someone to watch your back." His dark eyes danced with humor.

Lachlan slipped the note into his pocket without reading it, followed the direction of Niles's gaze, and fixed the burly valet with a questioning look, refusing to acknowledge the shorter man's insinuation that he might need physical protection from his wife.

The valet's grin broadened. "Quite the lady, my lord. She wields a rather mean poker."

The marquess raised his eyebrows. "You appear provokingly unharmed," he drawled. "I trust my wife is the same?"

"Aye, my lord. Nothing hurt but her pride. I didn't realize she was asleep in your bed when I arrived. We . . . Hmm." He paused as though searching for a properly descriptive word. "We *surprised* one another," he finished.

Lachlan gave the valet a long look. "My wife was not dressed when I left her, Niles."

"No," he agreed. "Nor when I arrived." He tilted his head toward the bed. "I imagine the maids will be wondering where the sheet has gone when they come to tidy up."

Lachlan's eyes roved from the bed, to the doors, and then back to his valet's amused face. "So you're telling me my wife held what she thought to be an intruder at bay with a fire poker while she was clad in nothing but a sheet?"

Niles nodded. "The poker wasn't her only weapon, my lord. She was also armed with a rather hot temper. With that mop of the thickest reddish-blonde hair I've ever seen in my life, are you sure she isn't Scots?"

"Quite sure," Lachlan answered over his shoulder. He had turned on his heel and strode toward the connecting doors.

"Well, I like her," called Niles at his master's retreating back. "I like her a great deal," he finished to himself, and returned to his task.

When Lachlan entered his wife's chamber he saw Charity kneeling on the floor before her giant wardrobe, muttering darkly to herself as she tried to find places for all the shoes her sisters had sent from London. He couldn't help but grin.

"Who in the world needs this many pairs of shoes, and why did I let them talk me into ordering them?" Without looking around, Charity reached back for another pair and then abruptly lost her balance, falling backwards onto her trim derriere. The location of her personal items in the mess she'd made unpacking her trunks was still a mystery, and she hadn't been able to properly brush her hair. With an exasperated sigh she shook tangles of her curly hair from her eyes.

Her gaze fell on the only sensible pair of footwear she'd been able to find, a sturdy pair of walking boots, and inspiration struck. She grabbed one and began pulling out the length of leather used to lace it up. Once the thong was freed from the eyelets, she gathered her tousled curls in one hand and began clumsily trying to wrap the unruly mass, intending to tie it all back at the nape of her neck.

She'd quite nearly managed when she felt the unexpected touch of a hand on hers. With a startled shriek she scrambled away, crablike, and crawled around one of the open trunks, trying to put something solid between her and the intruder. "I *knew* I should have used that fire poker on you!"

There came a chuckle, and at the sound of her husband's low laugh, Charity peeked over the top of the trunk. She scowled when she saw him standing there, the piece of leather she had dropped dangling from his fingers.

He composed his features and gave her an innocent look. "I was only trying to help." He glanced around. "From the look of things, you could use someone with more talent in that capacity."

Charity sighed and stood. "I had no idea I owned so many useless articles of clothing," she admitted. She held out her arms in a helpless gesture. "Most of those shoes wouldn't hold up ten minutes if I were to wear them out walking in this terrain."

Lachlan smiled. "It appears I married a very practical girl. What an unexpected delight." He took two long steps in her direction, reached for her chin and tilted her face up to his.

The last remnants of Charity's irritation evaporated, along with her ability to breathe. "You're so beautiful," she whispered, just before he took her lips in a long, soft kiss.

When he lifted his mouth from hers and turned her around so that he could see to gathering her hair, Charity closed her eyes, embarrassed by her inadvertent statement. Had she really told him he was beautiful? *Again?*

"There," said Lachlan. "A temporary solution to your grooming woes." He dropped his hands to her shoulders and pulled her back against him. "I need to go into the village today." He pressed a kiss to the top of her head. "Would you like to go with me? We could find you a proper lady's maid, and I could show you around."

Charity swallowed, not trusting herself to speak without blurting out more nonsense about her husband's beauty. Instead, she nodded.

Lachlan held her a moment longer, then let go and stepped away. He bent to pick up the boot from which Charity had removed the leather lace. "You made quite an impression on my valet, kitten."

At that statement, Charity found her voice and spun around, words suddenly tumbling over one another in their rush to escape her lips. "He sneaked up on me and . . . and . . . he *smirked* at me in the most horribly menacing way." She gesticulated wildly. "Why in the world do you employ someone who looks so frightening?" Shuddering, she leaned forward and lowered her voice. "And I was *naked*," she hissed.

Lachlan hid a smile. "Well, he likes you."

Taken aback, Charity straightened and closed her mouth with a snap. She frowned, her forehead furrowed in confusion. "Did he not tell you that I threatened him with a fire poker?"

"He did." Lachlan nodded, still struggling to keep a straight face. "I believe you threatened me with the same fate when I came into the room just now."

She blushed. "Well, it isn't my fault. Does everyone in this house intend to continue skulking about, sneaking up on people and scaring them half to death?"

Lachlan finally gave up and laughed. "You are exactly what this place needs, love. A bit of life and fire. Now let's find you a pair of reasonably serviceable shoes and get going. I'll send Niles to see if he can make sense of this mess while we're gone. He'll have to do until we get you a lady's maid."

The coach carrying the Marquess and Marchioness of Asheburton had scarcely cleared the gates of the keep when, unnoticed by the occupants of either vehicle, it passed the dowager marchioness's conveyance just returning from the village. The smaller carriage clattered over the drawbridge and circled around the drive, coming to a stop before the wide, shallow steps that led up to the great doors.

Lewiston, who had only just stepped inside after seeing Lachlan and Charity off, walked back out to help his mother alight. To his surprise, once Eloise Kimball was safely on the ground, another woman emerged from the confines of the carriage. He took one look at the new-comer's face and sucked in his breath.

"Mother," he hissed, "have you lost your mind?"

Eloise looked back at him, her eyes wide with innocence. "You remember Beth Gilweather." She smiled at the young blonde girl, who bobbed a quick curtsy in Lewiston's direction. "Of course you do, darling. Beth has graciously agreed to come be my lady's maid."

Lewiston glanced at the girl, a carefully blank look on her pretty face, but her green eyes were calculating and knowing, and she was listening intently. With an exasperated sigh he took his mother's elbow and pulled her a few steps away.

"Lachlan's going to know exactly why you've brought his former fiancée here, Mother."

"Of course he is," she returned in a reasonable tone. "He is well aware of the fact that I intended to find a lady's maid. You did tell him that's why I'd traveled to the village, didn't you?" She was unable to quite keep the look of triumph from her eyes.

"Yes," Lewiston bit out. "I told him."

Eloise laid a hand on her younger son's cheek. "Darling. You seem vexed. Have you had luncheon? You always become irritable when you are hungry."

Lewiston shook his head. "I wash my hands of this, Mother. You deal with Lachlan yourself when he learns what you've done." He turned away, nodded once at Beth, who smiled back sweetly, and strode inside.

Twenty-seven

"I think Scotland might be the most beautiful place in the entire world." Charity turned away from watching the passing scenery and smiled at her husband, her eyes shining with happiness.

"I tend to agree, kitten," he replied, giving his bride an indulgent smile that lent his normally stern expression an engaging boyishness. "If that is the case, it has only been made more beautiful by your presence."

"Charming wretch." Fascinated by the difference a simple smile made, Charity stared at him a moment and then tilted her face up to his for a quick kiss. "Tell me about the villagers, please," she said, picturing a small, intimate group of people not unlike the close-knit community of her childhood. Everyone knew everyone else in Pelthamshire, which could be provoking at times but was, for the most part, rather wonderful. "Are a great many of them employed by the keep?"

"The village exists to support the Marquess of Asheburton, which means it is my duty and responsibility to ensure their livelihoods are protected and secure." He tugged at one bright red-gold curl. "I don't, however, consider them employees."

The road beneath the wheels of the coach had gradually changed as they approached the village, smoothing out and causing fewer jars and bumps for the occupants. Charity pushed away from her husband and scooted back to the window, watching as they passed outlying farms and fields. Without fail, the people working in those fields looked up, smiled, and waved as the burgundy coach drove past with its coat of arms emblazoned on the doors.

Charity waved back cheerfully, and Lachlan shook his head, still smiling at the look of childlike wonder in her large aqua eyes. Young boys and girls appeared from no-where to run along the road a ways before falling off pace as they tired or were called back by their mothers.

It was, all in all, the most enjoyable day she'd experi-enced since leaving Pelthamshire for her London Season. Without warning, the coach turned off the road to the right. Thrown off balance, Charity plunked back on the seat next to Lachlan, and then leaned over him, trying to see where they were going through the window on his side. He laughed and tugged her across his lap so that she could see more easily.

"Relax, kitten," he told her. "We're going to stop here. You can get out and see all there is to see."

Sure enough, as soon as the coach stopped the door opened from the outside and a liveried footman bowed and offered his hand to help Charity down. She disembarked with a grateful smile, followed closely by Lachlan, who took her by the arm and guided her around the back of the coach. There, nestled into a copse of elm trees, was a quaint little gray stone church. A set of steps led up to the white oak doors, which stood open, inviting all who passed to come inside. Lachlan held out a hand.

"It's so pretty," said Charity, placing her hand in his. She followed him up the steps and into the dim interior.

Fifteen rows of wooden pews and kneelers flanked a wide center aisle that led to the chancel, three shallow steps up from the nave. A simple lectern stood to the right on the chancel, and a pulpit to the left. Though the building itself was small, the windows were not. Three soaring stained glass windows depicting biblical stories marched along both sides of the nave, topped with half circles of clear glass to allow natural light to flow through during the day. Charity looked around in wonder, fascinated that such a beautifully simple structure existed in the rustic area.

Lachlan led her down the aisle. "Father Bartholemew—"

"This church is Catholic?" interrupted Charity.

"Not precisely," Lachlan said. "Father Bartholemew came to Ashton not long after I met Gregory, my unofficial tutor, and I have always suspected he came from England at Gregory's urging." He stopped and pulled Charity up against his side, curving an arm around her shoulders. "Before that, Ashton did not have a church. A small group of Christians met each week in homes and shops, but there was really no formal religion. Some residents were pagan, and some held no beliefs at all.

"I never attended church as a child," he admitted. "Neither of my parents were spiritual. Even if they had some belief in Christianity, my mother would never have taken us to worship with the people in the village she viewed as common. What I now know of religion I learned with Gregory, at first from his many books and then from his example. He was devout, and mentioned to me once that he studied to be a vicar. He never told me why he gave up that plan. I strongly suspect he fell in love and lost her for some reason, but I never asked him personal questions. We had rather an unspoken agreement that such things were not to be discussed."

Charity rubbed her cheek on his jacket. "I love it when you speak of your childhood."

Lachlan kissed the top of her head and sat down in the

first pew, pulling her down onto his lap. "One day, when I arrived at Gregory's cabin, there was a stranger visiting him. He wore the robes of a man of the cloth and smiled kindly when I walked through the door. I apologized for interrupting, but both men encouraged me to stay. Gregory introduced me to Father Bart, and then gave me my daily assignment. I sat down to study at my little table but kept one ear on the conversation, the first of many such conversations to which I avidly paid attention.

"They were talking about building this church on the outskirts of the village. The project was to be privately funded, though they did not discuss from where the funds were to come, and there was to be no intention of changing the way the villagers currently chose to worship. Rather, Father Bart would offer himself and his church as an alternative to the unorganized congregation that already existed.

"Before long, most of the villagers who were inclined toward Christianity began to attend services on Sunday. My family still did not, but my religious education continued in Gregory's cabin, just like all my other lessons, with Father Bart frequently joining our discussions. After Gregory went home to England, I found myself stopping here."

Charity chewed on her lower lip. "Won't Father Bartholomew be disappointed that you did not get married here?"

"Why, yes. He is both surprised *and* disappointed."

Startled by the voice that came from behind them, Charity twisted around in her husband's lap to see a tall, thin gentleman in a simple black robe coming down the aisle from the doorway. Both she and Lachlan stood, and when the clergyman drew near, Lachlan stepped forward, a broad smile wreathing his face, and embraced the older man.

He turned back. "Father Bart, please meet my wife, Charity Kimball."

Charity was still unused to hearing her new full name spoken, and for a moment it did not register that Lachlan meant her. When the men eyed her curiously, she gave a little start of surprise. "Oh! You mean me, don't you?"

Both men laughed, and she blushed a little, smiling along with them. "Forgive me, Father." She wrinkled her forehead. "I'm not really sure if I should curtsy or . . . ?" Her words trailed off, and she turned her hands palms up and shrugged. Her religious upbringing had been cursory, at best, since the death of her mother when she was three. Before that, the family had attended the small church in Pelthamshire headed by the dour-faced Reverend Teesbury who, when children saw him out, inspired them to run the other way so that they wouldn't have to address him.

Father Bart took both of her hands in his, stepped forward and pressed a kiss onto her cheek. "You are delightful, my child." He glowered in Lachlan's direction. "I can't say the same for your husband."

The marquess looked unperturbed. "I thought it best that we get married at the border for a couple of reasons."

Bartholomew crossed his arms. "They had better be *good* reasons."

Charity laughed, loving the sight of her powerful husband put in the position of explaining himself.

"Well, in the first place," said Lachlan to the tall, spare clergyman with a dampening look at his wife, "I was not entirely sure Charity wouldn't change her mind if I gave her too much time to think about it."

"Is that so?" she asked, her eyes dancing impishly.

"Quite." His expression softened. "And I was quite determined, you see, to have her as my wife."

Although his words were directed at Father Bart, Lachlan was still looking at Charity. Her heart did a happy little flip.

Father Bart noted with satisfaction the way they were looking at one another. It appeared the many worried conversations he'd had with Gregory about their fears that Lachlan would never find a suitable mate had been unnecessary. He had no intention, however, of letting the boy off that easily. "The border is a very short drive from here," he admonished.

"Yes," agreed Lachlan. "But I thought it best to arrive at the keep already married."

"Ah." Bartholomew nodded. "Well, I cannot disagree with that." He turned back to Charity. "It is a decided pleasure to meet you, my lady."

"And you as well," she returned with a warm smile.

Soon enough they were on their way from the church, Charity promising to drop in any time she felt the inclination. They clattered in their coach across a wooden bridge atop a small stream and entered the village proper. It was neat and orderly and charming in every way. Lachlan escorted Charity to many of the shops and businesses along the main street. Without fail, the villagers greeted her with warmth and open friendliness, and she could tell they had nothing but affection for their young lord. Lachlan went out of his way to ask after family members and livelihoods, taking the time to genuinely listen to each and every person with whom he spoke.

Charity remembered his previous words. In the millinery, she admired a pretty little hat on display. When the hatter offered it to her as a gift, she sweetly thanked the woman but declined, saying she had no clothing that matched. Instead, she ordered one just like it with apple green trim to match the dress she wore. The hatter beamed happily as Lachlan paid for the purchase in advance.

They visited the bakery, the blacksmith, and the tanner, and then finally the general goods store at the end of the road. When they emerged back into the sunshine, Charity, clutching a wrapped box that contained a new hairbrush, comb, and mirror for her vanity, noticed a group of children playing next to a wooden building that could only be a school. Lachlan followed her gaze and smiled.

"Would you like to see my contribution to the village?" he asked. He held out his arm and also took her package from her.

They strolled across the street to stand at the open gate of the fenced building.

"Gregory built the church, but you started a school," she realized. Her heart warmed.

He nodded. "A proper school, with up-to-date educational materials, a lending library, and two teachers. No child in Ashton will ever have to go without an education again."

Charity watched the youngsters play for a few moments before she noticed a boy of about ten sitting alone under a nearby tree, a crutch propped against the trunk. She let go of her husband's arm and walked over to him. When he saw her approaching, he started to get up, but Charity quickly closed the distance and crouched before him so he wouldn't have to struggle.

"Good afternoon," she said, holding out a hand. "My name is Charity."

The boy regarded her with serious brown eyes from under a disheveled mop of dark brown hair. After a moment, he placed his hand in hers. "I'm Tommy." He looked over his shoulder at Lachlan, who still stood beside the gate and added hastily, "My lady." The marquess hid a smile.

"It's hard to play with the other children when you have to use a crutch, isn't it?" Charity's eyes were kind.

Tommy nodded, clearly wondering where her ladyship was going with this.

She sat down beside him with little regard for grass stains or dirt on her pretty frock. "When I was a little girl, I was sick a great deal of the time," she confided. "I used to sit in my bedroom window and watch while my sisters and friends played outside, and I would get so angry that I couldn't join them. Do you ever feel that way?"

Tommy chewed on his lip and nodded. "But only sometimes." He gave her a proud look. "I can read now, so it isn't so bad. Someday I'll—"

"Tommy!"

Charity looked up to see a young woman hurrying across the street from the apothecary shop. "That's my sister, Enid," said Tommy. He pushed himself up and reached for his crutch.

The newly arrived girl bobbed a quick curtsy as she passed Lachlan and then hurried through the gate. "I'm so sorry I'm late." She curtsied again in Charity's direction. "The shop was busy this afternoon."

Charity grinned. "Your brother and I were having a little chat. Do your parents own the apothecary?" The girl didn't look old enough to be out of school herself.

Enid's face clouded. "No, my lady. I just work there during the day."

"Our parents are dead," offered Tommy. Enid looked down at her feet.

Charity glanced past her and found Lachlan watching. She tilted her head toward Enid, and Lachlan nodded imperceptibly.

Sensing the girl wouldn't like to be considered an object

of pity, Charity kept her voice deliberately light, although her heart went out to the pair of young siblings. "Oh, it's too bad you already have a position with the apothecary. I came to the village to find a lady's maid, and I was really hoping to find someone like you, who is closer to my own age." She leaned forward and added conspiratorially, "Asheburton Keep is rather dreary, you see, and I'm accustomed to having my twin sister around to keep me company."

Enid looked up swiftly, searching Charity's face for signs of pity. When she found none, she said hesitantly, "It would be difficult to meet Tommy after school if I worked so far from the village."

Pleased that Enid was considering the opportunity and mindful of the girl's pride, Charity affected a look of confusion. "But I thought if you decided to come you would simply bring Tommy with you. It would be a simple matter to get him back and forth to school with one of the footmen." She stopped, afraid that if she offered too much, Enid would see it as a charitable gesture and refuse.

"I've never been a lady's maid. I don't know how to go about it."

"Well, then, we can learn together," said Charity. She glanced at Lachlan again and lowered her voice, confiding, "I have absolutely no idea how to go about learning to be a marchioness, either."

The village children looked at one another, Tommy's eyes pleading with his sister to accept the offer. After a long moment of silence, Enid glanced at Charity and nodded, her eyes huge with grateful tears she struggled not to shed.

"Excellent, then," said Charity briskly. She looked down at Tommy to give Enid a moment to regain her composure.

The boy gave her a tentative smile. "I'm going to be a doctor," he said.

"My sister is married to a doctor, so that means I will know two doctors," she replied.

Enid spoke up. "We should go home to dinner, Tommy." She addressed Charity. "I'll just give my notice at the apothecary, my lady, so they have time to find someone else."

Charity nodded. "Of course. Send word to the keep when you are ready."

Enid nodded and curtsied, and the pair of children left.

Lachlan smiled as they passed and waited for Charity to join him at the gate. "Did I just hire a lady's maid, or did I adopt two children?" he joked.

"I didn't have a mother for much of my life," said Charity softly. "But I had a father. They have neither, and she strikes me as a brave, strong girl."

They walked down the street toward their waiting coach. Lachlan provided some background information: "From what I recall, their mother died years ago, their father more recently from an excess of drinking. He never really recovered from losing his wife. Enid's never been to school. She's worked at one job or another since she was Tommy's age."

They reached the coach and climbed in. Charity sat in pensive silence until the conveyance began to climb the hill back to the keep. Finally, she looked at her husband. "Thank you," she said, tilting her face up for a kiss.

Lachlan pulled her close, folded her in his arms and softly took her lips. His mouth moved over hers, coaxing her lips to part. When they did, he dipped his tongue inside to taste her sweetness. Charity kissed him back, touching his tongue with her own until they both went wild. She pressed herself closer and ran her hands along his chest, slipping one inside his jacket and around his waist.

Lachlan tugged down one side of her bodice until a rosy-tipped breast popped free. With a groan he covered it with his hand and began rolling her hardening nipple between his thumb and forefinger. Jolts of sensation shot to her core, and Charity whimpered, her hand wandering down his torso and between his legs. She found him hard and ready, and tore her mouth from his.

"Make love to me," she said.

"Here?" he asked breathlessly, astonished again by her uninhibited ardor, her willingness to embrace new experiences.

"Yes, please," she murmured into his neck. Her lips found his earlobe. "Here."

Lachlan pushed her back into the velvet squabs, following her down. He drew her breast into his mouth, sinking his teeth ever so slightly into the hard nubbin at its center. His hand worked its way beneath her skirts to find her moist center. He was just reaching for the button on his trousers when, without warning, the coach gave a great lurch and the front half crashed to the ground, tossing them both forward.

"Are you all right?" Lachlan reached for Charity, who nodded. She struggled to straighten her clothing just as the door opened from the outside and one of the footmen stuck his head in, an anxious look on his face.

"We're fine," said Lachlan, helping his wife up. They climbed out of the coach and took a turn to survey the damage.

"What happened?" asked Charity. Her voice was slightly shaky, both from their interrupted lovemaking and the accident.

Lachlan knelt and peered under the vehicle. "Looks like an axle broke." He frowned. "Odd. The coach is nearly new." He stood and began issuing orders. "Unhitch the team and see what you can do to move the coach off to the side of the road. We'll walk to the keep and send back help." He held out a hand to his wife, which she took without question, peering the short distance up the road to the drawbridge. They were nearly home.

They set out, the coachman and two footmen already busily following the marquess's command. "Good thing I wore sensible shoes," Charity remarked, her tone cheerful.

Lachlan smiled at his stalwart little bride. "It most certainly is." He pointed to a trail they were just passing that led down toward a ravine. "If you follow that pathway and walk along the bluff for a bit, you'll reach Gregory's cabin."

Charity nodded. "Perhaps you can show that to me tomorrow. Does anyone live there now?"

He shook his head, and Charity's thoughts turned back to Enid and Tommy. It might be the perfect place for the children to live so that they could feel as though they weren't entirely under the noses of the Kimball family at the keep. She made a mental note to ask Lachlan when they visited it.

Lachlan watched his wife's expression turn thoughtful and wondered what was going through her fertile mind. After a moment, though, his thoughts returned to the accident. Bothered by an inexplicable sense that something wasn't quite right, he frowned. The axle should have been fine. He'd bought the coach when he arrived in London, and the entire vehicle had been inspected before the purchase. He'd have to take a closer look when they managed to get it back to the keep.

Charity looked up at her husband and noted his troubled look. Thinking he was worried about her, she decided to take his mind off what had just occurred. She reached up and tapped him on the shoulder. "Race you back to the keep," she said, her eyes twinkling, and then she took off running before he could respond.

Twenty-eight

With a shout of laughter, Lachlan ran after his wife, catching her just after she crossed the drawbridge and had almost made it to the steps of the entryway. "Oh, no you don't," he said, grabbing her around the waist before she could make it inside. He was sure she'd hide somewhere, waiting to jump out at him when he passed. Swinging her up into his arms, he intended to take her to his chamber and finish what they'd started in the coach. He'd send Niles to deal with the logistics of the accident.

Charity laughed merrily. "Where are we going?" she asked as he carried her inside, headed purposefully toward the great room and the wide staircase that led to the upper levels.

"Upstairs," he said, his voice stern. "To teach you how a marchioness is supposed to comport herself." But his eyes were twinkling, taking any sting from his words, and Charity tossed him a jaunty little smile.

He suddenly stopped walking, a scowl making its way across his face. Charity twisted her head around to see what had caused his mood to change so suddenly, and Lachlan set her on her feet beside him. Across the room, Lady Eloise stood talking to a young blonde girl. They both glanced in Lachlan and Charity's direction, and began walking toward them.

A few steps off, the blonde girl curtsied. "Hello, my lord," she said, her voice low and sweet.

"Hello, Beth."

Charity looked swiftly at her husband and then back at the girl. The air between them was thick with tension, and the blonde girl looked shyly at the floor.

"Charity, go upstairs and wait for me." Lachlan's voice was flat.

"But—" she began, and then closed her mouth. Uncharacteristically, she complied with the unexplained and high-handed order.

"Excuse us, Beth," she heard her husband say, and looked back to see him take his mother by the arm and propel her out of the great room and into the foyer. Frowning, Charity eyed Beth and found herself being watched, a small smile playing about the blonde's lips. Musing, she turned away and continued up the stairs.

The raised voices of Lachlan and Eloise followed Charity as she walked, but she couldn't quite make out what they were saying. Beth, on the other hand, heard every word.

"Don't think I don't know what you're up to, Mother. It won't work this time. Charity is not going to fall prey to your machinations. She's a bright, strong girl."

From her vantage in the foyer, Eloise could see into the great room and knew Beth was still listening. "Are you saying you don't think Beth is a bright girl, Lachlan? You claimed, at one time, to be in love with her."

"You will not sabotage my marriage, Mother. Take her back to the village. Now." Without waiting for a response, he stalked back into the great room and saw Beth standing there, saw the wounded look on her pretty face.

"I'm sorry, Lachlan," the girl said in a small voice. "I didn't imagine you'd be angry when I took the job your mother offered." She stared up at him with vulnerable eyes. "My father is struggling to continue working as he ages.

He's going to have to sell the blacksmith shop to someone younger. I thought it was a good opportunity for me to begin earning money of my own, so that I can care for him."

Lachlan sighed. "You're a beautiful girl, Beth. Surely you can find a husband to care for you and your father."

She shook her head. "Not if I stay in Ashton, and Papa has his heart set on that. My prospects are so limited here. Especially now."

Lachlan knew that she was right. The village was prospering, but because of the years of neglect before he began helping his father with investments, the village had lost an entire generation of young people who had left to seek opportunities elsewhere. The folk who remained were either elderly or married couples with smaller children.

The marquess found he was not proof against the look of helpless appeal in those wide green eyes. Though things had changed, he had indeed once felt for this girl. "Of course you can stay, Beth. It isn't your fault, in any case."

With a grateful smile, the blonde bobbed a quick curtsy and then impulsively stood on tiptoe to kiss his cheek. Taken by surprise, Lachlan reached for her shoulders to steady himself, but he only succeeded in pulling her against him before finally catching his balance. Charity watched from the top of the stairs. When she saw her husband's arms close around the blonde girl, she pressed her lips together and went to her room, trying to quell the sudden surge of jealousy that threatened to overwhelm her senses. Just days ago she would have reacted swiftly and loudly, a characteristic which had, ironically, landed her here in Scotland. Now, however . . . she found herself more and more often giving herself time to assess situations in an effort to better understand them.

Lachlan allowed Beth's kiss but then dropped his arms

and stepped quickly back. The girl's lips had lingered on his cheek, and he wanted no misunderstandings. "I said you can stay," he said evenly, "but no more of that." He turned away and went up the stairs, taking them two at time in his haste to explain things to his wife.

When he reached his chamber, she was nowhere to be seen. Cursing the events of the afternoon that had ruined a nearly perfect day, he crossed through the bathing chamber and knocked quietly on Charity's closed door. Without waiting, he turned the knob and pulled it open. His wife was seated at her vanity, brushing her hair, the room now neat and orderly thanks to Niles.

"Looks like I didn't need to purchase the new brush and comb after all, my lord," she said quietly into the mirror, her eyes seeking his in the reflection. "Is everything all right?"

Lachlan hesitated, not quite sure how to explain the situation downstairs. After a moment he spoke. "Beth Gilweather is the girl to whom I was formerly engaged, Charity." He watched her carefully.

Charity turned to face him, trying to get the image of his arms closing around Beth's shoulders from her mind. "Your mother brought her here to undermine our relationship?"

Lachlan nodded. "Our engagement badly. She had waited quite some time for me."

Charity chewed on her lower lip, wishing she could find a way to stem the tide of jealousy surging through her belly. "Do you still care for her?"

Lachlan met her eyes. "Only in the same way I care about the welfare and happiness of all those in Ashton. It is my duty."

Charity nodded, wondering at his sudden distance, but

she didn't ask again. If he wished to discuss his mother's new maid further with her he would, she decided.

When his wife remained silent, Lachlan bowed. "I'm going to find Niles so that we can see about getting the coach back up to the keep to repair the damage. I'll see you at supper, Charity." He crossed the room, pressed a kiss to her cheek, and left the room.

Twenty-nine

"It didn't break."

Lachlan looked up from the letter he was reading to see his valet standing in the doorway of his study. "I beg your pardon?"

"The axle. It didn't just break."

The marquess frowned, reading Niles's meaning. "It was deliberately tampered with?" He thought back to the scene at the inn and wondered if Anthony Iverson had been given time or opportunity to do such a thing after he'd let him go, but then he shook his head. The coachman and outriders had stayed with the vehicle until Lachlan sent them to London.

Niles nodded.

"Then, that means someone in London—"

"No, my lord," interrupted Niles. "The cut is fresh. No more than a day or two. It was sawed partially through, so that it would break while it was being used."

Lachlan steepled his fingers and pressed them against his lips, his gray eyes narrowed in contemplation. After a moment he picked up the letter he'd been reading and handed it to the valet. It was from Sebastian, and it simply said that they had lost track of Iverson after confronting him at a ball, and there were Bow Street Runners looking for him, but that Lachlan should be aware that the man could have traveled to Scotland. He'd made a threat just before he disappeared.

Niles scanned the contents and looked up. He chewed his lip, thinking. "I think we need to consider others as well, my lord."

"Others? Who would want me dead?" His mother's face danced into his mind, and he grimaced, loath to even consider the possibility that she hated him enough to go to such lengths. "It has to be someone like Iverson."

The burly valet shifted with discomfort. "Things would be very different here if your brother became Marquess of Asheburton," he said. He watched his master closely. The family seldom spoke of the madness that sometimes gripped Lewiston. It mostly manifested as a period of deep depression, but occasionally he would fly into a quiet sort of rage. During those times, he refused to reason with anyone, and the members of the household carefully avoided him until the madness passed.

"Lewiston has no interest in the title. He was horrified when I suggested abdicating so that he could inherit after the marquess died."

"I wasn't only thinking about him, my lord, and you know it."

Lachlan sighed. "Mother."

"She could manipulate your brother in ways she knows she cannot with you. And there is now the possibility that you will sire an heir with Charity, which would only further distance her from controlling these lands. You'll pardon me for saying."

Lachlan strummed his fingers on the desk and shook his head, then reached for a quill and parchment. "Keep an eye on her, Niles," he said brusquely. "I'll send a note to Sebastian asking him to visit. He and I will figure this out together."

The valet nodded grimly and left the room.

*   *   *

The next few weeks passed without event. Charity settled into her new role as Marchioness of Asheburton with ease, especially since learning it involved really nothing more than just being herself and enjoying the time she spent with her husband. And if Lachlan seemed distracted at times, she told herself it was only because he was back home and getting used to doing all the things he'd always done while at the same time managing a wife. She consoled herself with the fact that, even if she didn't see him during the day, he still made passionate love to her every night, whispering words of love and need. She still woke each morning curled in his bed, her body tingling in all the places he'd touched, and waited for him to return from his morning ride and teasingly kiss her out of the bed to begin her day. Inside, though, tiny niggling doubts were slowly eating away at her.

Everywhere she turned, it seemed, she saw Beth. If she went walking atop the walls, she saw the girl standing at a window, watching. When she went to the stables to acquaint herself with the gentle mare Lachlan provided for her to ride down to the village to see Father Bart, she encountered Beth on the way back. Ostensibly the girl was always on an errand for the dowager, but to Charity's mind she never seemed at all busy with any occupation connected to being a lady's maid. Enid had arrived, as promised, and she treated her position far differently, dancing attendance on her mistress, and being generally available to Charity at all times. The sight of the pretty blonde girl became so irritating, in fact, that Charity found herself on edge even when Beth wasn't around.

When Lachlan was busy, Charity took to spending time with Lewiston, who also seemed to dislike his mother's new maid. Despite his occasional tendency to become withdrawn, she liked her brother-in-law's gentle company and appreciated the pragmatic outlook with which he viewed life. To him, the simpler things were, the more he liked them, which was reportedly why he disliked Beth: she represented an unnecessary complication in a life that would run more smoothly, he felt, if she were absent.

"There's no convincing Mother of that, however," he sighed during one of their conversations.

Charity stroked Minerva, who was curled in her lap. The kitten was growing quickly and had the run of the house now that she had dealt with the dogs. She seemed to take great pleasure in spending time with Boris and Belle, actually, which amused Charity, since it also meant the kitten spent a great deal of time near Eloise, who, as it turned out, was allergic. Every sneeze that filtered through the keep was music to Charity's ears, unkind though such a sentiment was.

"I think your mother just doesn't really know how to let go of her disappointment in some of the choices she has made."

Lewiston raised his brows. "That's a generous assessment, given her treatment of you, Charity."

"I talked to Father Bart about it. She and I aren't so very different in temperament, you see." Charity's forehead wrinkled when she thought of some of her more impulsive moments, right up to the decision to drink too much champagne and trust Anthony Iverson. "I was fortunate that Lachlan was looking out for me, that he rescued me as he did. Your mother had to rescue herself."

"You really love him, don't you?"

Charity's lips curved in a winsome smile. "My sister Amity knew that I did long before I would admit it to myself. Again, showing my stubborn nature. But yes. I do. Very much."

Lewiston nudged her shoulder with his. "Then why are you sitting out here on this wall with me? Shouldn't you be spending time with him?"

"He's been busy," she said slowly. "I don't like to seem needy or bothersome." Charity stopped and laughed a little. "My family would likely be astonished to hear me say that." She shook her head in wonder at the changes in her temperament since her marriage.

"Go. Don't be a goose. I'm sure he'd love to see you."

Charity thought for a moment. "You know, I think I will," she decided with a nod. "Perhaps he doesn't know how I miss him. After all, we see one another at meals and at night. Maybe he thinks that is all I desire."

Lewiston watched his sister-in-law leave and made a mental note to ask Lachlan what had him so distracted. Although Charity didn't apparently know her husband well enough in this setting to understand his recent behavior was indeed odd, Lewiston did. And if it had anything at all to do with Beth, he had every intention of removing her from the keep. He'd do so even if he had to threaten his mother.

Charity walked through the great room to the foyer beyond, which led to the section of the keep that housed Lachlan's study and the extensive adjacent library. She had already spent hours in that room, astonished by the sheer number of books that lined the shelves from floor to ceiling on three of the four walls. She peeked inside, just in case Lachlan was there, but she didn't see him and turned toward the closed door of his study. Just as she raised her hand to knock, the door opened from the inside and Charity found herself face to face with Beth Gilweather.

They stared at one another a moment before Charity spoke. "Pardon me. I was looking for my husband." She lifted her chin and narrowed her eyes at the maid.

By way of answer, Beth pushed the door open wider so that Charity could see past her. Lachlan was seated at his desk, going over a book filled with columns of numbers. The maid gave her a smug little smile and brushed past on her way out.

Lachlan glanced up. "Charity," he said, standing up with a smile. "I didn't expect to see you until dinner."

Quite obviously, thought Charity, then instantly regretted the bitter thought. She put Beth's catty smile out of her mind and walked farther into the room. "I missed you, my lord," she admitted softly. "I wondered if you might like to take a walk?"

Lachlan glanced down at the ledger for a second and then closed it. "That sounds like an excellent idea, kitten." He grinned. "Are you wearing serviceable shoes?"

Charity laughed and lifted her skirts, showing him her walking boots. "They aren't very pretty," she said, "but at least I won't turn an ankle or hurt myself by stepping on a sharp rock."

They strolled outside and down the road to the side path that led to the bluff, talking companionably the whole way. Lachlan told her a bit about his recent investments, and how he'd neglected them during his trip to London.

"I'm sorry I've seemed so distracted. It was just a matter of catching up," he explained. He and Niles had decided she didn't need to know about the deliberate attempt on his life. It would only worry her and, given her impulsive nature, possibly place her in danger. They didn't want her to take it upon herself to investigate as well.

She gave him an impish little smile. "And have you caught up?"

Lachlan felt his body tighten, and he marveled at the fact that his tiny wife could arouse him with such ease.

"Quite nearly," he said, his voice low. He caught her hand and tugged her off the path to a patch of soft grass on the hillside, a familiar haunt of yesteryear. "I used to sit for hours here and listen to the stream down below when I was a boy."

Charity tilted her head to the side and listened. The water, unseen at the bottom of the deep ravine, sounded as if it gurgled and rushed over sharp rocks.

"Have you ever climbed down to play in the water?" she asked.

"Not from here," he said. "The cliff is sheer, and the bottom is nothing but stones and gravel." He paused. "We aren't far from where my father fell."

Charity glanced at him, sensing his melancholy. His eyes were far away, so she sat in silence for a few minutes to allow him time with his thoughts. Twisting, she looked all around. Her eyes roved the path and delved into a copse of trees they'd already passed, and something moved within. She leaned forward and narrowed her eyes, trying to decide if her eyes were playing tricks. She reached back blindly for her husband's arm and tugged on his sleeve.

"I think someone's watching us," she hissed. "Over in those trees."

Lachlan frowned. Under normal circumstances he would have laughed and pronounced it a rabbit, but things weren't very normal right now. "Are you sure?"

Charity nodded.

"Stay here," he said. He stood and walked back up the path toward the stand of trees she'd indicated.

She watched him go, hugging her arms around her midsection. She felt oddly queasy, though she didn't understand why. She looked around. The woods now seemed rather threatening, and the edge of the bluff far too close. She shuddered, disconcerted. She had never been a person afraid of the unknown. When Amity went through a period of eschewing dark places, Charity had always been the one to show her there was nothing to fear. She didn't feel that way anymore.

Behind her a twig cracked, and that was it for Charity. She stood and began walking up the path in the direction her husband had taken, her back crawling. Quickening her steps as she drew closer, wanting to reach him before he disappeared into the trees, she reached out and tapped him on the shoulder.

He spun. "Charity! I thought you were—" He took one look at her pale face and stopped walking. "Let's get you home."

"I don't know what's gotten into me," she admitted, a note of apologetic confusion in her voice. "I'm not usually this jumpy."

Lachlan shrugged and rubbed her shoulders. He had probably made his wife feel that way, himself, inadvertently infusing her with his own subconscious paranoia. They climbed together back up the path toward the keep. He vowed to calm her down in the best way he knew how.

Back in the trees, the watcher breathed a sigh of relief. There would have been nowhere to run if Lachlan hadn't turned around. This hiding place backed right onto the cliff, so the only option would have been to emerge and be seen.

"I was watching the entire time you were gone, my lord. She never left the solar."

Niles and Lachlan walked back down the path, hurrying to get there before nightfall. Lachlan shook his head. "Someone was there. Charity was completely spooked, and I felt it too. We were being followed at the very least, even if the person meant us no harm."

"I'm telling you," the valet said, "it wasn't your mother— unless she hired someone to follow you, which would be ludicrous. I don't think there's a single person in the entire village who would pour water on her if she was on fire, and she hasn't left Scotland in years."

They reached the trees and knelt, examining the ground leading into and out of the small grove. After a few moments Niles found what they were seeking: a footprint pressed into the soft earth. A man's footprint.

They looked around and found several more, the deepest ones very near the place Charity said she had first seen someone. Lachlan would have found him if his wife hadn't tapped his shoulder when she had.

"None of this makes sense," said Niles.

Lachlan glanced down the path. "We were sitting on that patch of grass when Charity grabbed my hand. I was looking down this way, toward the edge of the cliff where my father fell." He wrinkled his brow, trying to get a thought to coalesce. Something had been about to click into place when Charity grabbed his hand, something that should have seemed obvious to him.

"Do you think your father's accident was really an accident?"

"I'm beginning to wonder. He mentioned odd things that occurred in the months leading up to his death. A large rock fell from the outer wall of the keep and almost hit him when he was walking nearby. At the time we just thought the walls needed to be repaired, and I had that handled, but what if that rock was pushed?"

They turned and walked back up the path as darkness began to fall. Niles said, "You sent for the Duke of Blackthorne after the incident with the coach. Perhaps when he arrives we can begin to piece this together. He isn't so close to the situation, and might see things you're missing because you're so aware of the need to be vigilant."

Lachlan nodded. "He has a keen mind and an excellent feel for such things. In the meantime, we need to tell Lewiston. He can help keep an eye on Charity since she seems to enjoy his company. I can't help but feel she's in danger, too."

The valet looked grim. "If those footprints belong to that Iverson character, there's no telling what he plans. To follow you all the way up to Scotland . . . An obsessed madman is capable of just about anything."

Thirty

It took a while, as it turned out, for Lachlan's note to reach Sebastian. The messenger went first, as instructed, to Blackthorne Manor, where he learned the duke was not in residence. Having been instructed that might be the case, the messenger next made his way to London and presented himself at the Duke of Blackthorne's town house.

"His grace just left for Blackthorne Manor," intoned the haughty butler who opened the door.

The messenger sighed. "But I've just come from there!"

The butler raised his brows. "If you've been instructed to personally deliver that message, it appears you'll have to go back." Then he closed the door. The weary messenger turned and walked back down the steps. His horse needed rest. *He* needed rest. For that reason, he decided to stop for the night at the large inn he'd passed on the outskirts of London. He'd return to Blackthorne Manor in the morning.

Three days in a row Charity woke up feeling queasy. The first day she stayed in bed, hoping it would pass, but it didn't and she had to lunge for the chamber pot on Lachlan's side of the bed. By the third morning she figured out that she had time to make it to her own room if she got right out of bed and hurried.

Enid entered while she was still crouched over the bowl. Charity eyed her miserably. "I don't know what's wrong with me. I keep getting sick in the mornings, and then I'm fine for the rest of the day."

A smile appeared on the young girl's face, and she knelt next to her mistress. "My lady, you are with child."

"With child," Charity repeated numbly. "That is what's making me ill?"

Enid fetched a cloth and dampened it in the bathing chamber. She brought it back and pressed it to Charity's flushed forehead. "Your sisters have babies, my lady. Do you not know the signs?"

She shook her head. "They don't live near Pelthamshire, and I only saw Faith toward the end of her time." She stood up and then sat down heavily on the side of the bed. "With child," she said again, wonderingly. The reality finally began to sink in, and she raised delighted eyes to Enid. "I'm having a baby!"

The maid nodded and laughed.

"I have to find Lachlan and tell him right away." Charity took two steps toward the door and then looked down. She was still clad in only her dressing gown, and she looked a fright, having just been sick.

Enid sprang into action. "Let me draw you a bath, and then I'll lay something out for you to wear and send his lordship in to see you after a bit." Her voice faded as she walked into the bathing chamber and began drawing the water.

Charity stood and wandered over to the full-length mirror. She stood before it, staring at her midsection. It didn't seem possible that a baby could grow in there. She grabbed a pillow off the bed and turned sideways, holding it in front of her tummy. When that didn't help her envision the future, she opened the sides of her dressing gown, stuffed the pillow inside, and pulled them closed again.

"Are you planning a costume?"

At the sound of her husband's amused voice, Charity dropped the pillow and whirled. "You scared me!" she accused, but then smiled happily. She took a step toward him, but forgot about the pillow between her feet. Tripping, she fell in an undignified heap at his feet.

Lachlan laughed and held out a hand. Charity scraped the hair out of her eyes and accepted his help. Once she found her feet, she tilted her head to the side and regarded him steadily, a silly smile on her face and her eyes aglow.

"You look like you're just bursting with news, kitten."

"I am," she said, and then stopped, feeling suddenly shy.

He raised his eyebrow. "Well? Better out than in, I say."

Charity looked ruefully toward the chamber pot. "I'd have to agree," she said and bit her lip. "I—"

"My lady, your bath is ready." Enid emerged from the bathing chamber, saw the marquess, and curtsied. "Begging your pardon, my lord. I didn't realize you'd come in."

"It's fine, Enid." He smiled. "I'll help Lady Asheburton with her bath."

The girl nodded, exchanged a quick glance with Charity, and left.

Lachlan took his wife's hand and led her into the bathing room. He pushed the dressing gown back off her shoulders and watched as it slithered to the floor. "You . . . are beautiful, kitten," he said, awed as always by the sheer perfection of her body. Everything about his wife was petite but exquisitely proportioned, so that her legs appeared impossibly long although she barely came up to his shoulder.

He helped her into the hot scented water and then sat on the edge of the tub holding her hair up out of it so she could lie back. He draped the hair over the edge. "Now. Tell me this news."

Her lips curved in a smile, and her entire face was transformed by the glow that stole across her features. She raised eyes filled with wonder to his. "I think I am with child, Lachlan."

He drained of all color and didn't respond.

The smile faded from Charity's face when she saw his reaction, and she felt a tight knot form in her chest. She had been so sure he would be happy. "I mean, I'm n-not completely certain," she stammered, and then looked down so that he wouldn't see the tears that suddenly filled her eyes.

Lachlan realized his reaction was hurting her, when he was only concerned for her continued safety. If the person following them was after the title and his wife was now pregnant . . . "Oh, Charity," he said. He reached under her chin and lifted her face so that she could see his face. "I *am* happy. You just surprised me, that's all. It made me nervous. What if I'm a terrible father?"

"That's not possible," she said softly. "You take such wonderful care of me."

Charity finished her bath and he helped her out, wrapping her in a giant towel before ringing for Enid. The maid arrived, and he smiled and instructed her to never leave Charity alone. Ever. "Make sure that if you have to be elsewhere you've found someone else to stay with her."

"Lachlan!" admonished Charity, laughing. "I'm not an invalid."

"Still," he said, kissing her on the forehead. He left the room.

In the hall he stopped and stuck his head into his bedchamber, giving a cursory glance around, but he left when he didn't see Niles. Walking down the corridor toward the stairs, he covered the distance with ground-devouring strides. The need to find out who was behind the attacks had just received a sharp kick in the rear.

"You wanted to see me?" Lewiston stood in the doorway to his brother's study and glanced uncertainly from Niles to Lachlan. The valet, one hip perched on the edge of the desk, didn't say a word, but the marquess stopped in midpace and motioned him inside.

"I'm leaving for England within the hour, and I need you to help me with something."

Lewiston sat down in one of the brown leather club chairs facing the desk. "Of course, Lachlan. Anything." He watched as his brother circled around behind the desk and waited for him to speak, wondering what this was all about.

"I need you to keep an eye on Charity for me. There have been some . . . incidents since we've come to Scotland."

"Incidents?"

"It is possible the incidents were directed at me, but I can't be certain. Given the circumstances of my marriage to Charity, she might be the target as well. And there might be other reasons."

"Hold on, Lachlan. You're not making sense." Lewiston leaned forward. "I don't know the circumstances of your marriage, nor am I aware of any incidents since you've arrived."

"The axle did not simply *break* on my coach that day I took Charity into Ashton; it was sawed almost completely through so that it would come apart during the trip."

"Sawed through? That's insane. Who would do such a thing?"

"Someone who wanted to hurt either me or Charity, obviously. The bottom line is that I need you and Niles to keep her in sight at all times while I am gone. He can fill you in on the rest of the details, so that you understand why I think she might be a target. I need to get on the road, however, so that I can reach my destination and return as quickly as possible."

"I'll do everything I can. Are you going to London?"

"No. I'm going to get her twin sister and her brother-in-law. He's a doctor," Lachlan reported, as if that explained everything. Nodding to Niles and Lewiston, he turned toward the door.

"Wait!" Lewiston stood and faced the marquess, who paused briefly, an impatient look on his face. "Why are you going all the way to England for a doctor? If someone is hurt . . ."

Lachlan shook his head. "Nobody is hurt. Charity is pregnant. Gareth Lloyd trusted Dr. Meadows implicitly with his wife, and Charity won't feel so isolated from her family if her sister comes for a visit." He left the room, his booted feet echoing down the long stone floor until he turned the corner.

"Pregnant," repeated Lewiston in a stunned voice.

Through the night and with little regard for safety, the Duke of Blackthorne's coach made swift, inexorable progress toward Scotland.

"I will not stay in bed! This is ridiculous. I feel fine." Charity stalked through the bathing chamber into her husband's room, followed closely by her protesting maid. She found Niles standing there with his arms crossed. "Where is my husband?" she demanded.

"His lordship had to go out, my lady. He left orders that you were to get some rest," said Niles in his gravelly voice. He attempted a smile but then gave up and resorted to his more usual crabby expression.

"I cannot stay in bed for the entire pregnancy, Niles. Be reasonable. I'd like to understand what's going on around here." She glanced from Enid's worried and confused face to Niles's stubborn one and threw up her hands. "Fine. If you won't tell me, I'll find someone who will." She turned toward the door.

Astonishingly, Niles stepped in front of her. "Why don't you wait here and let Enid go find whomever you wish to speak with, my lady?"

Charity snorted. "So you can coach them into saying nothing upsetting to the nice pregnant lady? No, thank you. Now, kindly move out of my way."

Niles sighed and moved aside, and then fell into step beside her in the hall. "He'll be back in a day or so."

Charity kept walking. "What do you mean by 'or so'? And, where did he go?" She reached the top of the stairs and started down them, lifting her skirts slightly with one graceful hand.

"Please, my lady. Assist us a bit. You're making me wish I'd let you strike me with that fire poker the morning we met."

Charity suppressed a smile. "You won't be able to distract me, Niles." She swept into the great room and walked directly to the fire to stand before her mother-in-law. Beth rose from the stool beside her mistress's chair upon which she sat, legs curled beneath her.

Lady Eloise looked up but did not rise. She raised disdainful brows. "To what do I owe the dubious honor of this visit, Charity?"

"Where is Lachlan?"

The older woman sneered. "Oh, have you lost him?"

Beth giggled.

Charity glared at the maid and then returned her attention to Lady Eloise. "He wouldn't have left without telling me where he was going unless he thought the knowledge might worry me."

"Well, I can promise you I know nothing. Lachlan hasn't informed me of his comings and goings since he was ten years old and constantly disappearing to visit that old man on the bluff."

Charity tilted her head and regarded the older woman steadily. She thought she detected a thread of pain in her voice, so she softened her tone. "You really don't know, do you?"

Eloise looked toward the window. "No," she said. "I don't. Now, if you would be so kind, I was having a rather peaceful afternoon until you swept in here with your"—she flicked a glance toward Enid and Niles—"entourage."

Charity knelt beside her mother-in-law's chair. "I'm sorry we didn't come here before getting married, my lady," she said softly.

Lady Eloise furrowed her brow but didn't respond.

Beth stepped forward, eyes spitting green sparks. "You didn't come here before you got married because you *had* to get married."

Charity slowly stood, her eyes narrowed on the blonde girl's normally pretty face. It was now twisted with hatred.

"That's right," the girl said. "Lachlan told me everything."

Charity paled and said nothing.

"Do you really think he spends that time in his study alone? He trusts me. He's known me since we were children, and we were once engaged." Beth smiled slyly. "I know that he had to marry you after you ran off with someone unsuitable. He rescued you. Such the gentleman, isn't he?"

"Leave." Charity's voice was flat, and Enid looked at her

in surprise. Niles stepped up behind her in a show of support, a look of pride on his craggy face.

Beth shook her head. "You can't make me leave. I am employed by the Marchioness of Asheburton." She looked at Eloise. "Aren't I?"

Lady Eloise pressed her lips together and glanced first at Beth and then at her daughter-in-law. She lifted her chin and gave Charity a regal nod. "I'm sorry," she said, and then turned to Beth. "But I'm afraid Charity is the Marchioness of Asheburton. If she wishes for you to leave, then you must do so." She gave the girl a scathing look. "My reasons for bringing you here might not have been well intentioned, and of that I find myself unexpectedly ashamed. Your words and low common actions this morning fill me with contempt."

Surprised warmth filled Charity's heart, and she smiled swiftly at the older woman, who looked, for the first time, as though she had human feelings. Beth stared from one woman to the other before turning and leaving the room without another word. A second later the front door slammed.

"For the record," said Niles, into the silence, once again taking rather incredible license for a servant. "Beth was never alone in the study with Lachlan. The time you encountered her there, she was waiting when he came in and he sent her away immediately. Also, anything she might know about your marriage she's learned by eavesdropping on our conversations. I can guarantee that my master does not tell her anything."

Charity gave the valet a grateful smile. "Thank you," she said. "Now, are you going to tell me where my husband has gone, or do I have to go question the staff in the stables?"

"He's gone to get Matthew and Amity, my lady." Lewiston's voice rang out from the foyer, and they all turned to stare at him. "For God's sake, Niles. Can't you see *not* telling her is more upsetting than just giving her the truth? Why not just be honest with her?" He walked across the room to join the group and placed a hand on Lady Eloise's shoulder. "That was well done of you, Mother."

Before she could reply, they all turned toward the foyer at the sound of a deep male voice. "Excuse me. Where might I find the Marquess of Asheburton?" The Duke of Blackthorne stood in the entryway. He pointed down the foyer. "And you should know that the blonde maid who let me in wasn't at all helpful."

Everyone in the room burst into laughter.

Thirty-one

The Marquess of Asheburton entered the foyer of his home and found utter silence. No butler, no dogs barking, Minerva didn't even come running for attention, nothing. He walked slowly down the steps to the great room and stood in the middle of the floor, looking around. Even his mother, nearly always seated in her chair before the fire, was missing. It was as though the place were deserted.

After a few moments his guests appeared in the foyer behind him. Amity and Matthew eyed him curiously. Mercy, who had been visiting her sister when Lachlan arrived, popped up behind them, jumped down the steps, and looked around. "Fairly deserted castle you've got here, Ashe," she remarked.

"It's a keep," he corrected her absently. From far away, he finally heard something that sounded like applause. This was followed by a louder cheer. Curious, he turned toward the stairs that led to his mother's solar. She never entertained guests.

He took the steps two at a time. Mercy looked at her sister, shrugged, and followed.

He walked into the solar unnoticed by anyone except Sebastian, who leaned against a far wall, his arms folded across his chest. The rest of the household, staff and all, were gathered in a tight knot around a small table at which his mother and Niles were seated facing one another. He drew near and, because of his height, was able to look over the throng to see what was going on. It was a bit of a shock.

The unlikely pair was playing at a strange game, wrestling with their thumbs. He watched in astonishment as his mother deftly avoided having her thumb pinned by the stocky, powerfully built valet time and time again, until at last she managed to maneuver herself into position. With a cry of triumph, she smashed down on his thumb while the crowd counted gleefully to three, and then she threw up her arms in victory. Everyone cheered. Niles looked disgusted with himself.

"I'm telling you," crowed Lewiston. "She can't be beat!"

Just then, Mercy walked in with her sister and brother-in-law, and she let out a screech of delight when she saw Sebastian leaning against the wall. Everyone stopped and turned toward the door.

Sebastian groaned. "Sweet mother of—"

"Mercy!" cried Charity. She extricated herself from the throng and ran across the room to give her sister a hug. "My goodness, you've grown even taller since we left for London." She stepped around to hug Matthew and Amity, too, smiling happily at having rejoined some of her family.

"What's going on here?" Lachlan looked balefully around.

All the servants suddenly remembered they had duties they should be attending and scattered. Mercy watched them go with an irreverent grin. "Quite a talent you have there, Ashe. Are you going to frighten small children for your next act?"

Charity slipped arms around her husband's waist, thrilled that he had returned. "Your mother has the most formidable thumbs in all the land," she declared, before she remembered she was mad at him and pushed him away. "And why did you not tell me you were leaving?"

"I decided to save myself the hassle of hearing you argue that you did not need a doctor in residence." He peered around. "Had I known you'd turn my home upside down in less than a week, I'd have taken you with me."

"Actually," put in Matthew, "she probably doesn't need a doctor just yet. But it couldn't hurt," he amended hastily when his wife swatted his arm, cheerfully resigning himself to the fate of being carted all over the island whenever an Ackerly sister became pregnant.

Lachlan leaned down and kissed his wife on the cheek. "Forgive me?"

Too pleased to remain angry, Charity laughed and nodded. "You might want to rescue your cousin over there," she pointed out. Near the window, Mercy was chattering away at her hero, Sebastian, her hands waving wildly in the air as she apparently filled him in on everything that had happened since they last met. He appeared dazed.

"So, that's basically where we are now."

Lachlan and Sebastian were circling the perimeter of the keep, just beyond the walls, and the marquess had brought his cousin entirely up to date on the events transpiring since they'd arrived in Scotland.

"I think you and Niles may have hit upon something. There may indeed be a connection between the accident that killed your father and the ones you've experienced. It seems too much of a coincidence otherwise."

"If he was killed while riding . . . that would almost certainly point to Lewiston." Lachlan shook his head. "I just can't get my mind around that, him killing his father. He's always been adamantly opposed to inheriting. If you'll recall, I even offered to abdicate once I learned that Andrew Kimball was not truly my father. He flatly refused."

Sebastian nodded. "It doesn't seem to add up. Perhaps your mother? She's always been bitter that you inherited."

The marquess raised his eyebrows. "I got an earful about that from my wife. Charity decided that Mother was hurt by me as a child when I chose to spend time with Gregory and my father instead of her. She actually pointed her finger and told me to apologize."

Sebastian shook his head. "Ackerly logic."

Lachlan laughed.

"Spend enough time around them and you'll see what I mean. They see the world differently than any other people I've encountered. The only one who seems to have any sense at all is Patience, but she rarely leaves Pelthamshire."

They stopped walking near stone steps that led up to the drawbridge. Lachlan was thinking about his mother. "If it turns out Charity is right, then it's possible Mother did resent me but has now had a change of heart. Although, that wouldn't explain why she would want to remove my father, unless her prime motivation was for Lewiston to inherit. Then she would, through controlling him, regain her former position in the household . . . ?"

"I don't know." Sebastian shook his head. "This feels male. The footprints you found were male, and it would have taken someone strong to saw through that axle. If we can find a connection between your father's death and the attempts on your life, then I think we really need to look at Lewiston. If not him, it might be that Anthony Iverson has indeed made his way to Scotland and is attempting to hurt you and Charity both."

"Shh." Lachlan suddenly held a finger to his lips. "Did you hear that?"

Sebastian shook his head.

The marquess listened again and then quietly climbed the stairs to the drawbridge. He'd heard a distinctive scuffling sound, rather like a boot on gravel. The duke followed. Cautiously they looked around the corner and down the drive that led to the keep.

Coming toward them, clad in men's riding clothes, was Mercy Ackerly. Both men sighed and straightened.

"Hullo, Ashe," the young woman said in a pleasant tone, then smiled up at Sebastian, her eyes filled with adoration. "I came to see if you wanted to go riding with me," she announced, and then, before the duke could accept or decline, she turned back to Lachlan. "You'll let me ride Apollo, won't you?"

The two men eyed each other over the top of her curly auburn head. "No," said her brother-in-law, before reaching out to ruffle her hair.

Mercy scowled and ducked away from his hand. "When are people going to stop treating me like a child? I've just turned sixteen, after all." She tossed her head, turned on a heel, and stalked off toward the house, her long legs quickly eating up the distance.

"She's getting tall," remarked the duke, a fond smile playing about his lips.

Lachlan grinned. "Well, she's 'just turned sixteen,' you know. Before you know it she'll be on the marriage market and you'll be a doddering old man wishing you'd had the foresight to arrange the marriage before the Town dandies began crowding her dance card." He laughed and pointed to Sebastian's temple, where a short swath had begun to show on each side. "You're already turning gray."

"I blame that on the fact that my friends persist in marrying Ackerly women."

"You can only blame yourself, old man. If you hadn't tried so hard to mow poor Mercy down with your coach three years ago, none of us would ever have met them. And it's not as though you discourage her adoration."

Sebastian acknowledged the accusation with a reluctant nod. "Eh, the urchin amuses me. I admire her spirit."

They walked toward the house, following Mercy. "Well, you're going to have to set her straight soon," said Lachlan, "or you'll end up hurting her when she makes her debut and realizes you've never had any intention of offering for her or anyone else."

Their voices faded as they drew farther away from the drawbridge. When he was sure they'd gone, Lewiston emerged from the shadows beneath the structure and climbed the steps. He peeked around the corner and then quickly drew back his head. Amity and Charity were walking down the drive, arm in arm, deep in conversation. They strolled across the drawbridge and up the hill toward a little glade without noticing him. Their timing was perfect. Other voices were speaking, these in his head. They demanded he act.

He bent over, picked up a sizeable rock and tested its heft in his hand. It would do. He peeked inside the walls one last time and then followed at a short distance behind the sisters. It wouldn't be long now until his brother and his meddling friends figured out everything. The time to move was now.

Thirty-two

No, I had absolutely no idea what was going on," said Amity. "From Scotland, Matthew and I went straight to his home in Rothmere, and sent a note to Grace and Faith telling them what we'd done and where we were. Faith replied soon after, but she simply said that you ran off with Lachlan, and that they were happy for both of us. She didn't even *mention* the trouble with Anthony Iverson!" She gave her sister a curious look. "Do you know what became of him?"

"All Lachlan knows is that he apparently left London after Trevor, Gareth, Jon and his grace confronted him at a ball. It will be interesting to see if he turns up in London next Season." Charity's face glowed cherry red from embarrassment. "I was such a foolish girl, but Lachlan was wonderful. He took care of me and then asked me to marry him the very next day." Her chagrin faded, and she smiled at the memory. "Actually, he *told* me to marry him and then dared me to say no."

"And you finally realized you loved him and said yes, and now you're living happily ever after." Amity sighed with the beauty of it all.

Charity snorted. "Um, no. I actually did refuse him."

"You did *not!* After everything you'd both been through to be together?"

"Oh, you know me. I was stubborn." She smiled wryly. "But he convinced me, and now here we are." She pressed both hands to her flat abdomen. "Can you believe I'll be having a baby?"

They reached the crest of the hill and stopped, standing arm in arm for a quiet moment. Charity pointed down at the village. "I like to come up here in the morning because Ashton looks like a pretty jewel nestled in these green, green hills. I can't wait for you to meet Father Bartholomew and some of the villagers."

"You seem more peaceful and happy than I've ever known you, Charity." Amity grinned. "I'm so glad." She punched her sister playfully in the arm. "Now if you'd have just listened to me after he kissed you that first time."

Laughing, Charity turned to hug her sister. Her eyes widened. "Lewiston?" she said in confusion, and then screamed when he raised his arm and brought a rock crashing down on the back of Amity's head.

Her sister crumpled to the ground. Charity stood rooted in place for a moment, staring down at Amity, and then she looked back up at her brother-in-law. When he started toward her, she turned and ran in the opposite direction, down the hill and away from the keep.

With an angry snarl, Lewiston dropped the rock and gave chase.

Lachlan and Sebastian walked into the solar, still hashing out the situation in low voices. Niles stood in alarm when he saw them. "Where are the twins?" he asked.

Lachlan gaped. "They aren't here?"

"No. They said they wanted to take a walk, and when I looked out the window, the two of you were standing near the drawbridge talking to Mercy. I told them to go ahead, thinking you'd accompany them on their walk."

Lachlan stepped over to the window and looked down at

the wide courtyard. The girls were nowhere to be seen. He followed the drive with his eyes and then let them rove up the hillside where he knew Charity liked to take her morning stroll. Nothing. Then he saw it: a motionless scrap of pale pink near the crest of the hill.

"Matthew!" he bellowed, and sprinted out of the solar and down the stairs. Niles and Sebastian were hard on his heels, and the doctor joined them, looking confused.

"I'll saddle the horses," called the duke. He ran toward the stables while the other three men ran across the drawbridge and up the hill.

Lachlan got there first and knew instantly that it was Amity. He knelt and felt for a pulse, thankfully finding one, then stepped out of the way as Matthew arrived. Turning in a circle, Lachlan searched out any clue as to where Charity might have gone.

Sebastian rode up on his big black stallion, leading Apollo. Lachlan swung up into the horse's saddle. "Can the two of you get Amity back to the keep?" he asked the men without mounts.

Niles nodded. Matthew was gingerly feeling the bump at the back of her head and glanced at the bloody rock on the ground. "Go," he said to Lachlan. "Find your wife."

"Let go of me!" Charity clawed at the hand that half-covered her mouth while Lewiston dragged her toward the small cabin situated on the bluff. She kicked and struggled and dug in her feet, but because of her petite size Lewiston was able to make steady progress.

They reached the small structure and he opened the door, pushing Charity inside ahead of him. She stumbled and then rushed back at him, arms flailing. "What have you done?" she shrieked. The image of Amity falling to the ground was a terrible one, and she slapped at him in renewed fury.

Lewiston grunted and caught her wrists. He dragged her over to a table and grabbed the coiled rope he'd left atop it, binding her hands behind her back. "Your sister is still alive. I didn't hit her that hard."

"Bastard," she spat.

His eyes flashed. "No, my lady. *That* distinction belongs to your husband."

"Is that what this is about? You want to be the marquess?"

"Shut your mouth, Charity. You understand nothing. I'd have left you completely alone until we found out if that brat in your belly is male or female, but it turns out I may need you as a bargaining chip." He backed her away from the table and pushed her down into a wooden chair.

The second he let go of her, she tried to stand and run. Lewiston sighed and pushed her back down. "If you're going to make this difficult, I'll just go back and finish off that sister of yours."

She glared at him but stopped struggling, knowing he could get to Amity before she could. Lewiston grabbed the end of the rope that dangled from her wrists and began winding it around her ankles. He then tied the rope to one of the chair legs and took a step back.

"I don't suppose you'll sit here quietly while I go see what's happening at the keep, will you?" he asked. He hoped no one else had found Amity yet.

She stared at him in astonishment and then found her voice. "Of course I will," she said. Unfortunately, her eyes must have been burning with fury.

He shook his head. "There's entirely too much fight in you. Mother should never have interfered in Lachlan's relationship with Beth. At least that one was easy to manipulate." He untied his cravat and tugged it from around his neck. "This will have to do," he said. He covered Charity's mouth, tied the gag behind her head, and then left the cabin.

As Charity heard the key turn in the lock, she immediately began struggling to get free.

Thirty-three

Matthew and Niles struggled through the front door, carried Amity across the foyer, and laid her on a large sofa near the fire. Eloise and Mercy stood nearby, watching, their hearts in their throats.

Niles began to pace. He wanted to get out and help Lachlan and Sebastian but knew he couldn't leave the dowager and Mercy here unprotected, especially since Matthew was busy trying to revive Amity.

"What happened?" Mercy matched his steps.

"Charity's missing. His lordship and his grace are on horseback looking for her."

Mercy ran to the window, but on the ground floor could see nothing past the keep walls. She wrung her hands helplessly.

On the sofa, Amity moaned and tried to sit up. Matthew placed a hand on her shoulder. "Shh. Lay back, darling."

"My head hurts."

"I'd imagine it does." He laid a hand on her cheek.

"I don't know what happened." She opened her eyes in alarm. "Where's Charity?"

"They're looking for her, love. Do you remember anything?"

"No," she said. "We were just talking. She showed me the village." Amity closed her eyes. "Then she turned around and got this horrible look on her face . . . and then I woke up here."

Her eyes, filled with panic, flew open. She sought her husband's hand. He took it, and she glanced past him to the other occupants of the room. Mercy and Niles were pacing like caged animals and Eloise hovered near, a frightened expression on her face. "Wait," she said. She looked around again. "Where's Lewiston?"

Niles and Mercy eyed one another.

"Charity said his name just before I blacked out," Amity explained.

"I'll go," said both Niles and Mercy, then turned to glare at one another. "Stay here!" they said again in unison.

Niles grabbed at Mercy's arm. "You are *not* going out there. The marquess would have my hide, and his grace would finish off whatever's left."

"How well do you ride?" asked Mercy. When the valet's face fell, she tossed her head in a gesture of triumph. "Someone has to *quickly* tell them it's Lewiston," she said. "It'll be tough to even find them if you can't keep your seat."

As she spun and left the room, Niles stared after her. He turned back to the sofa and its occupants. "Is she always like this?"

"Yes," said Amity and Matthew.

Lewiston watched Mercy fly across the drawbridge on horseback and knew it was over. They'd found Amity, or she had managed to make her way back to the keep and likely told them it was him. At the very least, his absence would now have been noted. His only option was to find Lachlan and use Charity as bait to get his brother to the bluff. After that, it would be a simple matter of pushing both of them over the edge.

He sighed. It had been so much easier with his father.

* * *

Her heart in her throat, Mercy rode the hills watching for any sign of Lachlan, Sebastian, or Lewiston. It took nearly an hour before she caught sight of Sebastian coming out of the woods. She dug in her heels and rode to intercept him.

The duke scowled when he saw her approaching. He pulled up on the reins and said, "You should be back at the keep with Matthew and Niles."

She shook her head. "I have news. Amity woke up. It's Lewiston."

Sebastian's face was grim. "This is going to hit Lachlan hard." He gave Mercy a grave look. "Stay with me. We have no idea where the man is or of what he is capable." He wheeled his black stallion and headed back toward the area Lachlan had wanted to search, Mercy filling him in on all that Amity had said.

They were nearly back at the keep when they caught sight of Apollo standing near a glade of thin trees. Lachlan likely searched within, so Sebastian and Mercy pulled up and waited for him to emerge.

"What's *she* doing here?" Lachlan asked when he did, his voice tight with worry.

"Ashe . . . it's Lewiston." Sebastian's voice was pitched low.

"Lewiston? What's happened to him?"

Mercy's heart nearly broke as Sebastian shook his head. "No, he's not hurt. He's the one behind the accidents. Amity woke up and remembers Charity saying his name just before he hit her."

Pain flashed across Lachlan's face before he ruthlessly buried it. "In that case, I'm pretty sure I know where he's taken my wife."

He dug his heels into Apollo's flanks and headed for the

path that led to Gregory's cabin, Lachlan and Mercy following. The trio galloped along the bluff until the structure came into sight, and then Lachlan slowed and dismounted. He let Apollo's reins dangle free as he eyed the small building, knowing the well-trained stallion wouldn't wander off. Everything looked peaceful.

Sebastian pinned Mercy with his eyes. "Stay here," he commanded quietly. "Don't even think about dismounting. And for God's sake, if anything happens, run for the safety of the keep."

She nodded, her eyes huge, but then pointed up the path. Lewiston, on foot, was just coming into sight.

Lachlan and Sebastian glanced at each other. Lewiston saw them, and he veered off the path and into the trees, heading for the cliff behind the cottage.

Lachlan took off after his brother. "See if Charity is inside," he called back to Sebastian. He could hear the rushing sound of water far below, but closer, footsteps as his brother ran through the trees.

He emerged in a clearing to see Lewiston frozen at the edge of the cliff. Lachlan paused before taking a step forward.

His brother backed up another half inch, and he looked over his shoulder to the watery death that awaited. "You remember this spot, don't you?" he said.

Lachlan nodded, his eyes locked on Lewiston's face, who looked down.

"I didn't mean for him to die. I loved him." His brother's face contorted with sudden pain and he raised demented eyes. "I just wanted him to understand how I felt." His expression changed to one of blazing anger. "You aren't even his son! Sometimes it seems right that you inherited, but I have these terrible headaches. Sometimes things seem so horrible and—"

"I know," said Lachlan gently. "I don't know what's been going on, but we can work all this out. It can all be—"

Lewiston shook his head. "No. It's too late." He turned and stared downward. "He wouldn't listen to me. Told me you *earned* the right to be marquess. And these other voices in my head say that's wrong. Very wrong. I know that—"

"Lewiston, come away from the edge," Lachlan begged. "Tell me where Charity is. Tell me you haven't hurt her. It doesn't have to be any worse than it already is."

"She wouldn't listen to me either."

Sudden fear gripped Lachlan. Had his brother already thrown Charity to her death? He struggled to remain in control and took another step.

Lewiston held up a warning hand. "Don't come any closer! I'll jump . . . and then you'll never find her."

Relief flooded Lachlan, hope that she was still alive. His brother wouldn't be promising to show him her body, would he?

Sebastian appeared from the trees farther down the bluff, about thirty yards behind Lewiston. Lachlan kept talking, not wanting his brother to notice. The sound of rushing water below would help cover his friend's approach. "It isn't Charity with whom you're angry. It's me. Tell me where she is, and then you and I can work through the rest. We're brothers."

Sebastian moved closer and mouthed, "We've got her." Relief filled Lachlan.

Unfortunately, Lewiston saw his expression change. Following Lachlan's eyes, he turned, saw Sebastian, and sighed. "That's it, then." He glanced behind him and took the last step toward the edge. "I'm sorry," he said. "This is for the best." He vanished over the edge.

"No!" Lachlan ran toward the cliff.

Sebastian reached the spot first, grabbed his cousin and stopped him from looking over the edge. "Don't," he said quietly. Lachlan stared into his eyes, fighting tears. "Mercy took Charity to the keep. Go there. You don't need to see this. Think about the living."

Lachlan slowly nodded. He spared one last glance at the place he'd last seen Lewiston, and then he turned and ran back to Apollo, leapt into the saddle, and spurred on the horse back up the path.

He clattered across the drawbridge without slowing down and pulled up before the main doors, gravel spraying from the stallion's hooves as he skidded to a halt. His heart in his throat, he walked inside and through the foyer to the great room. Charity was kneeling next to the sofa where her sister reclined, the two hugging and crying with relief.

When she saw Amity's eyes flick toward the doorway, Charity looked over her shoulder to see Lachlan standing there, an expression of stark pain on his handsome face. Without a word she stood and walked to where he was standing. "I love you," she whispered. She took his hand and placed it on her stomach. "Your child and I are safe."

Lachlan fell to his knees, closed his eyes and wrapped his arms around her, burying his face in her abdomen. Tears streaking her cheeks, Charity stroked his hair and whispered soothing words of love and solace.

Epilogue

Spring, 1817

The day, nearly everyone agreed, couldn't have been more perfect for a celebration. The Marquess and Marchioness of Asheburton emerged from the tiny church. A moment later, Dr. and Mrs. Matthew Meadows appeared as well, and stepped up beside the first couple, followed by Father Bartholomew and all the members of their extended family. There were riotous cheers from the entire village. Their faces glowing, the twins clasped hands.

"We did it, Amity!" whispered Charity. "We finally had the double wedding we've always dreamed about." Amity squeezed her sister's hand in reply, mute with happiness.

After months of continued admonishment from the aging clergyman, Lachlan had finally grudgingly agreed that it was only right that they retake their vows in his church. Charity, who had been secretly conspiring with Father Bart to bring about the event, had instantly decided it could only be held on their twin daughter and son's first birthday, and that Amity and Matthew would have to come make it a double ceremony. Before Lachlan could blink, he found himself neck deep in plans—and Ackerlys.

"I'm not quite sure how this became such a circus," he said to the babies, who were supposed to be napping in the nursery. He had taken to slipping into the room just after the nanny put them down in the afternoon. It was the only room in the house where he could be assured a brief modicum of peace. "I thought it would be a simple matter of standing in church with my family and agreeing to spend the rest of my life with your mother, with whom I have already agreed to spend the rest of my life."

Charlotte giggled and pulled her blanket over her dark, curly head, but Charles stared up at his father soberly, as if agreeing and empathizing with his plight. He sat up and gave his sister a reproachful look.

"Best just go along with it, my lord," advised Tommy, who could typically be found near the twins. He'd appointed himself their protector not long after they arrived, and took his job very seriously. Lachlan hid a smile but had to agree with the young man's logic. Having one Ackerly in his household was disruptive enough. There was no fighting the lot of them.

He stood, kissed each twin on the forehead and ruffled Tommy's hair. "I'll go downstairs and see if I can sneak into my study to get some work done. This will all be over in just five more days, right?" The boy nodded agreeably and then opened the book he'd chosen and began reading the babies to sleep.

Miraculously, Lachlan made it to his study without incident. He breathed a sigh of relief, closed the door and then turned toward his desk, intending to catch up on some dreadfully neglected paperwork.

Charity was seated there, a determined look on her face. "We need to talk about your mother."

So much for working. Lachlan raised his brows. "What about her?"

"I would like you to ask her if she'll stand as witness with us when we speak our vows."

He scowled. Despite the close relationship his wife had developed with his mother, Lachlan had found it difficult to rebuild the emotional bridge Lady Eloise had spent his entire twenty-three years demolishing. Charity brought the subject up from time to time during the year and half or so they'd been married, but she hadn't forced the issue. Now, it seemed, she had decided it was time.

"Why don't *you* ask her?" he suggested.

Her eyes softened. "Because it would mean a great deal to her if you did it, darling." She watched his expression harden. "It would mean a great deal to me, as well."

When her husband didn't respond, she continued. "She's your mother. That will never change. Give her a chance, please. If you don't and lose the opportunity, I think you'll regret it."

"She should come to me," he grunted.

Charity stood and walked around the desk to lay a hand on his arm. "I know. But she's afraid. She thinks you'll reject her."

With good reason, he thought. But he stared down into his tiny wife's earnest aquamarine eyes and felt himself softening. He sighed, lifted one of her hands, and began inspecting her fingers.

"What are you doing?" she asked with a musical little laugh.

"They *look* like ordinary fingers." He kissed the tip of each and then pulled her into his arms for a kiss. She melted against him, and turned her face up to his. "But they can't possibly be the same sort the rest of us have," he said.

"No?" she asked.

"No." He shook his head and whispered against her lips, "Because I continue to find myself hopelessly wrapped around them." Then he kissed her until they both forgot, for a time, about his mother, about the ceremony, and even about the house full of visiting family.

Later that day, Lachlan *did* go talk to his mother, who joyfully agreed, with tears in her eyes, to stand with him as he renewed his vows. And five days later he found himself sandwiched between his wife and his mother, while Matthew Meadows stood between his wife and her father facing Father Bartholomew, who could scarcely manage to conduct the ceremony past the enormous smile on his thin face.

The celebration that followed took place on the grounds flanking Asheburton Keep, and everyone in the local environs was invited. Villagers trooped up the hill, following the coaches bearing their lord and his family, for a day filled with fun and games. The focus shifted quickly from the couples to the children, for this portion of the event was technically being given to celebrate the first anniversary of Charles and Charlotte's birth.

There was more food than anyone could possibly consume, and there were clowns and minstrels and gypsy fortune-tellers to entertain the guests. Music and laughter rang through the air as the lines between aristocrat and commoner blurred for one beautiful day.

Mercy was in heaven. She trailed after the Duke of Blackthorne, chattering like a magpie. "Perhaps we should have our fortunes told, your grace," she said with an impish smile. "You know, of course, that I am quite seventeen now. Not a little girl at all." She gave him a hopeful look.

Sebastian looked dazed. He stared over her head at the spot he'd last seen his cousin. He'd been in Scotland for only two days but was exhausted from trying to keep himself from ending up in a compromising situation with Mercy.

Not, he was sure, that she had any intention of forcing his hand in that manner. Quite the opposite. It simply didn't occur to her that they weren't already betrothed, and he had not yet been able to bring himself to kill the adoration he saw in her pansy blue eyes.

"Perhaps another time," he murmured, and stepped neatly around the table. Mercy followed. "But don't let me stop you from having *your* fortune read," he said hastily. Suddenly struck by an idea, he pulled a couple of coins from his pocket. He handed them to the gypsy and, grasping Mercy by the shoulders, plunked her down in the empty chair. "Come find me and tell me what she predicted for you," he commanded, and then he strode away before she could get up and run after him.

Sighing, Mercy stared across the table at the colorfully garbed old lady. Short of being rude, which didn't sit well with her, she was going to have to follow through.

As soon as the reading was over, she thanked the lady and hurried off after the duke. It took a while to find him in the throng, but she finally spotted him talking to Lachlan. Before she could reach the pair, however, the duke clapped his cousin on the shoulder, nodded, and began walking toward the keep.

Mercy quickened her steps.

"Hold on there, little sister." Lachlan stepped in front of her, a smile on his face. "You aren't leaving the party so soon, are you?"

She peered over his shoulder just in time to see her hero disappear inside the castle walls. "I'll be right back. I was just going to talk to his grace for a moment."

"Ah. You'll have to send him a letter. He's gone to instruct his coachman to ready the team. He wants to get an early start on his trip back to London."

Mercy frowned. "But he won't get far before night falls!"

"He's going to spend the night at the border." He slung an arm across his young sister-in-law's shoulders and began steering her back toward the festivities, trying to help his cousin out a bit.

Mercy played with her little niece and nephew for a while but kept one eye on the keep. Finally, unable to stand the thought of Sebastian leaving without at least saying good-bye, she slipped away. It was as she walked across the drawbridge that she saw the Blackthorne coach standing ready in the drive.

Inspiration struck. She waited until the coachman's back was turned, then sprinted the short distance to the coach, turned the handle on the door, and climbed quickly inside. Safely tucked away, she sat primly on the edge of the luxurious velvet seat and waited. Now Sebastian would be forced to see her before he left.

She listened, for a while, to the men working and talking outside. There were occasional bumps that jarred the vehicle as they loaded provisions and the various other items they had brought with them. Each time Mercy looked expectantly at the door, thinking Sebastian had arrived, but it never opened. Finally she slumped back on the cushions, wondering what was taking him so long.

The interior was quite warm, and she began to feel drowsy and a trifle irritable. She sighed and decided to count to one hundred. If Sebastian didn't show up by then, she'd have to get out and go find him. She had barely made it to twenty before her eyes fluttered closed and she fell asleep.

Darkness descended, and the villagers began making their way back down the hill to their homes. The Kimball family and various Ackerlys waved good-bye and went inside the keep, collapsing into chairs and onto couches in the great room, tired after the long and glorious day.

They talked quietly for a while before Patience looked around the room, brow furrowed with concern. "Where's Mercy?"

Everyone shrugged, and Grace laughed. "She's probably followed the duke wherever he went to try to get away from her."

Lachlan shook his head. "Sebastian left hours ago," he said. "He wanted to get an early start on his trip back to London, so he had his coach packed and then followed on horseback. I'd imagine he's at the border by now."

"You imagine wrong."

Everyone swiveled their heads toward the foyer in surprise at the sound of the Duke of Blackthorne's voice. He stood there, his hand locked around Mercy's upper arm, a look of long-suffering resignation on his handsome face.

"The urchin stowed away in my coach."

"I most certainly did not," Mercy cut in indignantly. "I fell asleep in your coach while I was waiting to tell you good-bye. It isn't my fault you decided not to ride inside the vehicle. I've already explained that to you a thousand times."

Sebastian didn't respond.

Trevor's lips twitched. "She *does* look rather well rested."

"Thank you," Mercy said, then scowled when the men in the room all burst out laughing. "I don't know why he's so cross about it. It's not like I was gone all night or my virtue was compromised and he had to marry . . ."

This time, the women laughed, too.

Sebastian looked horrified by the thought of being forced into wedlock, even though his cousin seemed perfectly happy after falling into his marriage in that very way. He cleared his throat. "Well, here she is, safe and sound. I think I'll take my chances on the dark roads and go back to the inn at the border." He glanced at Mercy and gave her a reluctant smile. "It's safer there. Behave yourself, urchin."

He released her arm, ruffled her hair fondly, and left the keep.

Charity slipped her arms around her husband's waist and looked around at all the people she loved most in the world. She lifted shining eyes to Lachlan. "Let's go to bed," she whispered.

"Our guests . . ." he started to say, and then stopped and laughed at the obstinate look on his wife's face. "I can see that you intend to have your way on this, Lady Asheburton."

Charity nodded firmly, grasped his hand and began leading him toward the stairs. "I intend, Lord Asheburton, to have my way with you for the rest of the night."

That, Lachlan promptly decided, was the most agreeable suggestion he'd heard the entire day. "Charity is . . . tired," he said to the rest of the room by way of explanation for their sudden decision to retire.

Cleo Egerton thunked her cane on the floor. "Bah! She doesn't look tired to me."

Lachlan stopped, a comical expression on his face, only to have his arm tugged again by his wife. "Good night," he finished with a sheepish grin. Then he turned, scooped his giggling wife up into his arms, and disappeared up the stairs, taking them two at a time.

CPSIA information can be obtained at www.ICGtesting.com
265548BV00002B/3/P